MUNDER WORLD

THE JESTER'S JOURNEY

MUNDERWORLD

KYLE SORRELL

4 Horsemen
Publications, Inc.

Munderworld

4 Horsemen Publications, Inc.
1497 Main St. Suite 169
Dunedin, FL 34698
4horsemenpublications.com
info@4horsemenpublications.com

Cover & Typesetting by S. Wilder
Editor Devora Gray

Library of Congress Control Number: 2022946466

Paperback ISBN-13: 979-8-8232-0073-8
Hardcover ISBN-13: 978-1-64450-732-2
Audiobook ISBN-13: 979-8-8232-0071-4
Ebook ISBN-13: 979-8-8232-0072-1

Dedication

Dedicated to my loving parents, Gary and Patricia, my little brothers Samuel and Jacob, and everyone else who put up with my weirdness!

Tall
the Minstrel

Fiddle
Cynkz

Table of Contents

Every Star
Near and far
Waits for us
To just
Reach out
And accept them

CHAPTER 1

EVER SINCE THE BEGINNING OF HIS STAY IN THE afterlife, far into the end of time and beyond the existence of the living world, Cynkz could recall that poem. Often, he would venture to a secluded spot in the open to look up into the perpetual night sky. His gaze pierced the thin, invisible layer between his world and the universe among the stars. He could hardly remember anything before the end, yet a simple poem weighed heavily from the very beginning, though its original meaning had long been lost.

Just as lost as he was, and just as lost as the world and life he once knew. Having lost whatever memories he had of his early life back on Peara, the world of po, he knew of little else to do but wander forward in Dulrot.

He appreciated the time alone to think upon the past, reflect upon his schemes and tricks, and laugh at prior victories and defeats, even if they mostly revolved around his plays and pranks in the afterlife. To a long dead soul bound to the nether, the depths of Munderworld, time was all one had, and paradoxically, the most valuable of resources.

"Cynkz! Hey, Cynkz!"

A sharp voice cut through the silence. It was welcoming and echoed across the star-lit fields.

"Why does your name have a 'z' in it anyway?" The little voice followed the slow reveal of a friendly imp through the dark knight as it approached. "People are gonna think I'm talking about a bathroom sink or something when they hear me yelling for you."

A miniature, husky creature presented itself to the stargazer. The light tone of its voice made its presence cordial, despite the little imp's coarse skin and scruffy impression. Small, bony hands and small hoofed feet stood out from its round body. The deep red skin of its head and torso blended into deeper brown fur. Its wings stood out from its back and were comically tiny. From any given angle, one hardly noticed these appendages flapping helplessly to keep the round body afloat. Its face, a bundle of rough and soft edges, signs of many lifetimes spent in joyous pranks, coincided into a pleasant expression.

"I knew I'd find you here, Cynkz!" the imp said, his voice toppling with glee.

"How are you tonight, little friend?" the stargazer replied.

"I'm well. But what are you doing out here again? We muns like the dark, but this is a bit much. Your black braid blends into the dark of night!"

"Yet you always find me so easily!"

Cynkz took a moment to think to himself, pondering his friend's words:

I don't know why he always says "we muns," when he knows for a fact that I am not one. Perhaps he does it to be endearing, to help me feel included with him in whatever group he sees himself a part of.

"Your pasty skin kind of gives you away. It reflects the starlight like a red-hot beacon!"

It was true, and Cynkz knew it. A slight chuckle slipped through, pushing his cheeks up into his eyes, nearly closing them.

Cynkz could not remember much, but he could recall the lessons of his old career in the po world as a court jester. He retained most of his worldly appearance in the afterlife. His tall, lithe figure, the way his clothing tapered down from his shoulders to thin wrists and thin ankles. The deep red and purple harlequin pattern, the colors of which were so similar in shade that they nearly blended together. His black cloak with its velvet-red interior caused his silhouette to pop out to the viewer's eye. His pointed hat followed suit; the deep red exterior's pointed edges led down to his sharp, pointed jaw that tapered toward a thick, black scruff of pointed hair on his chin. His black hair billowed out from beneath his cap into an excessively long braid that reached down to his feet when standing. The constant back-and-forth of sharp angles and blending colors of his outfit contrasted heavily with his pale skin and black hair. Such opposing elements forced the observer to look at him for just a bit longer than normal to truly make out his form. This was one of many of the jester's tricks—those extra seconds of looking at someone often made them that much more endearing, a staple in methods of charm and beguilement.

Cynkz looked back to his friend and noticed he was doing just that—getting in those extra few seconds of staring.

"It's always a pleasure to see you in good spirits, Cynkz," the imp said. "All this melancholy and star-gazing looks depressing."

"I know, Fiddle, I know. That is why I do it alone, to not sour our usual merriment."

"You think a lot about the old po world, don't you?"

Cynkz's gaze rounded, pulling down on his sharp eyes. He looked mournfully back toward the night sky.

"Yes, that I do. It'd be nice to remember what it feels like again: the faint gusts of wind, the pleasant warmth of the sun, the weight of one's body on another—"

"Bah!" Fiddle interrupted. "That was the one thing I hated about the living world. No matter what form you possessed, it was extremely heavy. After a mun spends a millenia as a weightless, floaty spirit, all that po muscle and fat pulling down on you was torture, I'd say."

"That is true," Cynkz said, "but it was always worth it, wasn't it? The chaos and fun you could cause among the po was priceless! Such as forcing a po to dig into their nose in public, dropping their trousers and dancing, or getting into fights! It always felt festive."

"Yeah, yeah, but when you were done, exorcized by some meddling priest or burnt alive at the stake, the instant shift in feeling heavy as a whale to popping up like a feather in Munderworld was traumatizing."

"True."

"You've been a master shapeshifter, far better than the average monster or mun. I'd say you never needed to possess anyone to pass for a po. Though unlike most of us, your forms were so heavy! You could disguise yourself as a mouse and the mighty thumps of your little footsteps would give you away!"

"Ha! True again!"

The two shared a peaceful grin before looking back up to the star-filled cosmos. Rows of dark fields and windless forests stretched before the two, the horizon nearly blending with the pitch-black sky. Silence created an air of tranquility to such a degree that one could almost hear the twinkling of the lights above.

Cynkz had known Fiddle long enough to know when something was on his mind. Normally, he would ask his companion what he was thinking but decided to let the peace sit and stir. He knew his friend would break the silence when he was ready.

"Wanna go explore a bit?" Fiddle said. "I heard an apostle is supposed to be venturing down here soon."

"An apostle? Another celestial here, so soon after the last one?"

Despite floating in the air, Fiddle rotated his body and patted himself down, as if readying himself to get up and go for a walk.

"Yeah, ever since the po world, Pear, was destroyed it seems they've been getting more aggressive with their missions. Each time they come down, they convert more po and uplift them to higher realms. I suppose whoever or whatever their boss is, they're trying to save as many souls as possible now that there ain't po alive to breed new ones."

"Hmm, how interesting," Cynkz said, perking up to rub the pointed black hairs that comprised his goatee.

"At this rate, there won't be any po left for us to mess with! I suppose we could always resort to pranking other muns for fun..."

"Ah, but that is not nearly as enjoyable, and you know it."

"Yep! Muns don't scare so easily, unlike po."

"Let's go then. If the rumors are true, a celestial's glowing form should be easy to spot in the dark of night."

CHAPTER 2

THE TWO DRIFTED EFFORTLESSLY INTO THE night, soaring with a smooth calmness one would expect from a leaf in the wind, if there was any natural wind to be had in Munderworld's uppermost layer.

Beneath the blanketing shadow of ever-lasting night, much life could be gleaned from the land below. The two entities were on top of their world. In the land of Dulrot, the highest and most peaceful realm of Munderworld, there was plenty of space to relieve oneself of their troubles. It was the most spacious territory, in that it was directly and incorporeally linked to the domain of the living, where the world of po once resided in the infinite black canvas of the universe. An endless variety of hills, mountains, trees, springs, and rocks covered the landscape in seemingly random and nonsensical order. The edges of the realms were constantly expanding, and the ground followed suit. It was a feature of Munderworld for things to make as little sense as possible, while paradoxically fitting together perfectly, akin to a jigsaw puzzle where the pieces constantly change shape.

The shifting of the land was a slow and gradual process, though to immortal beings a laboriously steady pace meant nothing. In fact, it was a favorite pastime for many a wandering mun to sit high up on a sequestered perch and look out to the horizon as it slowly crept away. The catharsis was enough to calm the most disturbed of muns, easing them into a meditative trance for at least a year or two. Dulrot, the land of dullness and stillness, lived up to its namesake in this way, despite for all intents and purposes being a place of punishment for po who were not deemed worthy enough at death to be accepted into a higher realm.

Faint hues could be seen peeking from the world below, signs of stray po souls going about their business. They emitted a soft, glowing aura that would normally be indistinguishable from average light, yet in the abyssal plane, they were distinct. It was more of a curse than a blessing, as it made concealment nigh impossible for the vulnerable souls.

From the above, however, the constant, twinkling dots of radiance dancing across the near-black ground resembled the star-filled night itself. As above and so below, a mun's view of the cosmos never truly faded.

On the formless horizon tiny threads of fierce white light cut into the otherwise placid landscape. They were both chaotic and frayed, yet they moved in unison with one another, as if with a singular purpose binding them together.

"You think that's it?" Fiddle said. "That's gotta be it! The apostle leading wayward po spirits!"

"Mayhaps," Cynkz replied. "Let's descend and fly low to the ground. It'd be best to remain unseen for now."

"Agreed."

Cynkz and Fiddle shifted a path against the treetops and gentle waves of sandy hills. They flew close enough to discern the source of the strange light and their purpose. They rested within the branches of a large, ash-textured oak and observed the scene.

"Look!" Fiddle said, exclaiming his remark with a pointed gesture. "It's an apostle!"

Hovering above a gentle collection of hills made of dark sand was an entity foreign to Munderworld. It could be described as an enormous fish, larger than any tree in Dulrot, and made entirely of light. Its scales were impossibly ornate and laid over each other in intricate patterns. Each scale poked out from the main body and formed rings that would bend back inward to overlay another scale that did the same. While the overwhelming radiance nearly burned out all color, faint hints of deep blue blending into vibrant greens and ending with varying tints and shades of gold filled in the outlines of its scales. Flowing through each scaled ring were the same threads of light noticed from the horizon, going in and out of nothing, appearing and reappearing in a never-ending rhythm. A dozen dark slits separated its body from its head, presumably gills of a sort. The head itself split into three; on either side lay half of its face, and in the center a new, fresh face emerged, cleaner and whiter than the rest of its body.

It moved slowly and deliberately, weaving through empty air like water. It swam in an orbital sequence, giving the impression of a swirling sphere of white and colored light from afar. It maintained this pattern as it moved forward, striking the eye with an uncanny sense of the being not existing presently in the same space as the world surrounding it, as if it were operating both within and without the observer's own plane of existence.

Below the light-bearing entity, a crowd of po trailed its movement. The po seemed as if they were a herd of lowly cattle being pulled along an invisible rail at the behest of their otherworldly shepherd. Most were garbed in simple, tattered rags, blending together in a sea of beiges and light browns. Each appeared gaunt and malnourished, as their sunken features and the dark crevices of their expressions contrasted deeply with their faint, radiating auras. Most of the muns in Dulrot were of a lesser breed, so few dared to attempt approaching the celestial. This in turn made the entity a sort of moving safe haven from the otherwise mild threats of the realm, prompting many po to follow and reach out for its light whenever it was near.

Despite this, a couple of the stronger muns, a class of sentinels tasked with guarding the edges of the realm, stayed near the entity's sides to maintain order. The two guards, while identical to one another, visually contradicted the divine spirit they escorted; each was lanky in form, with long limbs and strained, sinewy muscles wrapping around them, and perpetually hunched over, as if carrying a great weight. Their dull gray and purple skin forced bright pink scars to pop out. They were the lines of countless battles—or accidents, one could not assume either way—naturally leading the eye toward their covered heads. Long, gnarled snouts poked out from beneath loose hoods, concealing the rest of their features in a small shade. The asymmetrical off-white robes that wrapped around their bodies and led up to their crowns did little to hide their dour mood. Each clasped an absurdly long spear, their spindly fingers, bony joints, and dangerously sharp nails held their jagged weapons upright, often using them as walking sticks. Their combination of intimidation and gloom gave the impression that the guards had little patience for troublemakers, the one thing keeping the group of po following from acting out or fighting one another for the apostle's attention.

Fiddle slightly nudged his companion's arm and pointed a bony finger to the traveling group.

"Hey, Cynkz, look at the mun on the far side of the apostle. Isn't that Rackel?"

Cynkz noticed a familiar pink scar at the edge of the beastly mun's snout. It came from a small, deep cut along its lip, revealing the tiniest bit of yellowed canine.

"You're correct. That is definitely Rackel," Cynkz said.

"What are the odds, huh? Of all the dirty mun to be guarding this caravan, it had to be Rackel! You think he remembers the last time you—"

"Of course he remembers. There's not much else to do here than to distract oneself or think upon past grudges."

Cynkz reminded himself of past adventures. He could remember the first time he saw a sentinel, their frightening, thin silhouettes piercing the sky. He could remember hiding from them, in his fright discovering his abilities, and his eventual run in with Fiddle. Fiddle's nonchalant attitude toward the beasts put him at ease, and even led to the occasional conversation with them when alone. Rackel was the first and last time Cynkz could remember having a peaceful exchange with one of the beasts. Fiddle could not help but make light of their self-inflicted duty, and thus began the perpetual antagonism between himself and the sentinels.

"I guess that makes things a bit more interesting," Fiddle said with a strained, waspy breath. "I've heard stories about the apostles, and the threads of light constantly following them. Their power isn't like mun magic or our meager hexes. Apparently, a single thread from the lowest apostle can shape the world around it. Some say they can be used to enter dreams and shift time."

"That sounds like a tall tale muns share with one another to sound impressive."

"Maybe, but just think if we could get one! Wouldn't it be interesting to break it apart, see how it works? Maybe we could harness some of its power!"

"Harness its power?" Cynkz said, a tinge of bewilderment pitching his tone. "For what end? You plan on traversing the realms of Munderworld and usurping the King himself?"

"Ha! No, no. I was thinking we could make fireworks with it, maybe intimidate some po with bedazzling displays of holy miracles."

"Perhaps. It would make for a good story at least."

"Do you think we could pull it off?"

"Hmm."

Cynkz looked back to the apostle. The group moved in the opposite direction and slowly dragged countless heels across the sand, leaving a faint trail of raised dirt. Cynkz pulled at the coarse hairs of his goatee, then stopped, his grin revealing a self-assured thought.

"Old friend, I think I know exactly what we could do," Cynkz said.

"Really?! Splendid! How are we gonna do it?" Fiddle said.

"Adopt your smallest form and follow my lead. I'll disguise myself as a lowly po woman and blend in with the group. Once I begin a distraction, use the opportunity to swoop in and procure a thread."

"Perfect! Just ... be careful. Rackel will be looking for any excuse to cut you down, just like that tree from the cliff we dropped—"

"Worry not, my friend. None can pull a disguise like Cynkz the Jester!"

"Indeed! Let's go."

Fiddle burst into the shape of a tiny rodent small enough to fit in a child's palm. He was a drab mixture of coarse brown and white fur, body curled forward with an exceptionally long tail and relatively large, pink hind legs that pushed back and forth like bony springs.

Cynkz hovered to the desert's floor. His silhouette receded into colorless smoke. Out from the cloud emerged a small po woman bearing long, shiny black hair, dressed in dirty rags and youthful in appearance, looking of that awkward age between adolescence and adulthood.

Once settled, the duo drew near glowing formation on the horizon, beginning to act their roles. Cynkz, disguised as a young peasant girl, started to drag his heels and listlessly reach out toward the light. Fiddle stayed near his feet, occasionally twitching to clean his whiskers and skittering about, as if searching for food.

Cynkz felt the sharp sting of a whisker poking into his ankle and looked down to see what his companion wanted.

"Psst, Cynkz! Hey, Cynkz!" Fiddle whispered. "Your lead feet are sinking into the sand! It looks silly. Lighten up if you can!"

Fiddle was right. With each step, the frail-looking woman's legs sank nearly half a foot, leaving holes behind him. He began to deftly apply weight to his toes, then smoothly shifted his weight from the balls of his feet back toward his heel. The movement still left cavernous prints in the sand, but he was able to keep entirely above ground.

The overwhelming, all-consuming light emanating from the apostle revealed everything nearby. The two mischievous spirits knew that there was no room for error. Fiddle receded to the back of the group. He jumped onto the robes of a lumbering guard. Cynkz slowly made his way ahead, mimicking the gait of and occasional reaching gestures of the other desperate po.

Cynkz was squarely in the center of the group, surrounded by dozens of peasant and ragged po marching in unison. It was the perfect time to enact their plan. He lifted his foot and "tripped," falling to the ground. The po reacted, causing a wave of stuttered movement to disperse from the gathering of bodies. Everyone stopped. A couple of the po nearest to Cynkz reached out to help him up.

It was time to put on the show.

"Why…" Cynkz said, his voice sharp and light to match his disguise.

The apostle did not seem to notice but ceased its forward flight. The two guards perked up and shifted their spears to one hand so as to view the commotion.

"Why must we do this?" Cynkz continued. "Why must we suffer this?! Are we not worthy of salvation?! My mother, I haven't seen her in so long. Is she… is she even here…?"

"Quiet, little one," said one of the guards. "Be grateful you are granted the opportunity for salvation. If your mother is worthy, she will—"

"Worthy?!" Cynkz shrieked. "Who is so high on their own power that they get to determine who is and isn't 'worthy'?!"

The other guard, Rackel, curled his scarred lip, his grip tensing as he shifted his spear. He leaned forward, the glint of a fierce, peering eye shining as it focused on the source of the disturbance.

Fiddle, in his rodent form, prepared to spring for their prize.

Disorder rolled through the crowd. The shuffling of bodies and mumbling of voices grew to match the rising tension. Several began to express their own frustrations.

"Who is this wench?"

"In truth, I too wonder why we are forced into these rituals…"

"What right have you to question the Creator's order?"

"Silence, lest you spur the apostle's wrath!"

"Let the woman speak! She has the right!"

Rackel's patience, having reached its limit, compelled him to slam the blunt end of his spear into the ground with such force every po in range shook.

"Shut it! All of you!" Rackel said, hissing in his rage.

Cynkz, physically unfazed by the action, took notice of his companion as Fiddle was flung skyward by the blow and fell headfirst into the sand. He needed more time.

"You. I failed to notice your arrival. When did you get here?" Rackel said, pointing at the raucous young woman at the center of the crowd. "What spurred you to act out now of all times?"

"Well," Cynkz said, dusting himself off, "I didn't necessarily think of acting out. I'm just—overwhelmed by the—"

"Cynkz, that's you, isn't it?"

"E-excuse me?"

"I recognize your overacting anywhere. Your theatrics betray your shifting ability."

"I think you have me confused with someone else! I am merely a—"

"A scoundrel! I have not forgotten our last encounter! You and your lowly imp friend dropped a tree on my face!"

"It was an accident! Fiddle told you not to stand near the ledge!"

"Accident or not, your childish prank has left my beautiful maw scarred."

"Okay, look—"

Just as the argument between the two reached its peak, several other po focused their attention on the supposed young peasant woman standing before them. Countless whispers and mumblings echoed from the crowd.

"Is that … a mun?"

"A trickster lies in our midst?"

"What purpose would a mun have to hide among our kind?"

"Would a mun dare to seek salvation from an apostle?"

"What the—!? Something is crawling on my back!" the other guard screamed, stretching out and flailing at the back of the group.

Rackel, Cynkz, the downtrodden group of souls, and the heavenly entity focused their gaze on the sentinel swinging himself around in a mad fit. He reached over his shoulder with his bony limbs toward something on his back. A small rodent revealed itself near the brute's crown, caught with outstretched paws aimed toward the apostle itself.

Fiddle paused, then quickly turned his head to meet his gaze with dozens of wide, stretched open eyes as the po looked on.

A tense moment passed before the air was pierced with Rackel's wrath.

"That's it! I've had enough of these antics! Time to die again, scoundrels!"

The beastly guard slid his palms quickly along the shaft of his spear, using the momentum to slam the weapon toward Cynkz. Instantly, Cynkz burst into another cloud of smoke, narrowly dodging the spear's head as it struck the desert floor. The force was enough to send high walls of sand, and half a dozen po, flying into the air.

Cynkz slithered ahead at lightning speed in the form of a slick, iridescent serpent. He was sprinting to his friend, the small rodent still falling through the air from the shockwave of the prior attack.

Rackel's eyes followed Cynkz, and he called out to his fellow guard. "Hrike! Stay on guard! He's nearly at your feet!"

Hrike widened his stance, slid his feet apart, and shifted thrust his own spear at the serpent with lightning speed. Another wall of sand burst up, followed by another blast of that signature, colorless smoke. Just above the spear's head, another form faded into view—a crude approximation of the apostle! Cynkz, taking the form of a small, asymmetrical sea creature, spread out in the air and emitted a blast of blinding light. Rackel, Hrike, and the po still watching the altercation were disoriented with the overwhelming flash.

The true apostle was entirely undeterred, however, and focused its eye on Cynkz.

Cynkz, seeing his opportunity, returned to his original form. Just as he took hold of his friend, who had also returned to his own first form, a screeching wail pierced the air behind them. The apostle's three faces pointed directly at them. All of its light appeared to gather and fire in a single beam.

The blast cracked the ground at Cynkz' feet with such force Rackel, Hrike, and the nearby po were knocked back dozens of feet in all directions. Cynkz, with his friend in his arms, was shot up into the sky, and before long, the two disappeared into the cosmos.

CHAPTER 3

THE WORLD AROUND HIM WAS BRIGHT, SURREAL, and light. For a moment it was as if the weight of the world, and countless decisions and regrets, had been lifted from Cynkz's shoulders.

In front of him was a beautiful young woman, skin as clear and bright as a silk dress, shining brown hair that was dark as night, and two ice-blue eyes that pierced the soul. She was reaching out, the warmth of her palm resting upon his cheek. He caught her final few words.

"...to just, reach out, and accept them..."

He could feel his eyes widen, the skin on his brow and beneath his eyes compressing ever so slightly. His lips parted enough to allow words to pass when he was interrupted by a harsh clanging of wood as a deep, sad voice echoed from behind.

"My love! Lady Orilay! What is *he* doing here?!"

Just as he turned to greet the intrusive voice, the world faded into light, then receded beneath an instant curtain of darkness.

Cynkz could hardly tell whether he was still dreaming or not. The light was gone, but the same, weightless air lifted his body. He looked around to find himself floating aimlessly through space. An endless sea of radiant dots decorated the night sky. His scruffy companion was curled up and asleep by his side.

"Fiddle?" Cynkz said, nudging his friend's shoulder. "Fiddle! Are you all right?"

Fiddle's eyes crept open, followed by a stiff yawn and a jittery stretch, the kind one knows after a good nap.

"Ugh, finally," Fiddle said, half dozed and lethargic, "you're awake."

"What happened?" Cynkz asked. "I hardly remember anything after you…"

"Well, you came in to save me from the brutes, then the apostle—"

"The apostle?! And we're alive?"

"Yeah, you got us out of the way, though whatever force it used was immense. It sent the others flying and us into the sky. You were knocked out, but I kept an eye on you. You were asleep for a long time, so I decided to take a nap."

"I see. Thank you, and I'm glad you're all right, dear friend."

"I mean, it was *your* idea that got us into that mess. But you were also the one that saved me from obliteration, so I guess we're even!"

"If I recall, it was *your* suggestion to enact a plan to steal from the apostle, no?"

"Oh yeah! Ha!"

The two shared a chuckle, then a relieving sigh.

"Unfortunately, we seem to have failed in our quest," Cynkz said with a tinge of disappointment.

"Or *did* we?"

Fiddle pulled a fist from behind his back and turned it upward. Faint light seeped through the cracks of his digits. He slowly, dramatically, stretched his fingers to reveal a sliver of radiance clinging to the sandy skin of his palm.

"You got it!" Cynkz said. "You actually managed to pluck a celestial's hair!"

"It was pretty easy, what with all the chaos and distraction you were causing!"

"Well? Do you feel powerful enough to conquer the realms with a small piece of true divinity in your palm?"

"Actually, I don't feel anything. If I couldn't see it, I wouldn't know it was there."

"Truly? How bizarre..."

"Here," Fiddle said and offered the hair pinched between his finger and thumb. "You take it. Maybe you'll have a better idea of how to handle it."

Cynkz's curiosity peaked. If the thread had no effect on Fiddle, why would it be different for him? He reached out regardless and grasped the tiny sliver of light. Immediately, sensations ran through his fingers. Light tingles of electricity wormed their way into Cynkz's system like bugs crawling across his skin. The tickling worked its way to his head, and his mind was filled with several images: the woman from his vision, the sense of weight in the room the two were standing in, his emotions and even hers, and the dangerous aura of the voice that broke his dream.

His mind formed images of a king, perhaps several kings, lines of nobles and courtiers cajoling one another beneath colorful lights and glistening ballrooms. He was led to expansive green pastures in the countryside and could see simple people living simple lives within farmsteads. There was a family surrounding an elderly woman lying in bed, presumably sick and being doted on by her kin. Deeper in the vision, he could see a woman, the same woman who was lying in bed, but at a different time. She was being embraced by strands of light in corporeal form.

A light, raspy voice broke the vision, knocking Cynkz out of his trance.

"Cynkz? Hey, Cynkz! Are you there, buddy? Don't tell me you've fallen asleep again."

With a blink and a quick snap of his head, Cynkz was back in the void of space, a weightless soul drifting in the abyss. He stared at the thread, his mind swirling with thoughts, each like a finger grasping desperately for answers to his visions and his dreams.

"Are you okay, Cynkz?" Fiddle asked. "You're acting weird. Well, weirder than usual! Haha!"

"No I'm... I'm fine, thank you," Cynkz said.

"If you're ready, we should start heading back to Dulrot. Space is boring. I remember the way. Follow me."

Chapter 3

It was unclear just how long they had been drifting out in the void, then again, time meant nothing to muns. For what, to an observer, would seem like years, the two casually floated back to their home, passing countless stars and varicolored nebulas that painted the black canvas of space.

Not a moment passed on their journey where Cynkz did not ruminate on his experience. He was a naturally introspective, some would even say sensitive, soul to begin with. The recent happenings had shaken him to his core. He could hardly remember the po world, let alone his own time in it; his past, his family, his memories, even his parents or where they lived, felt wiped away like so many waves upon the rocky shores. The puzzle of the mysterious woman, or the unknown voice that barged in, nearly drove Cynkz into a fit. He needed answers, though he was not sure where to possibly begin looking.

Having endured enough, Cynkz accosted his companion with a mad idea.

"Fiddle…"

"Yeah, Cynkz?"

"When we were flung into the sky, and when I took hold of the thread, I was granted a dream, a vision…"

"Really?!" Fiddle jerked around to face his friend, his expression stretched. The whites of his eyes nearly consumed his pitch black irises. "W-what did you see? Do you think you were looking into the apostle's memories?"

"No, I think they were actually my own memories, back when I was a po."

"That's extraordinary! Who were you then?"

"I don't know… My visions were jumbled. None of it pieced together."

"Hmm," Fiddle exhaled, crossing his arms and rubbing his tiny, pointy chin with his fingers. "Maybe it was nothing."

"No," Cynkz said. "They were real. Somewhere deep within I could recall the specific feeling, the touch of a woman's hand on my cheek, and the same poem I have recalled since the beginning."

"Ah! A girl now? I figured you must have had someone sweet at some point in your existence. Did she… Did she have a sister, maybe?"

"Heh, no. I don't think so. Maybe she had a brother or perhaps was meant to marry someone else. I believe she was the one who first told me that poem. I don't know what to make of what I saw."

"Ah, that old nursery rhyme or whatever. There's not much we *can* do, aside from return home. That thread's a good keepsake of the experience."

"I think it's more than that, Fiddle."

"Hmm? How so?"

"I'd believe we could take this to the King himself at the bottom of Munderworld and wager for some answers."

"What?!" Fiddle screamed. "That's pure insanity! What makes you think a couple of derelicts, bums and scoundrels like us, could hope to pass through the lower realms? We'd surely befall a terrible fate, forced to die and relive the torment again and again!"

"You don't have to yell, Fiddle. I'm right here—"

"And if we *did* make it to the end, what do you know of the King himself? Who is to say he would not merely take the thread and throw us into the nearest pit?"

"True. Apparently, no one has seen the King in eons, long before the end of the po world."

"Exactly! For all we know he may not exist anymore, perhaps having fallen into whatever portal he used to bring Munderworld into existence."

"All the more reason to go forward with the venture. What are our mere pranks and tricks compared to a true adventure? We could become legends. We could conquer the ten realms of Munderworld, address the King himself, and—"

"Or," Fiddle interrupted, "we could trip and fall into the maw of a great chimera and be trapped by its innards for an eternity."

"We've gotten ourselves out of worse predicaments, Fiddle."

"I'll admit, all our time together, I've never seen you get injured or even die. It's really not so scary, as a mun dying in the Munderworld merely recollects their soul somewhere nearby. It feels pretty good actually."

"See? There's nothing to fear, old friend!"

"What? No! There's everything to fear!"

The riled imp stared into Cynkz's eyes. Fiddle was intense, nearly squinting, though he eventually relaxed, and let out a slow breath of relief.

"I know that look," Fiddle said. "When you're so sure of an idea, nothing can convince you otherwise, not even me. Fine, we'll try doing this 'adventure' of yours. But if it ends horribly, I will forever haunt your soul."

"Thank you, Fiddle," Cynkz said. "It means a lot—"

"I'm serious!" Fiddle said, interrupting Cynkz again, this time raising his arm to wag his finger in his friend's face. "I'll attach my tortured soul to your neck and whisper into your ear for all eternity: *Told ya so!*"

The two laughed, perhaps more heartily than they had before and began making their way toward the thin sliver of land on the horizon. The fields of Dulrot, the face of Munderworld, was in sight.

Chapter 4

"Het! Ghrey! In formation!"

The echo of a husky, rattled voice rolled into the darkness. After a moment's pause, two large figures could be seen flying toward the origin of the call. The figures revealed themselves to be sentinels, more of the drabby robed guards of the realm, each as scarred and long limbed as the last. With spear in hand, the two closed in on their leader, a larger sentinel bearing both a deep gray hood and various pieces of off-white plates of armor sat upon the beast's shoulders and arms. The cloth robe covering its midsection was cinched with a tight belt. Beneath the belt, the trailing ends of robe tapered into the air. It was a minor difference, but its plated garb was enough to distinguish it from its lesser peers.

"Did you find anything?" the commanding sentinel barked.

"No, sir," said Het, the shortest among the trio.

"What about you, Ghrey? Anything?"

"Afraid not, sir," Ghrey said, slightly taller and leaner than both his associate and his commander.

"Hmph. Let's go then. We'll trail the moving edge of Dulrot and skim for oddities."

The leader turned and flew toward the burning horizon with his two subordinates following.

Chapter 4

The trio flew in a triangle formation, soaring in perfect sync and at great speed, as if in a hurry. The tight form of their movements showed a sort of efficacy gained from countless years of experience. From below, many a single po and mun would look up to see the blazing trails of cloth cutting the sky. Most were prompted into hiding, afraid of drawing their attention, the same as smaller creatures and chimeric pests. From above, it looked little more interesting than seeing the occasional insect scurrying away when a larger creature walked into the area or overturned a rotted log.

The troupe reached the edge of the realm. A sharp, gnarled line of dark fire slowly burned into the abyss and revealed new land, expanding the realm into eternity.

"Why do we even bother with this?" Ghrey said. "What are we guarding anymore?"

"My thoughts exactly," Het said. "Who would be mad enough to try and cross to a lower, more dangerous plane?"

The leader stopped mid-flight, let out an angered sigh, and turned to face his followers.

"We do this because it is the order of the King himself. What we do here helps to maintain what little order holds Munderworld together."

"The King?" Het said. "No one has seen the King in eons! Who's to say he still persists? For all we know, he could have fallen into that pit he calls his throne, never to be heard from again."

"Our King, unlike you two, is bound and dedicated to his duty. This world is his, and he has no reason to abandon it."

"It's not much of a thing to brag about," Ghrey said. "The lands of Munderworld are beyond tarnished. His majesty's influence is hardly felt. What would he have to lose by merely going to the other si—"

"He would have everything to lose!" the leader snapped, a quick snarl interrupted the lesser guard. "One does not betray the Creator lightly. He knew what it would cost him to abandon His light to forge his own path."

Het and Ghrey shared a glance of worry before the shorter one looked back to his commander.

"You were there, right, Martus? When the King first broke off from the higher realms? Is what they say of the Creator true? That His light covers all, and pierces all, body and soul alike?"

"Yes," Martus responded. "Yes, it is all true. It is both the most beautiful and terrifying thing one could bear witness too. There is no hiding a*nything* from His eye."

"Then, how did the King do it?" Ghrey said, the nervousness of his demeanor showing from his shifting hands along his spear, trying to casually wipe away the sweat.

"I do not know how, exactly. All I know is that what you call the 'end of time' here, it was nothing compared to their battle. That was the one and only time I truly feared for the end."

Het lowered his own spear and curled his eyebrow, ready to ask another question.

"Then how—"

"Wait!"

Martus interrupted yet again, snapping his hand to signal silence. For nearly a minute the three intimidating muns were still in the air. A slight rustling could be heard from the darkened flora below.

Martus flew down first, fast enough to cause the wind around him to crash, and impaled his spear into the ground. Several trees and bursts of soil flew in all directions, leaving a hefty crater around him. Once he looked around, he noticed several ragged po cowering on the edges of the newly formed basin.

Het and Ghrey hovered over their leader, staring down the frightened souls.

"Hey! You little po scamps!" Het shouted, his voice rattling out of his snout like a powerful hiss. "You see anything weird lately? Heard of any muns scaring off an apostle?"

The group of po sat and shook in fear.

"Guess they don't know anything," Ghrey said with a shrug of his bony shoulders. "Though I wonder why they are so close to the realm's edge…"

Martus pulled his spear from the ground, making a loud thunk as a small trail of debris followed its jagged edge. He slammed the base of his weapon into the ground, then addressed the po himself.

"Leave and do not dare think of encroaching on the realm's border again."

The po merely sat frozen in fear. Martus, growing impatient growled, then lifted and slammed the base of his weapon into the dirt. The shockwave reverberating through the ground was enough for the po to shake, prompting them to get up and run off in the opposite direction, disappearing into the forest.

Once the sounds of their feet rustling through the foliage faded in the distance, Martus rolled his shoulders and readied more orders.

"Let's go."

Martus shot himself upward, Het and Ghrey shortly followed.

As the group flew closer to the edge of Dulrot, pitch black cinders and ash from the burning horizon disappeared into the dark sky above. Despite the massive scale of the phenomenon, the burning occurred slowly and made little sound. It barely registered to the flying beasts as they moved through the air, the wind pressing against their ears as they soared coating everything in a sharp hiss and whisking buzz.

"That is still the King's power, isn't it?" Het asked.

"Yes," Martus said. "So long as the burning edge continues to raze the abyss, we can rest assured that our King persists."

"How strong can he be to effortlessly cast such a hex from realms away?" Ghrey asked.

"Our King is indeed powerful. He was an Omun, after all."

"An Omun?!" Het shrieked. "An Omun? Like one of the apostles? Except way more powerful?"

"He was apparently a high ranking Omun, more powerful than even the apostles, perhaps even the strongest, second only to the Creator itself."

"For all we know, he could be doing this in his slumber," Het said.

"Perhaps, though I doubt he would deign to be so careless with his kingdom."

"Yet he refuses to reveal himself, to grant anyone an audience, to share the slightest shred of information as to his intentions?" Ghrey remarked, a bitter edge lining his skepticism.

"I cannot assume to know the wills or ends of higher beings. I am merely a sentinel, tasked with a most basic responsibility."

"Do you think he would know of the most recent apostle? And why it dispersed so quickly without taking a single po with it?" Het asked.

"More than likely, he is privy to all the goings-on in Munderworld."

"It's rare enough for an apostle to show up unannounced in Munderworld, and even more rare for one to leave empty-handed," Ghrey said.

"Who would be mad enough to disrupt the order of an apostle?" Het said.

"That is what we're trying to find out."

Just as they vanished into the distance, a group of frightened po rose from the shrubbery near the crater. "Hey, Fiddle! The coast is clear."

The several po bodies dispersed into a collective cloud of smoke, revealing a familiar pale jester with a long braid of shining black hair, his posture pushing out from his deep red and violet garb, and his stretched smile peeking from beneath his large, pointed tricorn hat, an expression of confidence he gained from a trick well done.

"That was close," Fiddle said, patting his hairy chest as he slowly flew out from behind a tree. "I always forget you can do that."

"Do what?" Cynkz asked.

"That you can split your shapeshifts into multiple parts. It really does the trick. No one ever seems to suspect it's the ruse of a single mun."

"That is true. Though you've got to be more careful, friend," Cynkz said. "When we're sneaking, even the slightest sound could alert every mun within earshot."

"Yeah, yeah, I know. It was a mistake, all right?"

"It was funny watching you sweat and trip over a mere leaf, just to fly into a wayward branch!"

"Psh, yeah, I bet."

The two looked cautiously at the burning horizon where the rift led to a lower realm.

"You sure you want to do this? There's still time to turn around and forget this mad pilgrimage," Fiddle said.

"No," Cynkz responded. "I've made up my mind. I'm tired of accepting things as they are, of bearing thoughts and guilt of things long past. I want to know more."

"Let's get to it, then. All we gotta do is fly past the horizon, and we'll be in the next realm. Do you remember what it was called?"

"The dark swamps of Gulligen."

"The land of infinite muck, the slow draw of tepid sludge that pulls the careless and negligent into unending silence."

"We'll have to be careful, Fiddle."

"Hey, we can fly, remember? How bad could it be? Hah!"

"That's the spirit! You may be a real adventurer yet."

Fiddle shrugged his small shoulders and smiled.

The jester looked back up toward the starry night sky, trying to recollect the fractured memories the thread revealed to him. The poem, the po in his memories, the lands that sprawled out before them. None of it made much sense but was intriguing enough to spur him forward.

The duo focused their eyes back on the rift and set forth as two red silhouettes disappearing into the abyssal border.

Chapter 5

A haze of yellow and green musk covered the sky, a flat and empty void blanketing the world in an oppressive, visual toxin. The swamp of Gulligen bore many legends, though few in Dulrot had ever experienced its perils for themselves. Still the tales of its bleak, all-consuming mire somehow spread far beyond its borders.

Beneath the clouded sky lay an infinite sea of black muck—countless, tepid waves of thick sludge ebbing and flowing to unknown forces trapped beneath. For scenery so ominous, the world was surprisingly calm. The soft ambience of slight bubbling and the quiet tapping of swamp bog slushing around permeated the atmosphere. Frail branches covered in glistening black and brown bark reached out like bony limbs writhing from the abyss. A dizzying variety of insects and pests flew in small collections of shining crimson and cerulean mixed with emerald greens and off-whites. Few of the creatures made any noise, and those that did barely registered the occasional humming in the distance. The static of numerous, tiny fibers flapping in the air harmonized with the crackling bubbles of the boiling mud. Everything was dark, slimy, and tranquil.

From the topmost layer of swamp, colorless vapors burst into the air, as if the mud was breathing. Two small reddish dots floated in the distance. The bog had visitors.

"There's no turning back now," Fiddle said. His tone was flat and failed to hide his unease.

"It will be all right, friend," Cynkz said. "Besides, what's an adventure without a little risk, eh?"

"I suppose you're right."

A number of oddly carved structures caught their eye. Clearly, they were manufactured instruments sticking out at random from the thick field of swamp.

"What are those things?" Fiddle asked, pointing to one nearby.

Cynkz squinted his eyes, focusing his gaze between compressed slits to discern as much detail from the foreign structures as possible.

Each stave was unique—every one a meticulous yet crude carving of long, asymmetrical bark. All of them expanded toward their top end, leaving room for a variety of trinkets and decorations: small animal skulls, teeth and claws, even some withered plants, though their luster had long since receded to time. Each one carried a small, tattered cloth loosely wrapped around it, usually beneath the jaw of the topmost skull. Their coarse visage showed careful planning behind their placement and were each given an uncanny amount of respect from the surrounding environment, remaining undisturbed no matter their location.

"There's an awful lot of them," Fiddle noted.

"They seem of a different plane," Cynkz said. "These carved sticks effortlessly resist the world around them."

"Who put them there? What purpose could they possibly serve in a place like this?"

"I cannot say. Perhaps we will meet their originators along the way."

"They'd have to be pretty tough, and obsessive, to go to the trouble of decorating a place like this with such efficacy."

"Ah! Efficacy!" Cynkz said, a quick turn of his shoulder to face his friend and expose a pleasing expression. "That's a good word. You're always picking up on them."

"I can't let you do all the fancy talkin'!"

A round of sharp chuckles rang from their chests, then simmered as the two resumed flight. Several minutes passed. The flat blocks of uniform color separating the black swamp and the yellowed sky blended together, rendering their progress less noticeable.

"We should try flying higher," Fiddle said. "Maybe we'll get a better view of where we are and if there's anything noteworthy that could lead us to the next realm. Maybe this place has a burning horizon like Dulrot?"

"Good idea," Cynkz replied.

The two arced upward, yet a hidden force kept them at altitude. The slow onset of frustration pulled their expressions inward as they wriggled and twisted to force themselves higher.

"Geez!" Fiddle exclaimed. "Why is this so hard? What's with this place?"

Fiddle looked to his friend, who appeared to be struggling more than him. The more Cynkz pushed, the more his body seemed to drag down toward the swampy sea. It took a moment before Fiddle realized what was going on. The thick vapors secreting from the bog were not as diaphanous as they appeared. Translucent streams slowly pushed up and around their bodies, forming a thin layer of near-invisible steam.

"The swamp!" Fiddle said. "It's pulling us down!"

"How in Munder is—"

"It's the vapor! Look! It's worming around us like a snake and weighing us down!"

Cynkz confirmed what his friend explained. Fiddle was animated, nearly spinning around completely, and flailing his stubby, red arms as if to fight the air itself. Cynkz looked to the sky, wondering if this would be their end, yet noticed something odd. High above them, a number of black birds effortlessly maintained their height. Cynkz could see the snapping of the raptor's pinions pushing the vapors away with ease. "Fiddle! I have an idea!" Cynkz said.

"Splendid! If you could hurry—"

Before the imp could finish his sentence, Cynkz spread his form and extended each limb of his body. His cloak burst into a great billow of colorless smoke, revealing two feathered wings attached to his back. First, he heaved them behind his body, then thrust forward, creating a substantial gale, strong enough to blow the vapors around them away into nothing. Both travelers jolted upward several feet like a spring action from excess weight being relieved.

"That was awesome!" Fiddle said. "How'd you figure that out?"

"I looked to the sky," Cynkz said between the occasional snapping of his own makeshift wings, "and noticed the birds were not struggling. They were pushing the heavy mist away with ease. I followed suit."

"Smart thinking," Fiddle replied.

Just as the two had grown comfortable, the tip of one of Cynkz's wings hit the swamp, scooping up a bit of the mud. A small portion grazed the end of Fiddle's foot, covering his toes.

"Ew, yuck! This stuff stinks!" Fiddle said. "It's heavy. Who'd have guessed?"

"My apologies, Fiddle," Cynkz said.

"Eh, no worries," Fiddle said, lightly waving his foot to shake off the debris.

The bits of muck hit the swamp bed and several bubbles formed around the area. Quickly, they gathered, and the cadence of their crackling grew in speed, forming a deep, echoing rumble that moved beneath the surface of the muck. It grew loud enough for Fiddle and Cynkz to notice from high up above.

"Hey, Cynkz, do you hear something—"

A great mass of bubbling mud pierced the flat yellow sky with a towering arc in an all-consuming bubble of noxious paint. Huge waves rolled from the rising mud, creating moving walls of muck that blotted out the heavens. A dragging slush echoed over the landscape, breaking the calm ambience with a blanket ready to smother the world.

Fiddle and Cynkz narrowly avoided the onslaught of sludge. They peered into the center of the chaos to see what had breached the surface.

"A chimera!" Fiddle screamed.

As the pool of black swamp matter settled, the top of a colossal beast appeared within. Its head was submerged and slowly receded away from the main body, a monumentally sized shell similar to a turtle's shell, except smoother, streamlined, and soft and leathery in texture. Its outline began broadly, then crudely tapered toward a rough tip. The rim of shell was serrated with lines of bony, deep yellow and orange spikes around the entire perimeter. At its tip, another broad, flat shape stuck out from below. A leather appendage, short and stocky, barely flapping out of the way to make room for its tail.

Perhaps the most impressive piece of the creature, its tail was flesh colored, shiny, and uniform in shape. The limb seemed to stretch out infinitely, poking brightly from beneath the dull, brown shell and disappearing into the swamp, hiding the creature's full length. One could only imagine the total breadth of the monster's reach, making facing its wrath a terrifying prospect.

At the creature's front, two large stumps crashed into the swamp with such force that it propelled forward at great speed. The shuffling of mud revealed a number of entities hanging on to the shell edge; countless po, a few small muns, and a mediocre variety of stumpy creatures and imps clung to the creature as it raced ahead. Gasps and murmurs accompanied the creature's movement as it moved like a train of the damned barreling through the abyss.

"What is it doing?" Fiddle asked.

Before Cynkz could reply, he took note of the creature's swerving motion.

"It's coming for us!" Cynkz said. "Move!"

With another thrust of his wings, Cynkz and Fiddle burst away from the monster, and the pursuit began.

Their red forms blazed across the yellow sky, parallel to the flat, black horizon. Smooth waves of mud gyrated behind the two. Cynkz and Fiddle, despite going as fast as they could manage, struggled with the constant, heavy vapors and gravity, a thick, invisible, perpetual pulling down of the body. Slowly, the pulsating mass of black swamp grew closer and closer to the two newcomers.

Fiddle slowed to lean close to his ally.

"Cynkz! I think we need to—*ack!*"

Something bright landed directly in Fiddle's mouth, most likely an insect flying about. Fiddle spun, desperately attempting to eject whatever it was from his throat. Spitting and crunching, he barreled toward the chimera.

"Fiddle! Hold on!" Cynkz yelled.

With a snap of his wings, Cynkz huddled into a ball, burst into smoke, and revealed his largest transformation yet. A massive serpent emerged bearing rows of emerald scales that faded into a golden-brown at their edges. Burnt orange hair flowed from his crown a third of the length of his body. Where the mane tapered off, a set of great wings extended, their thick, feathery forms contrasting with the smooth, scaly body. Each individual feather was a different shade: light oranges, dull yellows, harsh reds and smooth silvers. With each snap of the wings, their breadth nearly as long as the body, gales echoed beneath, pushing waves of muck and vapor away.

In this form, Cynkz's flight was powerful enough to shoot him toward his ally in time to catch him in his mouth, between one of his lower canines and a row of smaller fangs nearby. Before meeting the chimera head on, he was able to whip himself at a sharp angle. Cynkz skimmed off the top of its shell. Once Cynkz readjusted himself, he sped off in the opposite direction.

The chimera twisted around and leveled its entire body with the surface of the swamp. With another push of its stubby forelegs and a whip of its tail, it shot forth at an incalculable speed. The great serpent's flight left a significant draft behind it, aiding the swimming chimera in its assault. It caught up to Cynkz and Fiddle once again.

Both creatures streamlined their movement, moving parallel to the horizon. Just as the chimera was in reach of Cynkz, it poked its head out of the swamp and opened a pointed jaw. Cynkz twisted the base of his wings, forcing them flat against the wind. His body stopped midair and shot behind the chimera. Once above the beast's shell, Cynkz twisted his wings and leveled his flight.

Fiddle, who had his eyes shut tight, held on to Cynkz's lower canine. He forced himself to note the creature's back. The po were climbing on top of the creature's shell. He swore he could hear them chanting.

"All hail Andion of the murky abyss!"

"All praise Andion, the lord of sump and swamp!"

"Kill! Kill the usurper!"

"Uh oh," Fiddle mumbled.

The po began throwing sticks and mud at Cynkz. A few managed to form makeshift slings out of torn vines and cloth and hurled rocks.

"What's your problem?!" Fiddle screamed. He threw some of the debris back at the po, though most of it flew away once it hit the wind.

Several of the po bearing ragged robes and holding a small collection of twisted branches and vines, gathered and began chanting. Their words were indecipherable, a nonsensical collections of hums and random words and letters forced together. They synced their movements with one another, forming a single wave of motion in a small circle on the beast's back. They raised their crude instruments up and down, over and over, and slowly a thin mass of black muck gathered at their center.

Wow, are they casting a hex? Fiddle asked himself. *I figured only muns could do that!*

A shimmering ring bubbled around the po. t gathered and shot skyward, forming a great black sphere of reflected darkness. The po flung their arms toward Cynkz, and the murky orb flew in his direction.

Cynkz was well aware of the attack and shifted his wings to roll vertically, dodging the spell. Massive gusts of swamp vapor followed his maneuver.

By the time Cynkz readjusted his flight, the po were already huddled together, repeating the chant and concocting another incantation. This time, however, as they finished the final words of their chant, each po spread out in every direction. The black bubble forming between them splintered. Each fragment formed dozens of tiny orbs. Their arms flew up in unison, and a hail of muddy spheres were shot toward the flying serpent.

Cynkz rotated the base of his wings backward, flattening their span against the wind, causing him to brake midair and shoot back to the base of Andion's shell. Just ahead of him, the countless orbs fired into the sky, barely missing him. Once again the group of po immediately gathered and redoubled their efforts.

"Cynkz!" Fiddle yelled. "Get in close and I'll take care of 'em!"

Cynkz abided Fiddle's request. Fiddle quickly drew in a large breath and spat out a wave of bright orange fire along the shell. Most of the po merely flew off from the impact of the flames. A few burned, and in their smoldering state, they called out to their lord.

"Ahh! Andi-Andion! Murky lord! H-e-e-e-e-l-l-l-l-p-p-p-p…"

"Andion! Oh, Andion!"

"My lord, save me-e-e-e-e-e…"

One by one the po fell back into the swamp. Soon everything was clear, save for the large scorch marks on the chimera's shell.

"Yeah! We did it!" Fiddle said.

The swamp lord finally noticed a burning sensation and began to twist and torque its body violently. Cynkz flew up to avoid getting hit. He stared at the creature, unsure of what it was doing. A massive, looming shadow expanded above them. It was the chimera's tail! Its entire form was out of the swamp and curling toward Cynkz and Fiddle at full speed. The slow rumble of the mighty appendage grew like the shifting of rock during an earthquake.

Fiddle ran to the side of Cynkz's mouth and leaned out as far as he could.

"Cynkz!"

Cynkz realized what was going on. He whipped himself to his right, moving with such speed that the gust of wind from his wings created a booming crash against the swamp. He was not fast enough, and Andion's tail clipped the very end of his left wing with enough force to send Cynkz spiraling into the bog.

The beast instead hit its own shell, hard enough to send an ear splitting crack through the air. The impact left a massive, gnarled scar along the top of the creature's shell, revealing an oozing, glistening pink mass of guts and muscle underneath. It lifted its head to scream in pain before jerking itself around to begin disappearing into the swamp. Fiddle jumped out of Cynkz's mouth and looked at the chimera, watching carefully to make sure it was leaving. Cynkz returned to his own original form, holding his left arm, the wing that had been struck.

"We did it!" Fiddle yelled. "We did it! We did it! Looks like we're safe for now."

Fiddle looked to his friend, still holding and rubbing his arm.

"Are you okay, Cynkz? It looked like you took a hit."

"I'm all right. Just took a bump to the arm is all."

"That's good. Now we just need to—"

A slowly rising hiss grew beneath the two as mud was pulled away. A great crash of wet muck exploded, and the meaty appendage, the beast's tail, flung directly at Cynkz and Fiddle.

"Watch out!" Fiddle screamed.

Fiddle and Cynkz split apart. The beast's tail swung just between them, carrying huge chunks of swamp matter with it. The muck doused Fiddle and Cynkz entirely, and the two globs fell to the swamp, completely submerging them into a dark, silent fate.

CHAPTER 6

THE WORLD WAS DARK. EVERYTHING WAS blocked out by an impenetrable abyss. Cynkz tried to look around but could neither see nor perceive anything. The swamp had rendered him completely blind and deaf.

It was impossible to discern the direction he was going. Slowly, the weight of the mud around him pressed him into a curled position. He was suffocating, as if a great hand had clasped his entire body. His mind wandered, lost in the abyss. It was infinitely dark and quiet, more so than any perch up in Dulrot. Even then one could always look to the stars for some relief or guidance. Here, there was nothing beyond the weight of one's own body being forced to collapse unto itself.

Breathing was difficult; the pressure weighing down on his chest as he swirled through the muck only seemed to press down more as he tried to swim. With a final gasp, his anxiety turned to calm as he was left with no choice but to surrender himself to the heaving mire.

He could recall the face of the woman from his visions: her bright skin, piercing blue eyes, pitch black hair darker than the abyss in which Cynkz currently sat. He recalled the final lines of her poem.

Every star, near and far...

Waits for us, just...

Reach out and accept them...

To reach out for what? Cynkz thought to himself. *The stars? For warmth? For guidance?* Without context, it did not make sense to him, and it made even less sense that the poem had stuck with him for so long.

At that moment, he felt the small tug of something against his thigh.

The thread! Cynkz thought.

He slowly forced his arm through the muck and clasped the thin sliver of light. Somehow, amidst everything else, he could clearly perceive the thread in his hand as he pulled it in front of him. It felt as if something, or someone, were pulling relentlessly on the string. Something was guiding him.

That must be the way forward, Cynkz thought. His mind raced to find a way to move or push through, then he thought of Fiddle. *He can't be far. He was right next to me before we fell into the swamp, and I refuse to abandon my friend!*

Cynkz conceived a crude and simple solution. He would meet force with force, his weight against the void.

From above, the swamp's surface, for a time, was nearly flat and undisturbed. A quiet rumbling shifted the muck as pockets of air bubbled from below. An expanse of black mire shot upward and dispersed in all directions, revealing a new creature.

A massive hard-shelled reptile crashed against the sky, dragging waves and waves of black slime with it. Cynkz, now in the form of a great, though simple looking, turtle looked around desperately at what his transformation had unearthed from the swamp. Within the cavity rows of small po could be seen gasping for air. Dozens and dozens of small, emaciated bodies reached listlessly for the hazy yellow sky. Against the pitch-black swamp, their little lights resembled dim stars in the night sky. Branches, withered stones, and torn vines and plants provided some texture to the otherwise blank sea. Further inspection revealed tiny creatures, small muns that resembled alien critters, varying amounts of bony peach bodies with wiry limbs that stretched out tiny claws honed from years of swimming through the muck.

Desperate, Cynkz turned his leathery head back and forth, trying to find his friend. The corner of his eye caught the glimpse of a particularly energetic mass of deep red skin and brown fur coiling in circles—It was Fiddle! The large turtle swiveled in Fiddle's direction, then reared back and thrust into another burst of colorless smoke. From the dusty cloud emerged a large snake, nearly as long as the turtle, with a wide shovel-shaped head. The serpent swam toward Fiddle and wrapped around the small imp's waist, before shooting them farther into the swamp. Cynkz could feel the thread pulling him along, directing his path. He slithered his way through as fast as possible, with enough speed to avoid the collapse of surrounding swamp matter. The sensations guiding Cynkz were the pressing and shifting of the slime around him and the slight tugs of the thread.

On and on he made his way before suddenly bursting through a final layer of black matter into a great expanse. The serpent and the imp were now hundreds of feet in the open air. The quick release of breath was soon replaced with the internal pull of gravity that dragged the bodies to the newly discovered ground below.

CHAPTER 7

THE WEIGHTY SHIFTING OF MUCK WAS REPLACED with the hiss of air passing by as the two fell. Fiddle appeared to be unconscious, and Cynkz's eyes were still adjusting to the new light. His weightlessness was abruptly interrupted by the harsh crashing of their bodies against stone. As Cynkz regained a sense of where he was, he noticed a consistent rattling in the distance. Slowly, he rose and looked out onto the world before him, trying to parse what was in his line of vision.

They were resting on top of a huge mountain, a great, blocky stone that looked man-made. The landscape consisted of rows and rows of gray and white block stones, each one slowly shifting back and forth. It was as if they were resting on top of something living, and its breathing caused the structures to sway. The sky was a strange, desaturated blue and gray haze covering everything in sight. Farther up, they could see a thin black line covering the world like a murky ceiling, occasionally dripping black wet drops from its underside. The slight trickling of dark rain stained the otherwise smooth, light stones, though the usual splatter of their force hitting the rocky surfaces could not be heard over the constant rumble of mountains hitting mountains.

Cynkz noticed his friend, still curled and half-covered in black sludge. He rushed over to his companion and simultaneously brushed him off and nudged him. His jittery motions and the slight crack in his voice hinted at his fear: what if the imp didn't wake?

"Fiddle? Fiddle, come on. Wake up!" Cynkz said.

He continued to clean him off and rocked the little furred body back and forth before resting his hand on Fiddle's shoulder. Slowly, Cynkz pulled his hand back to his chest, his lips flattened, his eyes compressed and sparkled.

The silence was broken by a small huff and a cough.

"Fiddle!"

The imp began to hack and cough, spitting up several globs of ooze that hit the pavement hard enough to mimic the tapping of the trickling rain.

"You're alive!" Cynkz exclaimed. "Well, as alive as a mun can be, anyway."

Fiddle pushed himself up and rubbed his eyes in between several soft breaths of relief.

"I'm guessing you—" Fiddle said, interrupting himself with a cough. "I'm guessing you got me out of there. I had my big mouth open, and before I knew it, everything went black. I was suffocating or choking."

"It's fine, my friend," Cynkz said. "We're safe for now."

"Where are we?"

"I'm not certain. My knowledge of Munderworld's depths is limited beyond the first two layers."

"I've heard some of the sentinels, like Rackel, talking about some of the deeper levels."

Cynkz began to twirl the sharp hairs in his goatee, his mind pondering.

"Really?" Cynkz said. "What have you heard? I never expected Rackel of all people to carry much knowledge."

"Apparently, most of the sentinels come from here. Some of the lesser sentinels, like Rackel, are born here but don't stay. This realm is supposed to be a giant tomb for the legendary giant, Horgafell."

"Horgafell?!" Cynkz exclaimed. "The one true giant? Large as the moon? He who stood against the Munder King himself at the end of time?"

"That's the one. Most can't recall what the great giant looked like. Some of the sentinels believe it was the Munder King who decided to erase any immediate memories of his adversary from all beneath him."

"The Munder King seems incredible, if he can even alter people's memories."

"You think he could give us answers about the thread? And your weird visions?"

"Hmm."

Cynkz looked to his side, recalling the diaphanous string of light in his pocket and its effect in the swamp. He paused for a moment, reflecting on the troubles they have faced in such a short amount of time, and of the purpose of their journey.

"Cynkz?" Fiddle said.

"Ah, yes," Cynkz said, breaking from his trance. "I do believe if anyone would have answers for us, it would be the King himself."

"With the trouble we've been causing, I'm surprised he hasn't personally beckoned us!"

"Indeed! Yet our journey is far from over. Let's go cause more trouble."

"Fun, fun, fun, for the man and the mun!"

Cynkz sat up and drifting from the stone mountain, looking back to Fiddle.

"You still remember those old mun nursery rhymes?"

"A few, just the catchy ones."

"Let's head out and see if we can't figure out a path forward."

The two drifted along the gray horizon. From below, they hardly stood out; two small dark spots gliding along the even darker swamp centered in the sky above. Other than the great stone structures swaying to and fro and the light trickling of black rain, there was little to distinguish the landscape. It was a cold, barren, and overwhelming view all around.

Movement caught their attention. Faint lights scurried across the mountains.

"Look!" Fiddle said. "More po! What are they running from?"

As the faint lights scattered, a large, dark silhouette rose from a ledge of stone blocks; it was a sentinel, particularly bulkier and darker, though tall and sinewy. Deep purple skin poked out from beneath light blue cloth wrapped around black armor pauldrons and chest pieces. He carried no weapon, only a shield on his left arm. It was a giant rectangular slab of black and yellow that shined against the dim gray air.

"More sentinels… great," Fiddle said.

"I suppose the stories you heard held some truth," Cynkz said.

"I hate being right."

Cynkz smiled. "Let us go down and slither amongst the rocks. It would be best to not draw attention to ourselves."

"Good thought."

Cynkz and Fiddle flew along the edges of the moving rocky mountains and hid along their walls. They peered around a corner to observe the menacing figure.

The sentinel went after the small po, who were climbing and scurrying from the crevices between the stones like insects. The sentinel remained silent, and merely would focus its beady eyes on a po and come crashing down, either landing on top of them or sending them flying into the space between the stone blocks to be crushed. Not much could be heard from the po themselves, aside from the occasional bit of panting or crying. The terror in their eyes and the tension in their breath expressed pure shock. Again and again, the brute would fly up before crashing down again on his shield, mostly causing the po to spread and fly apart.

"What is he doing?" Fiddle whispered. "I've never seen a sentinel deliberately go after po, at least not without a good reason."

"Good question," Cynkz whispered back.

Once the group of po dispersed, the sentinel stopped and stood still, tilting his head upward. It appeared as if he was listening for something.

He coiled his legs and burst toward a seemingly random set of stone blocks about to collide into one another. He dove right between them and disappeared beneath their ledges. The shifting of the stones ceased and screaming could be heard coming from the crack.

Groups of po scrambled out from the ledge. Countless thin and frail limbs waved and scratched as they pulled their bodies above and ran. The sentinel ascended and repeated his assault on the new group. The trickling of heavy rain, followed by scraping of tiny po hands and nails against stone, capping off with the thunderous heaving of heavy metals as it crashed upon them; this was the steady rhythm of silence and chaos defining the realm.

"Looks like po are trying to hide," Cynkz said.

"Who knew the sentinels were strong enough to move mountains like that?" Fiddle said.

"We may be dealing with a new form of sentinel, one reserved for the deeper layers."

"Maybe that's why Rackel is always angry? Because he isn't strong enough to handle a place like this?"

"I believe his anger has more to do with *us* than anything else."

"I mean… Yeah, that makes more sense."

The sentinel raised his head again and listened, this time for longer. Eventually, he flew up into the sky and off into the distance, disappearing behind the rows of shifting stones on the horizon.

"Let's continue," Cynkz said.

They continued along the ground, flying between countless boulders and blocks. They drifted upward again and into the sky, giving them a broad view of the world. From on high, the ground looked like a series of tiles being gently pulled and pushed across one another.

Something stood out to Cynkz; in the distance, another pale light could be seen ascending the side wall of one of the stony blocks. Something, or someone, was climbing up toward the edge of a nearby cliff. Cynkz quietly drifted toward the light, revealing a young po woman desperately trying to climb the vertical surface. Her hair was long, almost reaching the middle of her back. It was straight and shining, and nearly as black as Cynkz's own hair. Her skin was bright and supple, and her thin wrists and ankles gave her the appearance of a growing youth. Her nails were bloodied, and the bottoms of her feet showed several scars and were covered in a thin layer of dirt. It seemed as if she had been climbing for a while; to where, and for what reason, Cynkz did not know, but his curiosity was piqued.

A small crack pierced the air. Several rocks broke away from the wall, bouncing off the wall before falling into the crevice. The woman's body stuttered, then began to slip. She tried to claw at the wall but it was too late; her hand slipped. Soon her foot followed suit, and her entire body fell back.

Cynkz flung himself as fast as he could toward the falling woman. He could see her reddened hands reaching through the many strands of black hair and her tattered gown flying upward. He grabbed her hand, easing his flight so as to not pull on her limb excessively, and began flying them up the mountain wall.

"You really should be more careful, madam," Cynkz said.

She was still breathing heavily but settled once the realization she had been saved became apparent. She looked up to the stranger holding her, who was still looking toward the top of the cliff.

"Don't worry. I can take you to the top of this boulder," Cynkz said. "But what exactly are you trying to do—?"

"Let go of me!" she screamed.

Cynkz's flight skittered, completely unprepared for such a reaction.

"Madam, please, we're almost at the top. Just let me—"

"Let go!" she screamed again. "I don't need some strange man's help! Let go! I can do it myself!"

Just as the two reached the top of the wall, the woman twisted and torqued her body violently. Cynkz reached down with his other hand to try and get a hold of her. Just as his hand came down, the woman scratched Cynkz as hard as she could. Her bloody fingernails sank into his pale skin, leaving a gnarled trail of deep red and pink lines on the back of his hand. He recoiled from the slight pain, releasing his grip, and dropped her on top of the stone surface.

Cynkz gripped his hand and glared at the woman. Fiddle came flying as quickly as he could manage, stopping at Cynkz's side.

"Cynkz! Are you okay? What happened—" Fiddle noticed the scars on Cynkz's hand.

Cynkz looked at the po woman, his squinted stare meeting hers.

"I don't need anyone's help," the woman said beneath her breath.

"What?" Fiddle asked.

"I don't need anyone's help! I can become one of the Sisters on my own!"

Fiddle flew in front of Cynkz and down to eye level with the woman. A raised eyebrow replaced his previously worried expression.

"Sisters? What are you talking about?" Fiddle asked.

"Don't play stupid with me," she said. "I'm not falling for any more tricks!"

She began to walk backward, away from the two, both of her hands up to her chest and clasping one another.

"I *will* become one of the great Sisters," she said. "And when I do, I will curse the both of you to the deepest pits of—"

Her heel sank into a small puddle of black ooze, causing her leg to fly up as the rest of her body tumbled backward. The slick of wet sludge swooping up was followed by the thumps of flesh and bone rolling along the ground. Soon the woman was falling over another ledge.

Cynkz's eyes widened. Instinctively, he reached for her, but it was too late. The woman fell off the ledge and was halfway into a deep crevice by the time he reached her spot on the cliff. Cynkz and Fiddle watched her fall into the darkness just as the two rock faces pressed together.

Cynkz stared in silence, his brow pressing down, and his cheeks pulling on their bottom lids into his mouth, now slightly open and breathless.

"Well," Fiddle said, before looking at his friend. "I figured you were better with the ladies, Cynkz! Guess you can't win them all…"

Fiddle noted his friend's expression and the complete lack of response to his teasing. He placed his small, clawed hand on Cynkz arm and patted it, trying to comfort him.

"It's all right, Cynkz," Fiddle said. "You did what you could. Don't blame yourself for trying to help."

Cynkz took a small breath and lightly nodded.

"Come on. Let's get out of here," Fiddle said. The two turned and drifted into the sky once again.

After some time drifting in silence, Fiddle decided to start a conversation, anything to get Cynkz's mind off of what happened earlier.

"What are the 'Sisters' supposed to be?" Fiddle asked.

"I'm not sure," Cynkz said.

"I've never heard of any 'Sisters' before. Whatever they are, they must be pretty secretive, or live somewhere deep into Munderworld."

"Even here, in this nonsensical world, word travels far."

"You think they're some kind of monster? Maybe it's a giant, pregnant spider chimera! With a million arms leading to a million hands with faces, all women, all 'sisters,' and maybe the body is chunky and it's constantly spewing out babies and—"

Cynkz glared at Fiddle, his eyes pressed into thin slits over a raised eyebrow.

"Or maybe I'm just rambling," Fiddle said. "I'm sure we'll happen across them at some point on our adventure."

Just as the two shared a smile, a thundering crash echoed from afar. Screams and wails followed, interrupting the slow, rolling ambience of the rocky landscape.

"You think it's another sentinel hunting po?" Fiddle asked.

"Most likely," Cynkz said. "Let's investigate again. One of them has to lead to something—"

"Psst! Hey! You two! Get down, will you?"

Their eyes darted back and forth as they turned their heads to find out who was speaking.

"Hey! Down here! If you stay out there, you're gonna give away our hiding spot!"

Cynkz and Fiddle looked at each other, then straight below them. Deep within one of the crevices, a faint light flickered from its depths. The frame of a small po man motioned his arm toward them. He appeared to be leaning out from a cave embedded in the mountain.

"If you two need somewhere to hide, we have plenty of room in here. Just hurry up and get out of the sky!"

Fiddle leaned against Cynkz and whispered, "You think it's a trap, Cynkz?"

"Mayhaps, though we have no other leads right now. He may know something, and I doubt he's in any way affiliated with the sentinels."

"Agreed," Fiddle said. "Let's go see what he's got for us."

The two angled downward and flew below the ledge of the stone structures. The po retreated into the opening, and Cynkz entered the cave first. He was greeted with a group of eyes staring back at him. There was just as much variation in their expression as their physical builds. Some of the po possessed much darker skin, with equally dark hair and eyes—features that contrasted with their ragged robes and the signature faint bright light all po emitted. Several children huddled together in a corner. A much older po woman with particularly ratty blonde-gray hair clumped like lumps of dried wax and enough lines around her eyes to make her face look grainy, glared at Cynkz.

The inside of the cave was dim, only lit by the sliver of distant light from the world above. A small shadow broke the light as Fiddle entered and revealed himself to the group. Fiddle looked around and, for once, was not quite sure what to say.

The po man who called to them stepped forward with a calm, relaxed gait.

"Hello, travelers," the man said. "Welcome to our temporary home."

"I suppose you all are hiding from the sentinels above?" Cynkz said.

"Ah, so that's what they're called," the man said.

"Well yeah," Fiddle said. "That's what everyone calls 'em, or at least what everyone has called them for as long as I can remember."

"We don't exactly have time to ponder such things here," the man said. "But you'll have to excuse my manners. My name is Kadd."

"Kadd?" Fiddle said. "That's a pretty weird name for a po."

"What is your name then, little one?"

"I'm Fiddle!"

Kadd smiled, the crevices around his nose deepened as the corners of his lips pressed his tanned cheeks into his eyes.

"Fiddle?" Kadd said. "Like the instrument?"

"I mean, it's just what everyone calls me. It stuck, you know?"

"I understand." Kadd looked at Cynkz, his brown eyes taking an extra second or two to look the jester up and down before settling back on his gaze. "And you, good sir?"

"My name is Cynkz, a pleasure to meet you all," Cynkz said.

"Cynkz? How is it spelled?"

"C-Y-N-K-Z!" Fiddle said. "It's said like 'sink,' but the 'z' is silent."

"Well, now *that* is a peculiar name," Kadd said, turning his head slightly, his eyes shifting back and forth as he tried to think the information out in his mind.

"It's the name that he came with," Fiddle said. "I like it."

"It's also one of the few things I remember from my time in Peara, the po world," Cynkz said.

"You were a po? What era? You look like you were an old jester of some sort," Kadd said. "I was born in the south Polenic region in 1681."

"That is correct. I was indeed a courtier and a jester," Cynkz said as he slightly adjusted his cloak and evening out the seams along his shoulders. "Though I believe you may have been born ahead of my time."

"Really? Both a courtier *and* a jester? You were intent on rubbing shoulders with the highest nobility, weren't you?"

"I believe so, yes."

"You truly do not remember much of your time alive, do you?"

"Unfortunately, no."

"You speak well. And considering your proclaimed titles, you were obviously educated."

"Yeah, he talks smart, sometimes," Fiddle said. "Though he comes up with the silliest ideas."

"Really?" Kadd said, perking up an eyebrow at the small imp. "Silly ideas? Such as what, if you don't mind me asking?"

"Like wanting to leave the cozy air of Dulrot to go looking for some king at the bottom of this cesspit of a world." Fiddle half-spun in midair, as if getting out his frustrations the way a child would throw a tantrum.

"King? What king?" Kadd asked.

"The Munder King! The Overseer of Munderworld! He Who Peers Into the Darkness!" Fiddle appeared to grow agitated, flailing his stubby arms as he spoke.

"So this place has a king. How strange…"

"Your king can go rot, for all I care," a raspy voice hissed from the back of the room, leading all eyes to the wrinkled woman sitting alone.

"Harla, please," Kadd said. "There's no need to be rude."

"Pah!" Harla scuffed. "What place is there for politeness in this wretched place? We are like insects, forced to scurry like ants to avoid getting attacked by those monsters. All just so we can fall into the depths of these caverns to get crushed by these nonsensical, giant slabs of rock."

"Is there any way out of here?" Fiddle asked.

"Why would I tell you anything, you scraggly mun?" Harla exclaimed. The tinge of bitterness laced her voice with a trailing hiss.

Fiddle gritted his teeth and inhaled a sharp breath through his flared nostrils. "Who are you calling scraggly?! You old—"

A crash thundered from the roof of the cavern. Their eyes widened and looked up to the pebbles and dirt falling from the ceiling. Several heaving thumps moved toward the thin sliver of light coming from the opening. A bulky shadow broke the center of the thin ray of light, and the space between the cavern's entrance and the wall of the mountain began to spread.

"Quickly," Cynkz whispered, turning to the group behind him. "Everyone, get against the wall and remain still."

The large shadow descended toward the cavern. Another large sentinel stretched his snout into the cavern, followed by the glint of a beady black eye. His own growling was nearly as loud as the rumbling of the shifting boulders and echoed throughout the small cave. His eyes darted, looking for signs of life, yet his vision was greeted with nothing but an empty, rocky space. He stared, then slowly rose out from the crevice, and his shadow disappeared back into the light.

The silence soon returned to the constant rolling of moving mountains, of rock grinding against rock. The room burst into clouds of colorless smoke, revealing Cynkz, Fiddle, and the po pressing against the dim cavern walls.

"W-what was that?" Kadd asked.

"Cynkz is a master shapeshifter!" Fiddle exclaimed. "It's the one thing he's good at."

"Just one thing?" Cynkz said with a raised eyebrow and a half-smile.

"I didn't mean it like that. It's just your master stroke, that's all!"

Cynzk chuckled, then looked at the group of po.

"Is everyone all right?" Cynkz asked. "Transformation is a bit uncomfortable for—"

"Ack!" Harla shrieked. "What spell did you cast on us, monster? It felt as if the weight of the world was bearing down on my chest."

"It's heavy, right?" Fiddle said. "I'm always telling him his disguises are so heavy."

"You two are quite the dynamic duo," Kadd said. "Thank you, good sir. You have bought us a bit of relief, though probably not much."

"What are you two trying to do, anyway?" asked one of the other po in the back of the group.

"We are trying to get farther down into Munderworld," Cynkz said. "We are trying to reach the King."

"But why?" the po asked again.

"Well," Fiddle said, "we got a hold of a piece of light from an apostle who—"

Cynkz raised his arm in front of Fiddle, prompting him to stop.

"Our reasons are our own," Cynkz said.

Kadd looked Cynkz directly in the eye, his own weathered squint leveled with Cynkz's sharp eyes and stern brow.

"I see," Kadd said. "We will pry no further then. Actually, perhaps we can assist one another."

"How so?" Cynkz asked.

"I've spent many, many years here. Once you grow accustomed to running for your well-being, and getting crushed either beneath the heel of the beasts or between the mountains, you begin to notice some things."

"You're wasting your breath, Kadd," Harla snarled.

"Harla!" Kadd snapped back. "Please, it is better if we can work together."

Harla glared at Kadd, then pulled herself into a curled position back in the corner of the cavern, resting her head in her arms. She mumbled something under her breath, but Kadd turned back to Cynkz.

Kadd continued, "The 'sentinels,' as you call them, will regularly gather together after a time. After their meeting, they will disappear, giving us a slight reprieve."

"Where do they go?" Fiddle asked.

"I am not sure," Kadd said. "But I believe I have heard murmurings of a portal of some sort leading to the lower realms. Specifically, they seem to look forward to their time of leave in the neighboring realm."

"I suppose nearly anything is preferable to the infinite swamp above or the dull grayness of this place," Cynkz said.

"Perhaps," Kadd said. "If there was a way to sneak by and observe them, to follow them as they are leaving to see where this 'portal' is, it could very well be your ticket out of here."

"Why would you want to help us, anyway?" Fiddle asked again.

Kadd smiled warmly at the imp before answering. "You ask many questions, little one. That is good! That is how you learn."

"I suppose so," Fiddle said. "Still, I wanna know why you're helping us."

"Because," Kadd said, "anything has to be better than this. I am willing to take the chance of whatever another realm may offer over this droll existence. If the beasts are going there for recreation, then it may very well give each of us a chance at something better."

"I cannot make any guarantees," Cynkz said, his brow flattening above his eyes.

"I know," Kadd said. "But it is something. It is an opportunity for something, anything, beyond this. I am willing to try and make something of it."

"So how do we go about tailing one of these guys?" Fiddle asked.

"Your friend here is a master of disguise, correct? Why not have him take on the role of a sentinel and try to blend in?"

"I'd rather not leave you all vulnerable," Cynkz said. "I can at least keep you hidden."

"Then what are we—Oh no..." Fiddle trailed off when he noticed Cynkz smiling at him.

"There's no way I could—"

"Fiddle," Cynkz said, "you do not need to disguise yourself. You possess several abilities, best of which is your skill for turning into shadows."

"Yeah, but it's a lot of work!" Fiddle exclaimed, pulling his hands and shoulders upward into a deep shrug. "It takes so much concentration, and if I mess up—"

"I know you can do it, Fiddle," Cynkz said. "You're more skilled than you know."

Fiddle looked around the room, noticing the different pairs of eyes staring back at him. Even Harla seemed to be looking on with a softer expression.

"Fine, fine!" Fiddle said. "I'll do it."

"Thank you, Fiddle," Kadd said. "You're doing us a great favor."

"Eh, it's what I do," Fiddle said. "Just ask Cynkz! I help him out all the time."

"Be careful, friend. If anything goes wrong, or you learn anything, return posthaste," Cynkz said.

"I got it, I got it. I'll be back before you know it!"

Fiddle drifted toward the cavern's opening. The shade within the cave grew dark and heavy, as if an invisible hand were closing over everyone inside. The imp's form faded into the darkness, where it gathered and slithered out into the light. As it left, the atmosphere lightened, leaving a comfortable—if dull—shadow behind it.

Chapter 8

In the center of the flat, gray sky stood a lone beast. It was a great sentinel built like a marble statue. His dark gray skin twinkled against the pale light of the realm. Darker still was his armor, black and rimmed with scratched gold—a sign of the many fights and scuffles he had gotten into over countless millennia. He was taller than most sentinels, and strangely bulky, with packets of dense muscle poking out between layers of armor, all loosely covered with his signature cloth. In his offhand, he held a thin spear, significantly longer than his own body. It appeared as a black rod of obsidian. He held the spear casually, comfortably, as one with experience would use a dangerous weapon.

The sentinel tilted his head back, opened his jaws, and out came a bellowing call. It shot off in all directions, seemingly for eternity. A deep, aural shattering of the air that rolled outward like waves crashing against the air. To the po, it was a frightening omen. Its sounds would rattle their small frail bodies from within, forcing their brittle bones with enough force to paralyze them. For sentinels, however, it was merely a call to action—their leader beckoning them to formation.

Several large bodies rose out from below the rocky mountains in the distance. Similarly, large sentinels came flying over the horizon, from behind mountains and ledges, and a few from the great black expanse in the sky's center. They gathered in front of the source of their beckoning. Floating in a line stood nearly twenty different sentinels, each a slight variation of the same form. Backs straight and chests puffed out, they were completely still save for the billowing of cloth trailing in the wind. From afar, it almost looked like a row of flags flowing against one another.

"Looks like everyone is here," the leader bellowed in a deep, guttural voice.

"We've done a pretty good job clearing out of the nearby caverns," another sentinel said, his voice much lighter and snappier.

"Not good enough," the commanding sentinel said. "I want everyone to do one more sweep of the area. No one gets access to the next realm's pleasantries until this place has been swept clean."

Complaints and whines echoed from the group. Some threw their arms around and another rubbed his eyes.

"Aww, c'mon."

"I swear I've gone in and out of these mountains a million times."

"I just want some time off. I need some of that good stuff from the next realm over."

"Silence!!" the commander barked. It was loud enough to shake the mountains shifting below. Every sentinel in the group shot up, their postures straightened like rods, their heads snapping up and looking forward. The commander inspected each of his soldiers, from left to right. His aura proved to be as heavy as his voice; one could feel the weight of his glare bearing down.

"We are done when I say we're done," the commander said. "Now go. Everyone split up and search as far as you can. I'll call you back when we are done. Dismissed."

Immediately, the group dispersed. The whipping of their cloaks in the wind mimicked the flapping of wings. Lanky bodies stretched out into the distance in all directions. The shadows they cast on the pale ground beneath fluttered and danced. The commanding sentinel remained still, watching his subordinates leave. The commanding brute slowly drifted to commence with his own search, yet a small part of his shadow remained in the crevice beneath.

What were they talking about? Fiddle thought. *Pleasantries? This seems interesting!*

The small shadow slithered along the rocky walls, dipping in and out of the shade of the crevices beneath the sentinel.

"Hmph," the commander grunted. "These sentinels are worthless. Hardly a worthy soldier among the lot of them. Young and spoiled."

Typical old man, Fiddle thought, grumbling complaints to himself. *What a loon.*

The sentinel continued his lazy flight. He looked halfheartedly, his head barely tilting to the left or right to give a good view of the world beneath him.

This is going too slow, Fiddle pondered. *He won't leave until he's riled up some po. I know! I'll find some and get them moving. Maybe then he'll be satisfied.*

Fiddle, still a flat, black shadow, weaved in and out of the crevices looking for any openings similar to the one Cynkz and the group were hiding while keeping an eye on the floating commander sentinel.

The scraping of small pebbles caught Fiddle's ear. Fortunately, it was faint enough to not draw the sentinel's attention.

That's gotta be a group of po! Fiddle thought.

His shadow slipped and crawled along several edges before happening upon a cavern with a group of frail-looking souls huddled inside. Each was just as ragged and sickly looking as the rest of the po with Cynkz; dark eyes with darker bags beneath them led to the harsh dents of sucked cheeks and gaunt faces. Their hair was just as messy and tattered as the rags they wore on their bodies. Fiddle never thought much of most po, though seeing them in such distress forced an emotion within him. He began to understand why Cynkz was sympathetic to them.

Fiddle slid to the top of the opening's ledge and peered down into the cave.

"Psst! Hey! You po! Want a better hiding spot?"

All of their sunken eyes widened, the whites surrounding their pupils lighting up like sparks in the dark. They darted their heads back and forth, looking for the source of the strange voice calling to them.

"Hey, I'm talking to you!" Fiddle said. "Oh wait, I should probably turn normal again."

A black sliver dripped onto the cavern floor into a plump approximation of the imp.

"See?" Fiddle said, stretching his small arms out. "I'm no threat! I just want your help."

"W-what are you?" a male po sitting in the front of the group asked.

"I'm Fiddle! But we can chat later. I need you guys to be a distraction, and—"

"A what?!" the male po said.

"Maybe that wasn't the best way to put it."

A small woman emerged from the back of the group, her tilted head matching the angle of her confused expression.

"What in Munderworld are you after, little imp?" she said. "Are you trying to lure us to those horrid beasts outside? What do you get out of it?"

"No! No, I hate sentinels. They're all so boring and angry all the time."

"So, you're not with *them?*" the man asked.

"For the last time, no!" Fiddle exclaimed. "In fact, me and my friend are working on getting out of here."

"T-There's a way out?" one of the po asked.

"Apparent—" Fiddle stopped himself, thinking it would be easier to convince the group to go along if he expressed confidence. Cynkz often spoke of "committing to your role" when it came to persuasion. "Yes! Yes, we've figured something out. But I need your help."

"Why should we trust you?" the man in the front said, glaring at the sharp glint of light out of the corner of his eye.

"Because what else are you gonna do? Sit here and wait to be crushed?"

The po softened their expressions. After sharing a few murmurings, they looked to the imp in unison. For once, Fiddle found himself caught off guard. He felt the bitter sting of anxiety as he was forced to bear the gaze of dozens of eyes. Both his brow and lips flattened, and for a moment, he nearly stepped back and tripped but steeled himself to maintain his air of confidence.

"Fine," the man said. "We'll help you. What do you want us to do?"

"It'll be easy," Fiddle said, thumbing the tip of his small, pointed nose. "Come out and help me create a distraction! I can take the brunt of the sentinel's force. Once he has had his fill, you will just need to hide for a bit and pretend to be scattered. The safe haven is a bit to the south, the opposite direction I move. You should have little trouble finding it."

"Are there others like us there?" the woman asked.

"Yeah, quite a few actually. You know a guy named Kadd?"

"Kadd?!" the woman said. "I have not seen him in ages. I see he is still trying to help people, no matter how futile it may be."

"He's with my friend, Cynkz."

"Who?"

"Um, you'll know him when you see him. He's tall, real lanky, and thin. Pale skin as bright as moonlight and a long braid of pitch black hair. Wears a dark red and purple jester's outfit with a pointy hat. He can shapeshift and is keeping everyone safe until I get back."

"How odd," the man said.

"I think he's kinda funny looking too, but he's my good friend. He's gooder than me! He'll keep you safe."

"Thank you, little one. Thank you so much."

"Don't mention it! Just be careful, and remember—"

"The opposite direction you move in, to the south, we'll remember."

"Good. Now I gotta try shapeshifting again…"

Fiddle stepped back, stretched out his little red arms, and slowly faded into a billowing cloud of black smoke. As the fumes dispersed, a new form arose: a short, pudgy po man with a bald head and stubby limbs. At a glance he seemed to be unremarkable, though closer inspection revealed little oddities. His brown eyes were too small and beady, his nose was too big, and his face appeared too big for his head, sitting upon a lumpy stump of a neck. His portly physique betrayed stocky limbs that appeared as if they had grown hard from overuse. His posture possessed a slight arch at the top of his back that lessened his height significantly and caused his large nose and head to shoot forward. His ears were small and round. A number of random little hairs stuck to their ends. It was a rather poor approximation of what someone might think a po looks like, while missing every necessary detail.

As Fiddle drew his first breath as a po, he opened his eyes, only to be greeted with the half-smiles of the group before him. Sharp cackles of restrained laughter shot out from the center of the group. Fiddle's brow and lips flattened as he parsed everyone's reactions.

"What?" Fiddle said, in a huskier voice that rattled phlegm as he spoke. "What's wrong? I look like a po, no?"

"Y-yes, you do," the man said. "We'll wait for your signal, then we'll climb out and try as best we can to aid in your distraction."

Fiddle nodded and turned to the cavern's opening. He waddled carelessly to the precipice and began to claw upward. A thought ran through Fiddle's mind: *Geez, I can never get used to how heavy it is to be a po.*

As soon as he reached the top of the stone structure, Fiddle peaked from the ledge and saw the sentinel sitting a fair ways in the distance. Fiddle leaned down, hanging on with one arm and tapping the rock wall with his other hand, prompting the group to poke their heads out. Fiddle gestured at the group to come forth, and immediately thin po hands and limbs ascended the wall.

By the time the group reached the top of the stone wall, Fiddle was sneaking forward, readying himself for his act. Looking over his shoulder, he confirmed they were ready, took a large step forward, and 'tripped,' falling to the ground. "Hwoof!!"

The sentinel stopped. Slowly, he peered over his shoulder. His stubby snout came into view, exposing more and more of his curled lips. His small, beady eye, the sharp reflection of the realm's dim light shone like a piercing star.

Fiddle, partly laying on the ground, stared the sentinel straight in the eye. is experience with Rackel in Dulrot had taught him a few things about sentinels, not least of which was their absolute intolerance for disrespect or obstinacy. For a lowly po to look a sentinel in the eye was like looking down one's nose at their king.

The sentinel whipped around, the twirl of the faded white cloth wrapped around his shining black and gold armor, and revealed his mighty spear. Fiddle ran toward the sentinel.

The sentinel dashed at lightning speed toward the seemingly corpulent po man who had the audacity to run at him.

Fiddle saw the po occasionally looking at him as they ran, hopping onto nearby ledges, but he had little relief. The silhouette of a tall, imposing beast bearing muscles like marble and an absurdly long spear was heading straight for his uncanny face. Just before the whistle of air from the spear's tip reached Fiddle, the imp ducked and dove for a nearby ledge.

The weapon crashed into the ground behind Fiddle with enough force to crack the stone surface. It was enough to push Fiddle over the ledge, causing him to fall into the depths. The sentinel landed on top of the ledge and dug his claws into the ground. He jumped off the precipice and dragged the entire structure toward another wall nearby. The grinding of stone and the shuffling of the mountain drown out everything else—the sentinel's beady eyes constricted, the adrenaline running through him focusing all his strength and senses onto his current task. Eventually he slammed the mountain in his hand against the opposing mountain wall. The following crash could be heard for miles—loud enough to shoot over the horizon, and forceful enough to split the sky.

Some of the po swore they could see the hazy black swamp bottom in the sky's center ripple from the sound. The sentinel stared down, then took a small breath of relief. He looked around and could only see the faint lights a scant few po falling into crevices far into the distance. He turned his head upward again, and listened; everything was quiet, or at least as quiet as the realm could be. The soothing hum of crawling mountains and crackling rocks on the horizon returned. He casually lowered his spear and repeated his call from before; the deep, gut-wrenching war drum echoed out into the horizon.

A group of lanky figures came flying toward the commander. They settled next to one another in formation, just as they had previously.

"We are done for now," the commander barked.

"So soon, commander?" one of the sentinels asked. Several others glared at him, and the one closest to him jabbed at his arm with a bony elbow.

"Yes," the commander said. "I've had enough of this place. I scattered a sizable group. Let's head to Eedoon."

Cheers emanated from the group, and the commander flew off. The others followed. Just below their meeting spot, the mountains slowly began to spread apart, and a small shadow crawled up the wall.

That was way too close for my liking, Fiddle thought. *Even as a shade, I can still feel these rock walls pressing on my face. Let's hurry this up. I'd like to get back and let Cynkz do all the shapeshifting again…*

The small shadow wormed out of the fissure and dashed toward the group of large sentinels in the distance.

The large mass of figures descended into a particularly mangled and vast crack in the ground. One by one, the sentinels disappeared into the gaping chasm. The whisk of cloth and clattering of metal armor trailed after them into the darkness.

The familiar small shadow inched toward the edge of the crack in the ground. When everything seemed quiet, he dipped into the darkness.

This is it! Fiddle thought. *I did it! I need to hurry back and let Cynkz and the others know!*

The shade shot out like an arrow from the abyss, slinking along and across every wall and ledge with reckless abandon.

CHAPTER 9

"SO WHAT OF THIS HORGAFELL?" CYNKZ ASKED. "What legends do you know?"

Kadd said, "I know he was considered the 'one true giant.' A being with a body of stone, said to be as large as the moon, and powerful enough to tear into any of the realms."

"How is that possible? How could one, by strength alone, 'tear' into another realm?"

"I don't know much, but I have my suspicions; I suspect that the realms are not as ephemeral as we'd like to believe. This may be an extension of the physical world."

"Dulrot, the topmost layer of Munderworld, lies just beneath a proper night sky, and if one can fly, they can go out into space."

"Into space, you say?" Kadd said, scratching the bottom of his scraggy chin with a wrinkled, bony finger.

"An infinite void filled with stars set at impossible distances from one another. It was the same space I would look at during my time in the po world."

"I see. Then perhaps it is not so far-fetched that one strong enough could force their way through the realms."

"The Munder King would not appreciate some rogue tyrant tearing apart his kingdom—"

"It would serve him right!" Harla sneered. "His 'kingdom' is nothing more than a grand cage filled with suffering. It is pathetic."

"Hmm." Cynkz scratched at the hairs on his chin. He could not think of a proper response to the old woman's outburst.

"He must have a reason for allowing all of this, correct?" Kadd asked.

"I would not know," Cynkz said. "The Munder King has been silent for eons now. No one has seen him. Some believe he may no longer be with us. His influence can be seen, however, as his power is said to be infinitely expanding the realms."

"How precisely is he a king? What subjects serve him? What does anyone gain from following his rule?" Kadd asked.

"The sentinels remain loyal to him, it appears to be the only thing keeping them going, their only motivation for doing anything," Cynkz said.

Another po leaned forward and spoke their mind through a strained, faint voice. "They seem to take great pleasure in torturing us."

"It's strange," Cynkz said. "In Dulrot, the sentinels are far and few between, and they seem to care little for what either po or mun do, so long as they do not encroach the burning horizon which leads to the next realm."

"This place makes no sense," Harla mumbled.

"I'd be inclined to agree with you," Cynkz said, "but I doubt the King would go to all this trouble for nothing. There must be something spurring him forward to continue as he does."

"What difference does it make? All I know is that his machinations lead to endless suffering for me and the rest of us," Harla said.

Cynkz shifted himself toward Harla, crossing his legs and placing his open palms in his lap, attempting to appear as open as possible to the old woman. "Do you know anything about 'sisters'? We happened across a spirited young woman who spoke of them."

"Ah," Harla said, slowly resting her arm on her knee and opening her body, though not toward Cynkz. "Yes, I have heard of them. The 'sisters' as you call them are more accurately known as the Sisters of Elm, an enigmatic order of elder women. They reside deep, deep within this 'Munderworld' and send out missionaries, known as 'maidens' of Elm, who recruit new initiates, all women, and establish new connections throughout the realm."

"Why do they need to establish anything?" Cynkz asked.

"If I knew that, I very well may not be here. I do know that they have the ability to traverse the realms with ease. Some say they have seen hooded maidens blinking in and out of existence through beacons set up over the realms. They essentially act as the Sister's eyes and ears."

"Beacons? By chance are they shaped like staves? Crudely carved pieces of wood with various cloth and animal skulls attached to them?"

"Aye, that is them, all right. How they operate, or what specific purpose they serve, no one outside of their order knows. Every now and then a maiden can be seen providing relief to poor souls along their journeys."

"I see," Cynkz said, his voice soft and trailing with a hint of contemplation. "Why have we yet to see any staves here? This seems like it'd be an easy enough realm to search for recruits."

"We joke that they really, really do not like the sentinels," Harla said. "The sentinels are often desperate for any kind of affection, and this is apparently a breeding ground for the beasts. The maidens avoid them at all costs…"

"Ah, they'd want nothing to do with this place. I do not blame them. I have yet to meet a sentinel that was not an obstacle of some sort."

"You and me both, stranger—"

"Harla, he has a name," Kadd said.

"Names are meaningless here," Harla said. "Who is to say once we try moving, we won't be crushed beneath the heel of a sentinel lying in wait for us? We will just reform somewhere else, far away from each other, to never see one another again—"

Kadd stood himself up, fists clenched and eyes narrowed into thin lines. "That is the very reason you need to learn to appreciate what little time you get to spend with others! Every peaceful interaction counts, Harla."

"Pah," Harla scoffed. "It counts for nothing here, and you know it. We *all* know it."

Kadd looked on at Harla, bearing down on her with an angry stare. Harla refused to look him in the eye and retreated to rest her head in her arms. The other po looked away, the angle of their faces accentuating the deep lines beneath their eyes.

Cynkz watched the group, his eyes following every sad wrinkle and crevice etched onto their faces. He thought of the young woman he saw get crushed when he arrived and wondered how often everyone experienced a similar fate, time and time again. He grew nostalgic of his easygoing time spent in Dulrot and the blissful ignorance he and Fiddle shared as they spent their time conducting pranks and staring at the beautiful night sky. He had not seen a real star in a long while, and kept likening other things such as the distant, faint lights of po to them.

A tense air kept the room silent for what seemed far too long. The uncomfortable tranquility was soon interrupted by the shuffling of rocks outside. The shadows of several pebbles fell, cutting through the thin line of light visible outside the cavern. Cynkz stood and faced the opening, holding out his arms to signal to the group to get against the wall and hold still, just as they had before.

A small, red face poked under the ledge, bearing a big, yellow grin.

"Cynkz!" Fiddle yelled, his sharp voice echoing through the small space.

"Ah, Fiddle. It's good to see it's you," Cynkz said.

"I brought friends," Fiddle said, gesturing a free hand past the ledge. Minor scuffles dragged against the rocks above. Small po hands and feet descended into the cavern. They greeted and were greeted by the current residents as warmly as one could in Munderworld: a few awkward glances, a single solid handshake, some of the new adult arrivals kneeled down to speak with the po children. Cynkz felt a certain warmth inside him. He never dealt directly with po, but he had wondered what a closer look might bring. Fiddle was the more social of the two, hence his propensity for learning new gossip and interesting words from fallen scholars and intellectuals. Cynkz found a deep satisfaction in providing comfort, however small, to a few lost souls.

"Have you told them what we're doing?" he asked Fiddle.

"Oh, um, well, not entirely," Fiddle said. "I just told them they could find a safe spot if they helped me out."

"Wait, what are you saying?" one of the new po said, looking at Fiddle with bright wide eyes from the dark circles surrounding their orbits.

"I knew you were leading us on!" another one snarled.

"It was a trap!" a third po woman screamed.

"Wait! I wasn't lying!" Fiddle said. "You're definitely safe here, especially with Cynkz looking after you."

"So," the first po replied, "what is going on?"

"Well," Fiddle huffed, sticking out his small chest and thumbing the tip of his pointy nose. "I found where the sentinels go and how they get to the next realm."

"It's true then!" Kadd said, the glint in his eyes lighting like the spark of a match. "The rumors were true! There is a way out of this wretched place!"

"Yeah, I found—" Fiddle stumbled at the sight of countless eyes staring at him. He thought he should be a bit used to the extra attention by now, but unfortunately, it was not getting easier. If nothing else, he did not feel his nerves pulling him back like last time. Fiddle took a deep breath and continued.

"I found the tomb where the sentinels go. They spoke of 'pleasantries' in the next realm, though they didn't say what exactly it meant."

"That's good enough for me," Kadd said, a smile breaking through the hard lines on his face.

"Still," Harla said, "who is to say these 'pleasantries' will be good for us? What if it is worse?"

"Do you truly wish to stay, and forever wonder about what-if's, Harla?" Kadd said.

"No," Harla said, her voice trailing off into a soft tone. "No, I do not."

"Let's get topside, then," Fiddle said. "Cynkz could carry all of you, if you don't mind riding on the back of a giant beast, that is."

Rows of confused expressions and furrowed brows followed several confused mumbles. Cynkz merely rolled his eyes and smiled, before floating out of the cavern.

The po followed Fiddle as he drifted out of the cavern and toward the top of the spire. Kadd was the first to see the beast—a massive, overlong serpent bearing emerald scales with golden-brown tints at their edges, a flowing bright orange mane, and sweeping rows of rainbowed feathers forming its wings. The beast's brilliant shine provided a contradistinction against the flat gray air. to the eye that forced it to obsess on its form for just a bit too long—that old jester's trick of adopting a visual look that demanded just enough extra attention so as to be entrancing. As Kadd stared in awe at the serpent, the rest of the po made their way out of the cave.

"Augh!" a rattled shriek rang out. "It's a monster! Greater than Horga fell himself! We're going to be eaten—"

"Harla!" Kadd yelled. "I-I believe it is just our shapeshifting friend. Right?"

Kadd looked at Fiddle, who was merely smiling, expressing a sharp, toothy grin that betrayed mischief.

"Yes, yes, it's just Cynkz," Fiddle said through a half-chuckle. "He likes to show off sometimes."

"Does he always choose such … ostentatious forms?" Kadd asked.

"Not always, though he does turn into a lot of snakes," Fiddle said.

"I see…" Kadd said, unable to look away from the entrancing serpent.

"Hurry and get on!" Fiddle commanded. "I'll point Cynkz in the right direction, then join the rest of you on board."

Kadd looked at the small imp with a twisted expression. "How exactly do we, um, 'ride' this thing?"

"Egh, it ain't hard," Fiddle said. "Just climb up and hold on to something. Try some of the hair up front."

Kadd looked back to the group of po behind him and greeted their gaze with a shrug. He began to ascend, using the space between its great scales as footholds. Once Kadd was up top, he settled inside the collection of bright orange fur constituting its mane and gripped a clump of it in one hand. A faint chuckle sprung out from within him, and he motioned the rest of the po to join him. The group of small bodies began to make their way up the beast's side, the pitter-pattering of their feet against the stone floor giving way to rounds of light taps on gripped scales. Harla was the last one to begin climbing. Her old age showed as she stumbled and struggled. Kadd extended a hand to pull her up. She looked at him for a second, then took hold of his hand. Kadd, along with several po, reached out to reel her up, where she crawled with a slight, anxious stutter to the center of the bright orange mane.

Once they were settled, Fiddle drifted up to Cynkz's eye and pointed a small finger toward the horizon. Cynkz's raised his serpentine form, quickly rising into the air. A row of awestruck wales echoed from his mane before he straightened into a smooth curve, then extended his wings. He crashed his wings, the gust from which crashed against the rocks below and shot the beast into the air. Another row of excited, if worried, gasps rang out as they slithered into the sky and toward the gray horizon.

The winged serpent flew smoothly and parallel to the horizon with swiftness. Its movements were elegant, fluid, and thoughtful enough to not disturb the small po riding on its back. "What exactly are we riding?" one of the po asked, looking to Fiddle the way one would the captain of a ship.

"Heck if I know. Cynkz loves old stories and legends. It's probably a deity of some sort," Fiddle said.

"How do you two learn about such things?" Kadd asked.

"Lots of different kinds of po end up in Munderworld," Fiddle said. "Dulrot is particularly big and lots of po end up there. It's also peaceful enough that you can find different po and ask them things."

"So you two are inquisitive learners, then?" Kadd asked.

"Inquisitive, inquisitive… Yeah, I supposed we are," Fiddle said as he looked off at nothing, his mind ruminating over the new word.

"How does Cynkz manage to form, I presume in his mind, a complete image of something he's only heard of from old stories?" Kadd asked.

"I have no idea. I just know he has a vivid imagination and is exceptionally talented at shapeshifting."

The rumbling of shifting scale and muscle moved the entire group. Everyone tightened their grip and gasped as the angle of flight turned downward. Fiddle, once he gathered himself, huffed and dragged himself forward up to the tip of Cynkz's head.

"Hey!" Fiddle yelled. "What's going on?! You're gonna scare everybody half to death!"

Cynkz tilted his head toward a collection of shifting rocky spires. Fiddle's eyes were drawn to a single faint light at the center of one of the rock faces. A young po woman, thin in body and languid in appearance lay on the ground, unconscious. Her hair was long and pitch black. Tons of small lights gathered together to reform her body, a process one underwent if one died in Munderworld; one's body would merely summon itself back nearby. No one fully understood the process. It appeared to be random, if nothing else.

"It's the po girl from before!" Fiddle said. "The one that scratched you!"

Fiddle looked on, thought for a moment, then slowly pressed his brow together and crossed his arms. "Hmph, who needs her?" he said. "We should just leave her and—"

Cynkz shook his head to jostle Fiddle's position, nearly sending him flying off.

"Hey! We don't—I mean why should we—She was—"

Fiddle's lip flattened, and he took in a breath to sigh softly.

"All right, all right. I don't have to see your face to know you're giving me *that* look again—the one where you refuse to take *no* for an answer. Let's go get her. I'll round up the po and get her on board."

The winged serpent circled around the unconscious woman before coming to a slow stop on the ground. To Fiddle's surprise, several po were already making their way down the side of Cynkz's scales. Kadd was in front and was the first to hold the woman up. The po still on Cynkz's back reached down and lifted the woman, dragging her to the center of his bright orange mane. Soon everyone was back on top of Cynkz's back. Fiddle turned back and patted the top of Cynkz's head, prompting him to lift his body and crash his wings, sending them into the air.

Fiddle grew excited. He could see the peculiar opening in the ground where the sentinels disappeared. From above, it looked like an enormous zigzagging line, or in another light could be compared to the gnarled tearing of an animal's flesh by a predator's claw.

Fiddle nearly fell off Cynkz's brow. "That's it! That's where the sentinels left for the next realm!"

The po perked up, hearing the imp's words. Everyone stretched out their necks to peer over the side of the beast to where Fiddle was pointing.

"It's massive," Kadd said. "It's not like any of the other crevices here. It's as if something was pushed through the ground…"

Cynkz angled his wings back, pushing against the wind to slow his movement. He sailed down and landed in front of the peculiar crack. The po slowly climbed their way off. Kadd and several others carried the still unconscious woman off.

"Man, is she ever gonna wake up?" Fiddle said.

"The process seems random," Kadd said. "She could be out for a while."

"Well, I ain't carrying her!" Fiddle exclaimed.

The giant serpent burst into a great cloud of colorless smoke, and from its center, Cynkz walked out, greeted by the stares of the po. He walked over to Fiddle and Kadd, who was still holding the woman in his arms.

"Is she all right?" Cynkz asked.

"Yes," Kadd said. "She's fine, but her body is still reforming itself."

"I'll carry her, then. You have done enough."

"Cynkz! You don't have to do *everything*," Fiddle said. "Also, what if she wakes up and scratches at you again?"

"It's fine, Fiddle. We'll play it by ear and manage things as they happen."

"Isn't that what we always do?"

"Precisely!"

Kadd chuckled and shook his head. "You two are such an interesting pair. You're much younger and more spritely than I, so it would probably be for the best."

Cynkz stretched out his arms and took the woman, pulling her close. He noticed the soft curves of her features and faint, calm breaths. Her similarity to the woman from his visions was uncanny, though the girl in his arms appeared younger, barely beyond the cusp of adolescence. Another thing he noticed was just how warm she was. It was not merely heat, but an inner warmth; the type of heat one feels inside when hugging a close friend or family. Cynkz looked back to Kadd and Fiddle, who were staring at the large opening in the ground. The group of po had gathered at the crack's edge and were pacing back forth, attempting to get a good look inside.

"Fiddle," Cynkz said, "you've looked into the cavern, correct? What precisely did you see?"

"Honestly, it would be difficult to describe," Fiddle said. "The inside of the crack is just a big slope of rocks leading down to giant stairs in front of the portal."

"Stairs?" Kadd said, his eyebrows raised.

"Yeah, it's really weird. The stairs are so big that you po will probably need to climb each step."

"How peculiar," Cynkz said. "Well then, lead the way, my friend."

Fiddle flew forward, sprinting into the depths. Some of the po began to traipse in behind him, and Kadd walked forward, prompting the rest to follow his lead. Only Cynkz and Harla remained outside, along with the young woman in Cynkz's arms.

"I'm watching you, scoundrel," Harla said, fierce glints beaming out from the corners of her sharp, gray eyes. "You do anything to harm that poor girl and I'll—"

"Ma'am, please, I only wish to help," Cynkz said.

Harla continued glaring at Cynkz, her eyes like daggers aiming straight for the soft, rounded expression in his face. After what felt like an eon, Harla blinked and began walking into the pit. Cynkz watched her fade into the darkness, and he moved to do the same.

The hum of weak winds dragging across the stone floor whistled through the dark. The tapping of small feet created an uneven rhythm in the air. The dim light reaching from outside could barely keep the ground visible. All that could be felt was the dropping thump of the body with each step, descending farther and farther until the entrance appeared almost entirely above in the air behind.

Shrouded in darkness, a sharp voice could be heard up front.

"Watch your step!" Fiddle shouted.

Cynkz could see a faint light somewhere deep in the dark; it appeared to be a ledge. The slope grew steeper, rockier, and bumpier. Cynkz could see the silhouettes of many of the po breaking the light ahead as they descended. As he stepped closer to the ledge, the aural hum of light winds dragging across the cave walls turned to heavy gusts. The crackling of the ever-shifting rocks returned, their sound amplified by the closed space. Sounds seemed to magnify as they reverberated against unseen edges in the dark. Cynkz approached the ledge and carefully made his way down, the unconscious woman in his arms forcing him to be more cautious than usual. The image greeting his vision caused him to slow down in an attempt to discern what precisely he was seeing.

A massive collection of huge stone slabs poked through the dark. Each stone appeared to be meticulously carved. They were layered one on top of another, creating a staircase. The stone steps were a different color than the others; they were an almost vibrant ice blue, nearly sparkling white and their shine ever shifting. It was as if chilled blood ran through them beneath the surface. The floor was coated with a soft, alien cerulean aura. It was similar to standing at the edge of a small pond at night, watching the moonlight dance along gentle ripples in the water. The slabs moved more erratically than all the other stones, as if matching the rhythm of one's breathing. They did not separate; instead, they expanded out, paused for a moment, then retracted back together, like skin stretching and compressing. The po made their move as they flattened. Then, once they would contract, the po would stop and wait until the next expansion.

Cynkz noticed the rock felt different beneath his feet. Each step was greeted with a soft, wet sound, whose echo quickly faded in the air. The cold, ice-blue stone beneath only made the warmth of the po in his arms feel that much greater.

Fiddle remained floating above the group, occasionally swooping down to observe the po's movements, and looking back at Cynkz to ensure he was with the group.

"Just ahead lies a grand opening. I saw the sentinels disappearing into it earlier," Fiddle said.

"I'm growing tired of descending into dark caves and 'openings,'" Kadd said.

"This one is different!" Fiddle exclaimed.

"We will see—" Kadd stopped himself mid-sentence to look ahead. "I'm guessing that's it, then."

In front of Kadd, the tip of a huge fissure began to form. As the eye followed this separation in the rock forward its edges expanded quickly, forming jagged lines that ran through toward the infinite darkness ahead. Beside its edges the stones took on more peculiar shapes; they dipped and curved at oddly natural angles, reminiscent of the bones of a person's chest and clavicle. Further out these shapes receded into broad, rounded slabs, appearing more like giant shoulders than rock. They shifted and moved as the stones breathed.

"Is this… Is this Horgafell?!" Kadd said. "It can't be…"

Everyone remained silent, allowing the grinding rock and deep beating air to enrapture everything.

"Where is his head?" Kadd asked. "What is keeping him trapped beneath the world? Is this dark pit, where his head should be, the way forward?"

"Yep," Fiddle replied.

"This place truly is bizarre," Kadd said.

No one quite knew what to do or how to react. Cynkz could see the frightened and confused looks on their faces; the twisted brows, flattened lips, and bunched cheeks betrayed an air of uncertainty.

Another sound began to rise out from the fissure ahead. Everyone immediately froze. The focus was tense enough to drown out the constant noise in the room. Fiddle slowly lowered toward Cynkz, his neck stretched out and his nose poking toward the abyss. As the new sound grew louder, Cynkz tightened his shoulders and gripped the woman in his arms, his eyes never leaving the fissure. The sound grew loud enough that it began to easily pierce through the tomb's ambience. The sharp tapping of metal colliding echoed in uneven layers. Just as the harsh sounds reached their zenith, it stopped, and the room returned to its calm state.

The soft hiss of cloth followed a deep guttural growl, and a dark purple snout poked through the darkness in the fissure.

"Oh no," Fiddle whispered.

"You!" a booming voice shot out from the snout in the dark. Everything rambled with his call.

A great sentinel revealed himself. His tall, bulky form towered over everyone, his black armor shined a light blue along its edges against the peculiar light radiating from the tomb's floor, and the gold lining disappeared entirely. He quickly stepped out and slammed his feet against the ground, sending a shockwave that rattled the po nearby. None dared to move, remaining frozen in shock, awestruck by the fearsome beast staring them down. The last thing to leave the shadow was the sentinel's signature spear, an exceptionally long and thin rod that almost disappeared into the darkness as he held it upright.

"How did you get here?!" the sentinel screamed. "How did you find this place? None are allowed to leave the tomb of Horgafell! None!"

A row of gasps and heavy breaths rolled over the po. The sentinel gave little time for as he readied his spear in both of his large, stony hands and thrust his weapon's end toward the group of po nearest to him. He put such force into his shoulders that the metal layers forming his pauldrons clashed hard enough to send ear-shattering waves of sound in all directions. In an instant, the silvery tip of his spear was in the ground, and the crunch of broken stone and whistling of flying rubble filled the air. Several small bodies were sent flying in multiple directions, their gasping wails trailing with them.

"Everyone move!" Kadd screamed. "This is our only chance! Run to the portal!"

"You dare!" the sentinel mumbled, turning his head to focus solely on Kadd.

Before the sentinel could shift his spear toward Kadd, a warm, bright orange glow crept from beneath him. Thick smoke wafted from his feet, and he could feel the curled tips of his toes char. He looked down to see a small imp blowing fumes of bright flames in waves against his feet.

"Pest!" the sentinel yelled, before twisting the shaft of his spear around to slam its blunt end toward the diminutive mun. The following crash created a small, deep crater next to his foot, and the small imp was sent flying off into the darkness.

Cynkz ran forward as fast as he could. During the distraction he jumped up and flew in behind Kadd.

"Here, take her into the portal!" Cynkz yelled. "Make sure everyone gets through. Me and Fiddle will deal with the sentinel."

Kadd caught the unconscious woman in his arms. "Thank you, Cynkz. Hopefully, we can meet again on the other side."

"Yes. Now go and stay safe."

Kadd shared a nod with the jester, then turned and ran into the fissure.

"Get back here!" the sentinel screamed, focusing on the small po running ahead of him.

Cynkz immediately jumped into a great burst of smoke that billowed into a massive cloud. From inside the cloud, a lumbering figure lurched forward. It had light purple skin wrapped around an exceedingly tall and lithe figure and wielded a large flat square black metal shield and a thick wooden club. When he landed, the slabs buckled under his weight, forcing them to spike and break apart. Cynkz could feel a flat, wet and fleshy texture poking through some of the cracks beneath his feet.

The sentinel stared at the new creature in front of him, his mind rattling around the image of the blunt approximation of his kind before him as he was forced to look up to its face.

"A shapeshifter..." the sentinel mumbled. "I see. There were sneaks among us it seems."

The sentinel widened his stance and braced his feet against the jagged slabs of rock. He twisted his spear and gripped its shaft and holding it close to his body. Not a single gesture was wasted. Cynkz, now towering above the sentinel, rammed his rectangular shield into the ground in front of him, and with his other arm, raised his club and swung it down. It was so heavy, and swung with such force, the wind around it could be heard whistling against the wind.

"Hmph, you look the part, but you have neither discipline nor training," the sentinel said.

He waited until the last moment before diving forward. Just as the massive bludgeon crashed into the rocks, he was nearly at Cynkz's feet. He shifted his spear parallel to his body, allowing him to slink past the inner edge of his opponent's shield. As soon as he was past the shield, he angled his body up and rammed the full length of his spear into Cynkz's shins.

An ear splitting crack forced Cynkz's legs to separate and buckle. As he fell forward, his monstrous feet dragged against the stone slabs, sending rows of rocks and debris in all directions.

Just as the sentinel aimed his spear at the colossus, a small orange light flickered in the darkness. A raving ball of fire expanded and flew into his face. The deep roar of flame could be heard hitting its target with a force similar to a boulder crashing into the ocean. The sentinel's body recoiled, almost falling into itself. As he growled and scratched at his burnt face, a small imp hurtled from the abyss.

"Cynkz!" Fiddle yelled. He threw himself toward the sentinel, his little arms bracing for impact. Before Fiddle could reach the sentinel, he lowered his free hand and looked right at Fiddle. The imp immediately stopped and froze in place as the warrior peered directly in his eyes. Before he could react, the sentinel's long palm was already flying at Fiddle, and he hit it with harsh smack, as if swatting away a bug. Fiddle went flying to the ground and rolled along the jagged floor.

A burst of colorless smoke exploded from below, filling the entire tomb. As it dissipated, a massive, slithering black mass of iridescent scales coiled back and forth out of the darkness on either side of the cavern. It whipped around as it faded into and out of the shade.

Cynkz, now in the form of a colossal, black serpent, continued to expand as he moved. He could feel the walls on both sides of his body, deep within the darkness. He continued to expand before he nearly appeared too big for the room. As the serpent moved, he banged against the walls and pulled up numerous slabs of vibrant rock in his wake. The ceiling, somewhere deep in the abyss above, began to crumble.

"You fool!" the sentinel barked. "You're going to cave us in! Stop—"

Before he could finish, a massive rope of leathery scales slid beneath and whipped toward him. The sound of heaving muscle crashing against the stony sentinel had barely enough time to echo out before he was thrust into the ceiling. What began as a mild rumbling turned to an immense quake as chunks of stone fell from the roof of the cavern.

Pale boulders began to fill the cavern. Fiddle picked himself up and began crawling toward the fissure. Another massive burst of colorless smoke emitted from the serpent. Another, much smaller serpent, no bigger than Fiddle's arm, swam across the stone slabs, weaving between countless falling stones.

"Cynkz, hurry!" Fiddle screamed.

He pushed himself up and threw his body into the fissure. The serpent darted in after him. The unconscious sentinel fell to the ground beneath a pile of rubble and was soon overtaken as the cave collapsed.

CHAPTER 10

TRAILS OF RUMBLING ECHOES FELL BACK INTO the darkness. The world turned and flipped forward. Cynkz could feel himself moving, yet everything remained dark. A powerfully sweet and pungent odor wormed its way into all of his senses. The darkness soon gave way to light flashes of color, his mind's eye revealed the saccharine musk of exotic plants and pollen. Cynkz, back in his original form, felt the crunch of damp grass beneath his feet. He could not remember when he transformed back, or what precisely he was walking on or toward. The fumes ahead of him seemed to rise from the ground, through his nose, and up to his eyes. The world was a haze of nonsensical stimuli. Amorphous blurs and streams of chemicals formed a maelstrom in his mind.

Eventually, his focus settled. Cynkz found himself hobbling through dense woods. The light was bright, and it took a moment for his eyes to adjust. In contrast to the rows of pale rocks and mountains of the previous realm, everything was overwhelmingly colorful. A motley assortment of plants and leaves surrounded him, from the bright, almost turquoise grass beneath his feet to the intense pinks and yellows of iridescent leaves at his side and above. The bushwood felt claustrophobic; airy thin limbs closed in around him. His vision was fogged but at least functioning. He staggered forward, noting how movement slowly brought his senses back to form.

In a thicket beyond him, Cynkz heard the murmurs of strange voices, and at least one sharp sounding voice he recognized. *Is that Fiddle?* Cynkz thought. He realized he had been alone for a time and was curious as to the whereabouts of the po he had traveled with. With nothing else to go on, he began pushing his way to the voices in the distance.

Cynkz approached a thick collection of dark leaves and branches. He reached out with both hands and parted the brush in front of him, creating a small hole of uneven light. Several po satin a disorganized circle in the bright green grass. Most he recognized from the cavern, though a few appeared to be new faces. They were agitated, restless and constantly fidgeting around as they sat and laughed. Deeper in the group, a couple of young po had their arms wrapped around a small imp; it was Fiddle! He appeared to be just as much out of his mind as the po did sharing their merriment with him.

Cynkz snapped out of his haze and ran to his friend, stepping over giggling bodies as he made his way forward.

"Fiddle? Fiddle! You're all right!" Cynkz said. "What happened? Where are the others? Are you—"

Fiddle listlessly wriggled as Cynkz shook him by the shoulders. He looked at Cynkz, grinned, belched, and returned to his chortling.

"Fiddle…" Cynkz said with an exasperated sigh. Happy as he was to find his friend unharmed, he was unsure of what to do of the current situation.

Cynkz had not fully realized how quiet the woods were until he heard crackling in the brush beyond. Along with the sharp snaps of twigs and leaves, he could hear strange, irregular clicking noises. Someone was approaching. Cynkz hastily grabbed his friend and flew up into the tree tops out of sight. Strange, humanoid creatures stepped into the grassy opening. They were short, monstrous amalgamations of brown and yellow skin. Layers of thick fleshy caps stuck out from their thin bodies. All over their bodies were bursts of open indentations, rimmed by thin, fleshy disks composed of countless rings of earthy colors: gray pinks, muted and dark browns, thin slivers of scratchy greens, even soft manilas and beige. Their cores were long, thin stims approximating a humanoid form. Several branchy limbs protruded from their center. Some contained the usual four limbs: two arms and two legs. Others contained many more, often an uneven and asymmetrical number of each. All of the strange creatures carried long walking sticks crudely decorated with colorful fungi.

Four of the fungal muns crept out from the woods and the half-conscious po strewn about. They made numerous clicking sounds, though they appeared to have no visible mouths or teeth. They traipsed around the listless bodies, looking back and forth between the po and each other, communicating all the while. Cynkz could not understand what precisely they were saying, but there was much he could infer from their mannerisms and body language. They were deeply interested and focused on the po. Several pointed toward the bushes from which they emerged. They were planning something.

Another fungal mun walked out from the same bushes, carrying a frayed, light brown sack that wobbled as he walked. At the edge of the pos, they opened the top end of the sack and spilled forth tons of small, black and slimy leeches onto the ground. The group of writhing, mucous-y parasites crawled toward the po and latched onto their skin. The fungal muns lined up, turned their backs, and began spewing erratic bursts of light pink spores at the leeches. The line of muns began to march back into the brush. The leeches followed, dragging the bodies with them.

What a disgusting fate… Cynkz thought to himself and scratched at the coarse hairs on his chin, considering how quickly the strange fungal muns were able to find and gather the new po.

Perhaps I should follow these muns, he thought to himself. *They may lead me to the others, maybe even Kadd or the unconscious woman.*

Cynkz tossed Fiddle beneath his arm and under his cloak in an attempt to muffle the occasional chuckles and hiccups Fiddle was making. Slinking across the treetops, he followed the po abductors.

The fungals walked briskly through the woods, which was impressive considering their meek appearance and frail-looking forms. Beneath a burning pink sky lay an endless sea of brown and green foliage. Unknown plants dotted the base of most of the trees; some contained huge crimson petals with yellow dots and others were thin and wiry, coated in speckles of burnt sienna and near-black hazels. Others barely looked like plants at all, poking from the roots like sharp rocks that had pierced their hosts. Papery leaves of every color glistened in the murky light, followed by thread for stems so thin one would never notice their color or form if not for the light reflecting off of them. Faint bursts of textured winds shot out from the plants, filling the air with intoxicating, mind-altering fumes. Nothing appeared to bother the fungals as they made their way with the po in tow.

They approached a low, flat expanse of shining dark water and fibrous debris, walking right up to and through the muck without hesitation. Cynkz, on the other hand, still carrying his intoxicated companion, was hesitant. It was difficult to forget the feeling of near suffocation from the last swamp he had delved into. He wondered if there might be more grand chimeras such as Andion or if there might be more hostile po looking to cast unknown hexes on him should he be found. The fungals trudged ahead without a care, which alleviated his worries, if only a bit.

Cynkz receded back into the trees, burst into smoke, then a small dragonfly with an infant latched onto its back came out and flew after the fungal muns.

A cacophony of trickling beats and rolling chirps bounced off of the air, weaving their way through the streams of fog and pungent murk. The slow dragging hiss of muck behind the fungal muns and the gusts of bright sandy spores contrasted against the sharp trickling of crickets and vibrating wings of beetles. Cynkz's wings buzzed lightly against the thick air. It was difficult to see far into the distance, but the horizon revealed itself, as well as what appeared to be the fungal mun's destination.

What stood out the most to Cynkz were the sheer number of frogs littering the place. Their croaks blended with the rest of the natural noises of the swamp, but when he stopped to look around, he saw countless amphibians hiding in plain sight among the marshland. Beady black eyes shone in the hazy yellow and pink light. Slimy, wart-covered balls of mouths and webbed limbs sat just below the water's surface. Tiny, lanky frogs latched onto nearby twigs and branches with faded green and peach limbs. Others had small, horned protrusions sticking out from above and around their eyes, and even around their mouths, giving the impression of cartilaginous fangs. Cynkz knew better than to get close; he did not want to test what may happen if he were to be eaten whilst transformed.

A dark silhouette poked through the mist. It appeared small, perhaps a rock or boulder. As Cynkz flew forward, its form carved through the veil. A large trunk extended into the sky, and countless tiny branches jutted from its side. The off-white fog gave way to scattered plumage in the sky; thousands of variegated dots waved in the wind, countless leaves mixing varying mixtures of dull yellows, faded pinks, light greens and blues fluttered and twinkled in the sky. The tree was so large that it seemed to warp perspective.

Cynkz struggled to determine how far away it was, no matter how long he stared at it. He landed on a small twig poking out from the swamp, not only to give himself time to rest, but to look on in awe at the sheet size of the plant. There were no significant mountains, and the horizon was an even stretch of muted treetops that caused the eye to naturally glaze over the landscape.

Once the great tree's presence was undeniable, the fungal muns reached out and clicked more aggressively. They spewed more fumes and spores, which caused the leeches dragging the poor po bodies through the shallow swamp water to wriggle forward quickly. Cynkz would have appreciated the increased enthusiasm if not for the off-putting details of the situation. He was also growing tired of maintaining his extended transformation and exasperated by having to carry his still inebriated companion. Anything to get things over with more quickly was a blessing in Cynkz's eyes.

CHAPTER 11

THE GUSHING OF SMALL BRANCH FEET ABRUPTLY turned into the slight crunch of grass and hardened dirt as the fungal muns carried themselves from the edge of the flat swamp into soft land.

The tree was close enough to nearly swallow up the entire sky. One had to nearly look to their back in order to see the sky. Details in its trunk could be discerned now that they were closer. Primitive carvings filled the wall of bark, varying in size and detail. Most of them depicted simple plants and frogs, as well as a number of strange, arcane symbols representing a language of some sort. Surrounding the symbols were similarly crude paintings; bold lines of white and brown paint splattered into forms depicting stick figures representing hunters, perhaps worshippers, it was difficult to tell. Above them all, was a significantly large illustration of a massive frog, one that towered over everything. It bore a yellow outline, somewhat faded and dull from time, forming a large, sloppy curve. Centered at the top of the arc, two tiny spikes sat above two dots. Just beneath a wide, thin line separated the yellow outline from everything below.

Cynkz's eyes followed the painted arcs before noticing the swift movement of billowing smoke coming from the woods. In the distance, he could hear the beating of drums and sticks, as well as the occasional howl.

We're finally getting close, Cynkz thought, though to what, he wasn't sure. He receded into shadow and transformed himself and Fiddle back to their original forms. The imp was carried to a large tree hollow nearby and nestled within it. Cynkz could still feel the mild influence of the constant fumes of strange plants and spores in the air but was unsure of what to make of Fiddle's predicament. Somehow Cynkz could resist the mind-altering effects of the plant life, but Fiddle was completely lost, half-asleep and drunk, his only signs of life being the occasional hiccup or odd mumblings under his breath. Cynkz shook his head and turned to continue pursuing the fungal muns.

Cynkz slithered across the treetops and through the shadows toward the billowing stacks of smoke and commotion. Crowded woods gave way to a wall composed of large, yellowed logs sticking out of the ground. They were bound together by dried, brown paste and wrapped with numerous black vines and sharp and curved bones. The wall itself was nearly as tall as the trees surrounding the encampment, and far off to one side, an opening parted for the fungal muns. Cynkz could see the faint glow of the po they were dragging. He decided to investigate further, remaining inconspicuous, and slunk back into the shade of the woods. The tiniest black bird flew to the top rim of the wall. The bird perched high and looked into the encampment.

Dozens of wooden huts stretched out as far as the eye could see. They were of similar coloring to the walls forming the perimeter of the settlement. He could see countless small bodies covered in various large fungi moving back and forth throughout the place. Many of them were carrying long sticks and staves with objects hanging off of them. Some carried hollowed animal skulls, others small bowls with strange liquids spilling out of them. Most seemed to be moving with purpose, eventually fixing themselves toward the tree.

Cynkz noticed tall, lumbering figures waddling near the base of the giant tree at the center of the village Sentinels! hey appeared noticeably relaxed and uncharacteristically at ease with their surroundings. All of the sentinels Cynkz and Fiddle had encountered in Dulrot had little patience for other creatures, particularly muns or any who associated with them. One of the sentinels was being pulled into a large hut by several of the small fungal muns. Another one was being handed a small bowl with vivid, bubbling liquids. He lifted it to his snout and consumed it.

Cynkz had an idea. He flew into the inconspicuous shaded woods and re-emerged as a new approximation of a sentinel; tall and lanky, wrapped in wiry, sinewy muscle and a loose, off-white and draping cloth, with lavender skin and signature snout. Cynkz could not bring himself to copy their usual yellow teeth, though he figured his guise would suffice.

Cynkz trudged his way toward the entrance to the village. After several steps, he noticed his feet sinking into the soil. Remembering Fiddle's suggestion he float, he lifted himself and began to step more carefully, shifting his weight from the tips of his toes toward the balls of his feet. Between impeccable teeth and heavy footsteps, Cynkz wondered if his shapeshifting technique was getting sloppy. Or perhaps the intoxicating air of the jungle was getting to him. Regardless, he continued on his way.

As he approached the village's entrance, a small group of fungal muns ran toward him. Their glee expressed itself through numerous clicks and clacks and sporadic bursts of expelled spores. Cynkz's eyes teared up from all of the plant dust shooting up around him. A few fungals from the group jumped up and down, then grabbed his large hands and began guiding him forward. Not wanting to seem out of place, he went along with them. They led him to a particularly large hut and held open the cloth drapes acting as doors. Cynkz had to hunch to fit inside the opening. Several other sentinels sat in a half-circle in the center of the room. Cynkz was shocked to see them actually relaxing, smiling even. Their laughs rattled like stones being tossed down a hill, thick and textured, like smearing gravel across mud. He remembered Rackel's words about his "acting ability" and tried to remain focused despite the merry atmosphere exhibited by the other sentinels.

The fungal muns guiding him pulled at Cynkz's large, stony fingers and led him to the edge of the sentinels sitting together. He sat himself down, and before getting a moment to look around, he was approached by a fungal mun holding a wide bowl filled with pink liquid. The fungal mun spewed spores into the bowl, glittering its surface and causing it to bubble. The other sentinels immediately stopped their conversations and stared intently at the bowl being presented to Cynkz.

Cynkz glanced around, then back to the bowl in front of him.

Well, he thought, *I appear to be fairly resistant to everything else here. What harm could this do to me?*

Cynkz lifted the bowl to his snout, tilted his head back, and consumed the bubbling liquid.

Cynkz smacked his thin lips and paused, trying to parse the flavors he just took in.

Hmm, tasty! Though perhaps I should not have guzzled the entire bowl, Cynkz thought. Light, airy, the liquid was almost like sweet grass or… or…

Words escaped him, his jaw slackened, and his vision fixated itself into empty space. He could hear the cheering of the fungals and the rumbling of the sentinels rallying, though it was muffled, as if they were some distance away. The light seeping between the crack in the drapes grew intense, like a hot beacon of burning heat cutting into the room. The foreground and background smashed together, as if depth no longer meant anything, as if everything were on a flat plane within his reach. Every color swirled and jostled within their borders, creating the faintest aura around everything in sight. The fungals flattened and danced. Several grabbed at his hands as they jumped up and down. The spores they shot out of their orifices came out as rainbows and carried music with their arcs.

A bright white light descended. Rows of flames circling an ornate chandelier basked a huge room of people below. Elaborate, swirling colors accented hundreds of exquisite dresses and puffed tudors. They spun and danced, their own motions matching the circling of the chandelier above and the marking in the shining floor underneath then. It was a ball, being held late in the night, burning against the darkness like a star, and at the center of this miniature galaxy was a man and a lute, stringing odd notes and telling odd jokes to a crowd of masked aristocrats.

Cynkz could feel himself smiling, his eyes careful moving back and forth, judging the reactions of the masked eyes looking at him. The warmth of the lights, the sharp pulls on his fingers as he played his instrument, the swaying of his cloak and sleeves as he moved around, every action was light and calculated. The masks everyone wore made it easier for him to pull his tricks. Small shapes of porcelain, molded into false, twisted expressions of extreme happiness, sadness, confusion, and everything in between sat in front as their cheeks balled up and mouths beneath stretched out to partake in the jester's regaling play.

As the jester frolicked through the ballroom, he looked to the front of the grand hall and saw a familiar face: a slender woman with pale skin, piercing blue eyes and shining brown hair that was as dark as night. She wore a mask consisting of a simple nose and two squinting eyes, pushed upward the way a smile would. Beneath the mask, it was easy to tell that her own feelings did not match her mask. Her face was desperate to maintain a proper appearance, but the weight of a heavy heart pulled down on her features. Seated in a grand throne next to her was a much older man, equally masked and even more ornate in his manner of dress; a puffed robe with billowing white fur and deep crimson velvet framed in gold lining surrounded him. Farther to his side was another man, younger and taller, with a solid frame. His clothes were equally ostentatious, though the softer blues and silvers receded behind the man in the throne.

The jester naturally adored the eyes upon him, though the soft tickling of the guest's attention quickly gave way to the daggers thrown upon him by the three distinguished individuals. He stopped and stared back for just a bit too long, falling for his own trick. Before he realized what he was doing and before he could turn his eyes away in fear of disrespecting his superiors, the soft glow of their faces faded. Thin rows of fungus overtook their faces, then their bodies, which melted into thin, bony stems. The throne remained, and the gold and brass broke apart to reveal wild arrangements of sticks and vines tied together to form a crude semblance of a royal's seat. The warm, circular lights flattened into a flat pink sky, and the once beautifully decorated ballroom floor became rough and grainy soil. The masked courtiers surrounding the jester lowered their heads beneath hoods, their faces receding into shadow and leathery snouts.

The pleasant rhythm of flutes and strings turned into harsh cacophonies of clicks and clacks, meaty drums and rattling beads. The false mask of artificial ostentation returned to the grime and dirt of a natural swamp.

Cynkz gathered himself. He was seated near the base of the massive tree. The king, the maiden, and the consort remained, though their roles were occupied by the monstrous visage of several fungal muns. The "king" in particular caught Cynkz's attention. He was a diminutive, scarred collection of fungi and mushrooms and bark held together into the form of a belligerently seated individual. He held a scepter that was much too long for him. It was a long, thin branch of dark wood with a bright pink bulb at its top. He wore a large and elaborately patterned red leaf with exquisitely placed yellow dots around his tiny shoulder. Despite not speaking anything resembling proper speech, his body language was as readable as a nursery rhyme. He was in charge, and he knew it.

To his left was a taller and thinner fungal mun, who bore red petals stitched together to form a loose, tapering gown. The mushrooms sticking out of her head were comically large, appearing as a gaudy approximation of an aristocrat's wig. To the king's right was an even larger fungal person, likely taller than Cynkz in his original form. He was draped in a simple, dark blue leaf cloak. He stood attentively with his arms, or at least what one could call his arms, behind his back.

What stood out the most, however, was what sat behind the king's throne. Cynkz had never seen a plant so large. It had a massive, fibrous crimson bowl, containing an impressive amount of boiling pink liquid. The inner walls were dull yellow leathery fiber bearing countless messy stains. At the edges of the flower's bowl half a dozen mighty petals billowed and curled back. Their base was a deep, inky crimson color with dark purple veins fading across the surface. The colors blended and lightened as they moved toward the petal's edges. The deep crimson became a more vibrant scarlet, revealing numerous amber and brown spots dotted evenly on its surface. The underlying shade of red became dark as it neared the edge, curling away from the observer.

Cynkz looked around to see even more fungal servants organizing beneath their king. They jumped and waved and clicked and clacked, all the while spewing overwhelming amounts of multicolored spores from their unique orifices. The sentinels seated next to him and behind him remained hunched over and in a state of torpor, perhaps a consequence of whatever drugs they had been given. Another slow glance revealed an abundant amount of small carvings on the nearby architecture. There were crude depictions of plants and frogs, similar to the ones on the tree. A carving depicting the large yellow frog stood out to Cynkz.

The group of fungal servants grew louder, their clicking more aggressive and constant, the sounds nearly tripping over themselves as the fungals tripped approaching the king. The dancing and antics escalated, reaching a zenith. An ear-shattering slam rang out from the king as he slapped his scepter against the ground. The wood beneath could be heard splintering from the impact. Everything stopped, and the nearby sentinels perked their heads to see what was going on. The silence was thicker than the mist weaving through the air.

That was when *he* came out.

Another fungal, smaller than most, though not quite as small as the king, pranced through the crowd. He was as thin and wiry as the rest of the fungals, though his body was wrapped in several layers of stringy vines. Each vine was a unique color, similar to the ones found in the giant tree's plumage, and loosely wrapped around him. His waist, wrists, and ankles appeared to have the most. They billowed out in bunches, and their many untied ends dangled behind him.

He had three arms: two long branches sticking out from just beneath his head, and a third poking out from his back. His third arm wielded a small, thick branch with various colored rocks tied to the end. The rocks collided against each other as he waved the instrument around. Flaps of short and leathery fiber draped down over his shoulders, and two comically long flaps extended from beneath, appearing similar to the coattails of a robe. His feet were small and pointy brown stubs that stuck out from his yellow, branchy body. Each had a large, green leaf tied around the top that curled inward at their tips. His head was a mass of billowing fungi, each one stretching out farther than the one underneath. The edges were covered in speckles of pink and blue lumps of moss that showered flakes as he danced. At his crown was a small, bright salmon-colored flower with three huge vines coming out of it that curled down and nearly reached his waist. The swaying loose material on his body caused every movement to appear exaggerated and confusing. He had the air of a jester, doing what they do best, staving off silence with merriment.

The fungus-ridden fool weaved his way through invisible obstacles as he made his way to the king, his propped-up wooden platform a perfect stage for an actor. He jumped up with the confidence of an acrobat, planted himself firmly in front of his king, and turned to face the crowd. He stretched his little arms toward the sky and clicked and clacked as loud as he could. None responded. Another short, awkward silence passed, and the unperturbed jester expelled a loud burst of colorful spores and right at the king's feet. Immediately, rows of raucous clicking echoed from the crowd. A festival of clapping branches and rocking mushroom heads shook the audience into mimicking a joyous festival. The maiden and the consort on stage seemed moved by the gesture. Even the sentinels took part and cackled through their snaggle-toothed snouts. The only one who did not react in any way was the king, who looked on with steeled nerves.

An ear-splitting crack cut through the noise, and everything went silent. Everyone, save for the sozzled sentinels and Cynkz, snapped to attention. The fungal fool on stage maintained his cavorting, the thumps from his dancing shooting from the stage.

Cynkz was not entirely sure what the king was doing, perhaps he was merely breathing, or perhaps he was beginning to huff and puff in a fluster. It was difficult to read the body language of such odd creatures. What Cynkz did notice was the king's grip. He knew a good tip for dealing with royalty was to observe their hands, which were often delicate and exposed, and would reveal much about even the most reserved of nobles. The king's grip, once a slacked bundle of twiggy fingers, had tightened into a dense ball around his scepter. It was so tight his knuckles were shaking and rattling against the accessory's shaft.

The king sat upright, pulled his scepter close to chest, then flung its bulbous end into the side of his daunting guard. The tall fungal immediately stepped forward, causing his tall, lean shadow to cover the small jester in shadow. A large and fibrous claw reached out and clutched one of the mossy rims on his crown. His body became a small blur as he was lifted and flung over the guard's shoulder like a sack of rubbish. The jester could still be partially seen as he was dunked into the boiling glop in the flower behind the stage. Thrashing and sizzling followed the poor fungal as he waved desperately for help, before sinking beneath the constant bubbles of the pink liquid's surface.

Oh my, tough crowd... Cynkz thought.

The king settled back into his throne, then motioned his free hand at the crowd. Part of the audience split apart to give room for several fungal muns as they walked forward, expelling bursts of pink spores behind them. Dozens of unconscious po were dragged forward by pitch-black leeches. Cynkz did not recognize any of them, save for one woman near the back of the group, a young po woman with dark brown hair and pale skin.

It's her! Cynkz thought. *The unconscious woman from the previous realm!*

One by one, the bodies were brought to the foot of the ramshackle stage. The king thrust his miniature hand forward, and his guard observed the po. Cynkz's heart began to race, fearing the worst. With lightning speed, the guard stretched out a long, lanky branch of an arm to grab one of the unconscious po, an older gentleman with gaunt features and practically no hair on his head. The guard brushed at the po's sides, flicking off the leeches still suckling on the po's skin. Once cleaned, the guard snapped his arm and tossed the po into the gurgling pink concoction in the giant fibrous bowl behind them. The po must have still been unconscious, as he made no noise or attempts to flee once taken by the liquid.

They're sacrificing the po! But for what purpose? If I don't do something, then she might—

All of the fungal servants in the crowd were bowing, and the sentinels hung their heads low in deference to the ritual.

"Hey, new guy," a voice called to Cynkz. "Bow down or something. We gotta respect their customs if we want them to keep giving us the juice."

Cynkz realized it was one of the sentinels speaking to him. He turned his eyes toward the stage and realized the king, his maiden, and his guard appeared to be looking in his direction. It was surreal, a twisted version of his drug-fueled vision brought to life, or at least what one could consider life in Munderworld. Cynkz could feel the same invisible daggers being forced into his soul. He recognized the look of bothered aristocrats, no matter their appearance. Cynkz tilted his head just enough to conceal his face in the shadow of his hood, but not enough to break vision from the group of po splayed out like meat. The guard grabbed another unknown po, the hefty thumps of his footsteps prompting the audience, both fungal and sentinel alike, to raise their heads and observe the next sacrifice.

Cynkz's mind began to race, feverishly flipping through thoughts and ideas.

I have to do something! What if they go for the woman next? Would it be unwise to transform and try to escape with her? What of the other sentinels? Can I outrun them? Can I defend myself, and her, against all of them? There must be something—

Cynkz's heart stopped. His mind grew quiet, and his beady eyes pushed against their edges, revealing the whites around his pupils. The guard was standing over the unconscious woman. Everything blacked out, except for the fungal guard and the woman. The overwhelming colors and hues and textures and smells of the strange swamp world dulled in Cynkz's perception. Time itself crawled. Images of what could and should not happen flashed in his mind. Cynkz was frozen. *What should I do?!*

The guard bent over and clasped the neck of the woman. He held her up and began to brush off the leeches pulling at her skin. The fungal observers assumed a prostrated position, and the sentinels relaxed their shoulders and lowered their heads. Only Cynkz remained upright, sticking out from the rounded silhouette of the kneeling crowd.

Cynkz could feel the dagger-like look of the king peering at him like invisible hot pins slowly pushed into his soul. He could not help himself, his focus remained fixated on the woman in the guard's grip. Everything froze, the only reminder of the passing of time being the beating of his heart as it knocked against his senses. He could see the fungal guard's thin twig fingers slowly pressing the skin on her neck, the fibrous layers of his wrist twisting and tensing.

"Hey! Hey, hey, hey, what kind of—*hic!*—party is this?!"

A sharp voice cut through the silence. It was welcoming, though dragged through a slight drawl.

The tension in the air loosened as all bodies presented lifted toward the strange new voice. A small red imp staggered forward, barely able to keep himself upright. The collection of fungal muns scrambled to get out of the stranger's way as he carving a line through the audience.

Fiddle! How did that foolish imp get here…

"Wha' happened?" Fiddle said. "Why's everyone quiet? *Hic!*"

A dense crackling rang out from the stage. The diminutive king stood and shook his scepter in furious swings. Deep red bursts of spores exploded from his head as he stamped around on his throne. As soon as he pointed at the imp with the bulbous end of his scepter, every fungal mun in the audience whipped themselves into a frenzy and charged the imp.

"Whoa! We're-*hic!*-dancing now? *Hic!*"

Fiddle danced his way around the mass of small yellow bodies crashing toward him. The scuffling of pressed grass and dragging dirt up filled the air. The rumbling of stone-like muscle shifting underscored the chaos as the sentinels joined the fray. Fiddle's sharp hiccups could be heard piercing through the mayhem. The king's guard had released the woman to run toward the crowd. The maiden was leaning forward, so much so that she nearly fell out of her seat. The king had run to the edge of this stage to stomp and flail at the sea of bodies rolling around before him.

This is my chance, Cynkz thought.

Cynkz slithered to the edge of the chaos before slinking into the shadows of a nearby hut. A quick burst of colorless smoke revealed a small iridescent snake dashing toward the stage.

A small red body bounced past yellow swarms and muscled pillars. The imp began to fly, his stuttered flight proving difficult for his assailants to predict.

"Ha! *Hic!* Can't catch me!" Fiddle said. "Hey, where's Cynkz, anyway?"

As the sentinels rose up to try to grab him, one of them mistakenly thrust his elbow into the face of another.

"Watch what you're doing, you dimwit!" the bruised sentinel said before swinging the back of his hand into the other's arm.

"Me?! How about you stay out of my way!" the other sentinel said, following up with a mighty push.

"Try me again, weakling!"

"Like this?!"

The shoving turned to striking, and their encounter brushed against the sentinels who had been ignoring the confrontation. Blows were exchanged, and the mass of bodies descended into a messy skirmish.

"Oh, a fight! This'll—*hic!*—be good!" Fiddle said, looking through half-closed eyes and dangling, relaxed arms.

Bangs of wood crashing into wood followed as the scrimmage expanded, colliding with several huts. Thundering echoes followed the mighty blows of the sentinels as they fought. Sharp wails and cries rang out from the small fungal servants caught in the middle and crushed beneath the imposing stone warriors. Fiddle's shrill laughter cut through the noise as he drifted down half-asleep into the sea of disorder. One of the sentinels noticed the imp and seized the opportunity to take hold of him, wrapping his massive, stony fingers around Fiddle's body.

"I got 'em! I got 'em—" The sentinel's joyful shout was interrupted by a swift fist to the side of his snout, forcing him to drop the imp to the ground.

The ground began to shake, forcing the world to rattle violently. Everyone stopped. The petals attached to the giant plant at the tree's base fluttered and danced. A dense mass of slime and leather slowly emerged from the bowl. A huge, yellow curve expanded past the bowl's rim, revealing a pitch black underbelly p. It was so large it appeared as if the dark of night were about to overtake the sky. Its mouth was a thick line neatly separated the two regions and appeared as wide as its body. At the center of the creature's top, two small cartilaginous spikes poked upward. Embedded within were two black, beady eyes. Just like the tree and the bowled plant, its presence nearly swallowed up one's vision.

The king, once tightened and fierce in action, immediately loosened and fell to the ground to prostrate himself before the creature. Both his guard and his maiden threw themselves down and followed suit. Every fungal in the crowd, still messy and scuffed from the fight, dropped down to join their leaders. The sentinels stopped their fighting to observe the source of their worship soaking up the sightline above the stage.

A single click echoed out from the king, then another, and finally a third before the fungals began to mimic his rhythm. All together the branchy, fibrous beings chanted together:

Click-click-Eeeeeeeeeeeeeeeeee!
Click-clack-Doooooooooooooon!
Click-click-Eeeeeeeeeeeeeeeeee!
Click-clack-Doooooooooooooon!

The great amphibian twisted and turned the tiny black orbs constituting its eyes. It focused on the unconscious woman lying on the ground, her thin form barely leaving an impression on the soil beneath. Then it torqued his vision to look at the small red imp resting in a slackened pose in the middle of the crouched and bowing bodies.

The great frog parted its lips just enough to draw in a sharp breath, then split them apart, revealing the odd peach-colored insides and its blue and gray spotted tongue. A piercing roar shot out; the trembles of the scream could both be felt and seen, as if the eyes of the observer were being repeatedly struck from behind their sockets. It grew in intensity and lowered in pitch, like an ever-increasing pull at one's bowels. Eventually, the sound trailed off, though its mouth remained open.

While everyone was occupied with curling themselves into the ground, the amphibian flung its sticky tongue out to the unconscious po woman and dragged her into the recesses of its bottom lip. Another tongue flicked out of the mouth, this time pulling in the small red imp. The snapping of thick, leathery lips jolted everyone left, causing them to raise their lowered heads.

Cynkz pulled down his monstrous form into itself to recoil enough force to send himself flying up into the sky. The force was so great that a thick wave of air rolled over the ground, pushing everyone but the sentinels away.

CHAPTER 12

A GREAT MASS OF SLIME AND CORIACEOUS SKIN flew up and across a canvas of dark oak. The whistling of parted wind could be heard miles away. The amphibian's rise eventually slowed and curved toward the tree, and it latched onto its surface with huge, webbed black and yellow feet. The deeper timbre of its body crashing against the bark of the massive tree carried a similar distance through the air. The frog began clawing its way up before disappearing beneath the dull rainbow plumage.

Cynkz made his way farther up the tree before noticing a massive opening above, another tree hollow, similar to the one he first put Fiddle in before entering the village. He pulled his heaving mass up to its ledge and spat out the contents of his mouth. The po woman and Fiddle slid onto the wood and settled within a pool of textured, clear saliva. A cloud of achromatic smoke ruptured from the amphibian's skin, and the lithe jester descended from the cloud's center. He nearly fell to his knees, exhaustion pulling him down like a cumbersome anchor. Through several tired breaths he looked to his friend and the po woman, then attempted to look to the horizon. The world was covered by a field of leaves hanging down from the tree's top. The numerous dots of dull pinks and greens and yellows danced against the tiny holes of light peering between them. The way they flickered like small moments in time reminded him of the twinkling stars back in Dulrot. He closed his eyes and let himself succumb to his weariness, the darkness brought on like a comfortable blanket being softly pulled over his head.

The jester could see the night sky he so admired from a balcony. The city streets below radiated with such light that a warm, orange glow bled through the horizon. The sky itself was a soft blank sheet of midnight, the stars obscured by the artificial lights.

A regal figure leaned against the sparkling frame of the balcony, looking up to the sky. As Cynkz approached the noble po, he turned around, scepter in hand and close to his chest, to greet his visitor.

"Ah, my good jester!" the king said.

"Always a pleasure, your majesty," Cynkz said. "To what do I owe the pleasure of this meeting? The night is still young and the festivities have plenty more to offer."

"I wanted an outsider's perspective on something."

The whites of Cynkz's eyes shrank, his pupils nearly enveloping the dark brown circles at their center.

"There is no need to be concerned," the king said. "I know you are a foreigner, though you've done an excellent job of disguising yourself among my people."

"I see… You seem to think somewhat favorably of me, or else you would not have invited me up here to speak with you alone."

"As shrewd as ever, I see." The king relaxed his shoulders and rested the bottom of his scepter on the ground near his feet. "I'd like to think of myself as a good judge of character, and I have judged yours to be an amicable one."

"If I may be so bold, can I ask what brought you to that conclusion?"

The king turned himself back toward the ledge of the balcony, placing his free hand atop the frame and looked up to the blank night sky.

"I deal with political sorts every day. As king, I see many faces, and have become attuned to the slight twitches and expressions that often unveil the true intent beneath. I see the deep ridges of teary-eyed peasants as they bow before me. I see the pudgy, rounded faces of lifelong courtiers and advisors as they look at me with the sharpest of looks. Their soft, spoiled features barely hide keen intuition. You, however, are a strange one."

The king turned to peer directly into Cynkz' eyes, focusing his gaze into the light behind them.

"In you, I notice a collection of sharp, refined features and opposing angles. Yet in your eyes, I see an uncharacteristic softness—the kind of softness one garners from leaving oneself vulnerable to the needs of others."

Again the king lifted his scepter to his chest and approached the jester who, despite being nearly a foot taller, imposed his presence as a superior would their subordinate, or a parent may their child.

"From what land do you hail from, stranger? You can be honest with me."

Cynkz looked at the po, softened his lips, and drew in a small breath of relief.

"I am from the small country of Hirlwe, my lord," Cynkz said.

"Ah, I see. That is what I was afraid of."

"My lord?"

"You know my nation is steeped in conflict with the Delnitian empire. Ours is a war that has raged on for nearly a century. I owe it to the good rule of my father and my father's father that we have defended ourselves so well."

"Of course, your highness. Your lineage goes back thousands of years and gained such renown that tales of your family's deeds reach my corner of the world."

"I appreciate your kind words, but you need not flatter me, jester. Or, excuse me, I should at least respect your name. What was it, again?"

"Cynkz, Cynkz Krullowski II, my lord."

"An appropriately odd name for an odd man, I suppose. Regardless, your small country lies directly between me and the Delnitians. I know that yours is a most fertile land, perhaps *the* most fertile of lands, and supplies crops throughout the year to all nearby. If the Delnitians were to get hold of it, either to increase their own rations tenfold, or perhaps raze the land and salt the soil to deter anyone else from making use of it—"

"My lord, please! I ask that you will protect the land, and most importantly, the people within it. My family, my mother, sickly as she is, have roots there that cannot be taken out—"

"So I should waste my time, my resources, the lives of the men in my army, to protect your farm? I should potentially expose my forces to the enemy to keep safe your patch of soil in a far off land?"

"If it is so valuable, so fertile, then why not take hold of it for yourself? There is no need to tear the land asunder just to spite your foes. You are more than powerful enough to—"

"What do you know of power, jester? What makes you think it can be so easily laid out and spread? For generations, my family worked to undo the Delnitians. We have won the last half-dozen battles, but that is no reason to give them an advantage. The only blow that matters is the final one. It would be efficient to turn the land to waste and march on to the Delnitians, to finish what my grandfather started."

Cynkz looked away from the king, his eyes pressed to the floor as their edges twinkled in the soft glow of night. Then a thought ran across him, lifting his brow into a sharp arch above his eyes.

"My lord," Cynkz said, his tone as refined as a blade's edge, "why not use Hirlwe as a trap? Make it appear as if you are unsure of yourself, your forces moving sloppily in front, to give the enemy the impression of weakness? Having lost as many skirmishes as they have, your enemies will be desperate for a victory, no matter how small. Lure them in, then surround them and wipe them out. Such a blow could very well be the final strike needed, the final blow."

The king's piercing gaze rounded as he contemplated the jester's words. He lowered his scepter and scratched at the tip of his delicate chin.

Cynkz continued, "This way, you would save the fertile lands for yourself, have yet another advantage over the foe, perhaps the final victory, and save the vulnerable peoples of a nation, who would most certainly feel indebted to you."

His eyes darting around and his chin still in his hand, the king turned and walked to the balcony's edge. He stood with his head down for what seemed like an eternity before turning around to speak.

"You've put some thought into this, haven't you?" the king said.

“When one is concerned for the wellbeing of their family, it is all one thinks about.”

“That is understandable. I will speak with my advisors in private. I know that they are hungry for a swift victory. If they could, they would gather every capable hand and place a sword in it to march on Delnitian coast. I do not want to win at any cost. Victory needs to leave room for prosperity if I am to leave a proper legacy behind.”

“So you will do it? Truly?”

“I will consider it. Thank you, Cynkz. A foreign perspective was perhaps just what I needed.”

Cynkz could feel himself smiling, the corners of his lips pressing up into the bottom of his eyes, a sharp v-shape overtaking his expression. In an attempt to conceal his delight, if only a bit, he closed his eyes as he lowered himself into a curtsy.

“Thank you, my lord.”

As Cynkz’s eyes closed in the memory, he could feel the embrace of darkness taking over his body, his mind being dragged into a slumber.

Cynkz heard a faint tapping deep in the distance of the abyss. He parted his lids, slowly pulling away the veil to reveal his two companions upright in a wide, thin pool of dried spittle. Cynkz’s eyes widened and his lips parted into an open smile at the sight.

“Fiddle!” Cynkz said. “You’re all right! You caused quite a scene down there.”

“Man, Cynkz, I just had the wildest, longest dream ever,” Fiddle said, his head still in small hand.

“You’ve been out for some time. Whatever haze is smothering this land affected me as well, though I was able to remain sober.”

“Wait, I’ve been drunk this whole time?!”

“Not necessarily ‘drunk’ but intoxicated in some form or another.”

“Huh, neat.” Fiddle looked up at the colored plumage above and over the edge of the tree hollow’s ledge below. “Where are we, anyway?”

"I believe we are at the center of this realm. There was a tribe of strange muns performing some sort of sacrificial ritual at the base of this tree—"

"Sacrifice?!" Fiddle shrieked. "Sacrificed to what? I was almost sacrificed?"

"Not you, necessarily. Though you did start a fight with a group of sentinels."

"Huh, nice."

"Indeed, how you escaped unharmed is beyond me." Cynkz shifted his focus to the po woman sitting nearby, her face covered by a curtain of drooping, dark brown hair. "She was the one nearly sacrificed."

Fiddle turned around and looked at the po woman, who seemed to be not yet aware of where she was. She still had numerous red marks forming rows along her flesh, the result of the leeches, keeping her sustained for who knows how long.

"Hey, it's you!" Fiddle said. "It's a good thing Cynkz here likes you, or you would have been sacrificed! Whatever that would have entailed…"

The woman slowly turned her head to look at the imp. Her brow pressed down, at first unsure of what to make of what she was seeing. Her eyes shifted to Cynkz, and her eyes widened.

"Y-you…" she said. "I remember you…" She dipped her head, her eyes receding into shade beneath her hair. "I remember falling into a stone pit and being crushed. I was dreaming, but I could feel myself being carried, flying through the air, then being dragged through the mud…"

"You have been through a lot recently," Cynkz said. "But you need not fret. Just know that you are safe for the time being."

"Where are we?" she asked.

"Yeah, I don't really know where we are," Fiddle said. "You're not good at explaining stuff, Cynkz."

"Well, we are in a new realm, far beyond Horgafell's tomb," Cynkz said.

"What?!" the po woman exclaimed. "You mean, I'm finally out of that wretched land of rocks? For real?"

"Yes, but we have not become properly acquainted. What is your name, madam?"

"I am Orla… Who are you?"

"I'm Fiddle!" the imp said as he jumped up and beat his chest. "And he is Cynkz."

"Cynkz? Like, a sink in a kitchen?" Orla asked Fiddle.

"See? I told you, Cynkz. Everyone thinks that when they hear your name," Fiddle said.

"How is it spelled?" Orla asked.

"C-Y-N-K-Z, but the 'z' is silent," Fiddle said.

"What a strange name," Orla said.

"I always say it's the name he came with, so it's what we call him," Fiddle said.

"Does your friend always do this much talking?" Orla said, turning her attention to the jester.

"I prefer to watch and listen more than I speak, plus Fiddle's good with people," Cynkz said.

"You're damn right I am—"

"Fortunately," Cynkz said, interrupting his companion, "I'm equally good at getting him out of whatever trouble his words get us into."

Fiddle glared from beneath a furrowed brow. Orla chuckled, causing Fiddle to lighten his own expression and play along. Cynkz looked on and gave a wry smile of his own.

"Orla," Cynkz said. "You mentioned, back near Horgafell, about joining the 'Sisters.' Who are they?"

Orla pulled her knees to her chest. Her face softened as she stared at nothing in particular, thinking over her next words.

"I have seen them," Orla said, "the maidens they send out across the realms. I heard that they move across the realms to observe, offering assistance and comfort to the suffering as they expand their influence. I know that they recruit women to their order and figured if I could find my way forward, maybe I could reach them and join their ranks."

"It's better than nothing, I suppose," Fiddle said.

"It wasn't much, but it gave me hope, something to look toward. I did not want to sit around and suffer. So many others give up and do nothing here. I hate it."

"I knew that Munderworld was not a particularly nice place, but the scale of the dangers and suffering are beyond anything I could have imagined," Cynkz said.

"So what about you two?" Orla asked. "Are you trying to see the Sisters too?"

"Well actually—"

"Well actually!" Fiddle said, interrupting Cynkz. "We're trying to get to the bottom of Munderworld, to gain an audience with the King himself!"

"The King?" Orla said. "This place has a king?"

"Yep! He created Munderworld a long, long time ago. His power is what continues the infinite expansion of the realms."

"For what purpose? Is he aware of all of the suffering occurring in his realm?"

"He sees everything that happens in Munderworld. I'm sure he is aware of everything going on."

"Why doesn't he intervene?"

Fiddle looked at Cynkz, then at Orla.

"In truth, no one has seen the king in eons. Many believe he may have perished, or he may be asleep. As of now, no one knows," Fiddle said.

"What makes you think you will fare any better at finding him? What could you possibly have to offer him that would make him care enough to give you attention?"

Cynkz reached beneath his cloak and revealed the thin sliver of light. Orla's eyes widened, her lips parted ever so slightly as she looked on in awe of the radiant thread.

"W-what is that?" Orla asked.

"It's a thread from one of the apostles," Cynkz said.

"Yep! I snagged it back in Dulrot," Fiddle said.

"We almost perished trying to get it," Cynkz said.

"I don't know. I think we had a good handle on the situation."

"We were blasted into the cosmos, Fiddle."

"We lived, didn't we?!"

"True."

"The cosmos?" Orla said, her eyes pressed into a fierce squint. "You mean outer space?"

"Yes," Cynkz said. "In the uppermost realm of Munderworld, in Dulrot, you can see the night sky and many of the stars within in it."

"The same night sky as—"

"Yes, the same night sky that was visible from the po world," Cynkz said.

"The po world? You mean Peara?"

"Hmm?"

"Peara, the living world," Orla said. "Were you not a living po once?"

"I think I was, but I lost my memory long ago," Cynkz said.

"I still remember when he first arrived," Fiddle said. "He had no idea who he was or what happened. He remembered his name, at least. Then he got scared and started shapeshifting better than anyone I had ever seen and—"

"Shapeshifting?" Orla said. "You can shapeshift?"

"Yes," Cynkz said.

"He's the best!" Fiddle said.

"Is this your original form? How do I know you're not trying to pull some trick?" Orla asked.

"Transforming requires quite a bit of exertion," Cynkz said. "I get exhausted if I do it too much or for too long."

"I see. So right now you're relaxed? This is your 'resting' form?"

"More or less, yes. Though I never gave it that much thought."

"He can transform others too. He could turn us into lizards or blocks of cheese if he really wanted to!" Fiddle said.

"That sounds like an amazing ability," Orla said.

"It has its limits," Cynkz said.

"Yeah, your acting is terrible. Even Rackel could see through your disguise last time," Fiddle said.

"Rackel? Who is that?" Orla asked.

"Pah! He's just a dumb mun, a sentinel we cross paths with up in Dulrot."

"A sentinel?" Orla said.

"Those big, skinny stone muns with the cloaks and weapons and such."

"So that's what those beasts are called…"

"Yeah, we don't like them much either. They're so boring and always wanna fight."

"They've done nothing but torment us, chase us out like cockroaches."

"It's certainly strange, considering up in Dulrot they are not particularly aggressive at all, unless you give them a reason," Cynkz said.

"We never gave them a reason, yet they still tortured us…" Orla said.

"I'm sorry. I didn't mean to—"

"It's fine. It's nothing to worry about. I'm just glad to have a moment of peace," Orla said.

Everyone fell quiet. Orla looked at her feet, and Cynkz looked up to the leaves twinkling in the breeze, like grains of sand sparkling in the sun. Fiddle looked around, unsure of what to do with himself in the tranquility. He scratched at the hairs at the end of his long ears and sighed.

Fiddle said, "Where do we go from here?"

"I believe we need to go down into this tree," Cynkz said.

"What makes you think that's a good idea?" Fiddle said, pouting as he blared his question at Cynkz.

"I'm merely following the thread, the same as I did back when we got lost in that swamp."

"Huh? What do you mean?" Fiddle asked.

"When that chimera knocked us into the swamp, I could feel the thread pulling us to where we needed to go."

"Oh… Oh! So that's how you got us out of there! I didn't think to ask about that before."

"No worries. Here, watch the thread yourself if you need proof."

Cynkz held out his palm, the thread of light at its center. It moved ever so slightly toward the center of the tree, as if being pulled into the abyss within.

"How is it doing that?" Orla asked.

"I am not sure, but it has not led me astray. At least, not yet," Cynkz said.

"I can't believe we're taking directions from a magic string," Fiddle said.

"It is not as if we have any other leads, and I doubt this realm harbors beings sane or sober enough to guide us."

"I guess I can't argue with that," Fiddle said.

"You're really going toward the center of this mad world," Orla said. It wasn't a question.

"Of course," Cynkz said. "We've come this far. There is no reason for us to quit."

"What will you do with me, then?" Orla said.

"You could come with us!" Fiddle said. "We're probably your best bet at finding the weird old ladies."

"I agree, and I doubt there's anything worth seeing here anyway," Orla said. "And it's not as if I have anywhere else to go."

"It may be dangerous," Cynkz warned.

"I know, but that doesn't worry me. Ultimately, we can't die here..."

"But you could end up lost!" Fiddle said. "There's no rhyme or reason to where your body will reform when you die. You could end up materializing deep underground, or in the jaws of a great beast, or in quicksand, or—"

"Fiddle!" Cynkz said. "That will be enough. She is well aware of the danger ahead."

"All right, all right," Fiddle said.

"Let's go," Orla said. "I'd like to keep going and find the sisters as soon as we can. Who knows? If they accept me, I may even be able to assist you two further."

"Good thought," Cynkz said through a soft smile as he picked himself up. "If you two are ready, I'd like to start moving ahead."

Orla looked puzzled at the jester, then down into the black pit inside the tree. "Wait, how are we going to—"

A puff of colorless smoke covered everything nearby. A large bird revealed itself; it stood nearly three times as tall as Orla, the top of its small, rounded head having to crane itself down to look at the woman and the imp. A mass of white billowed out from its chest, fading into a pitch black rim. Its wings swooped back into pleasant curves, their tips dancing gently in the wind. Its eyes were two shining brown beads that pierced into the soul.

Fiddle rested on its back, settling into a soft spot at the nook of the bird's neck.

"Hop on! Cynkz will carry us. He's good at this. No need to worry," Fiddle said.

Orla remained frozen, her eyes refusing to leave the glint of the large kestrel's stare. She was like prey before a predator. Fiddle noticed her trepidation, then looked at Cynkz.

"Hey Cynkz, you're scaring her! Try to look less intense, will ya?"

The bird swiveled his head to the side to look into the darkness. Orla continued staring before finally letting out a breath she had been holding in for far too long.

"A-are you sure about this?" Orla said, trying as hard as she could to hide the trembling in her voice.

"It's fine!" Fiddle said. "Man, the other po had an easier time adjusting to Cynkz disguised as a dragon than you do with a bird. Look at how fluffy and soft he is!"

Fiddle playfully patted at the feathers on the creature's back, and the bird pushed its shoulders out before shaking its body; a wave shot back through its feathers from its head to its tail. Fiddle nearly fell off but caught himself, doing everything he could to keep steady.

Once Orla was close enough, she reached out and grabbed onto the bird's plumage, pulling herself next to Fiddle. Her body formed a neat dent in the dark feathers beneath her. Despite being black, Orla could see their edges twinkling in the light, dancing around like stars. She had not seen a proper night sky in ages, though she could remember the feeling like it was yesterday, at least when she looked upon the bird's form.

Once settled, the large bird flung its wings to appear as if their tips could touch each end of the tree hollow's opening. Cynkz lowered his body, coiled his legs back and pushed himself into the abyss. The flapping of his great wings almost drowned out Orla's screaming as they steadily drifted down into the darkness.

CHAPTER 13

SNAPPING WINDS TRICKLED DOWN FROM THE darkness above. As it grew loud, a faint, white form slowly faded into view. It descended toward a collection of large roots hanging from the darkness and settled on one that twisted and stretched nearly to the ground. As soon as it landed, the bird crouched and leaned to its side to allow its passengers to step down.

"Guess we're here," Fiddle said. "That took forever. It felt like we were hanging out in a void for hours."

Fiddle drifted away from the bird and turned to look at Orla. The woman held herself tight to the bird's back. Her grip was tight enough to cause her hands to shake, though she may have been trembling from fright. She kept her head pointed forward, her lips pressed together and her brow heavy and flat against the top of her eyes.

"Hey! Orla! You can let go now," Fiddle said. "It wasn't that bad. I thought Cynkz gave us a smooth ride down."

Orla slowly loosened her grip, the tight bundles of feathers in her hand expanding. She took a deep breath and slid off Cynkz's back. As she exhaled, he dragged herself to the edge of the bird she nearly tripped, jutting her foot out before quickly recoiling it back in to press into whatever she could to use as a foothold. Her feet tapped the surface of the dark root once she was down, and she finally let go of Cynkz and stepped back, holding her clasped hands close to her chest.

The giant bird burst into smoke, concealing its form entirely before revealing Cynkz's thin frame within the cloud.

Cynkz's vision was greeted with a vast desert. Waves and waves of black sand ebbed and flowed against the horizon. The sky was a simple, blank sheet of darkness. Cynkz found it unnerving—a pure night sky without a single star. The ground looked more like a proper night sky than anything, as the infinite grains of sand twinkled like stars in the light.

Despite the world being shrouded in dark air, everything was well lit—Cynkz could easily see himself, Orla, Fiddle, the surface of the tree's great roots hanging from the sky, and the sand-filled floor beneath them. He had grown accustomed to Munderworld's refusal to make sense, though he found his own patience being tested by the ever-increasing oddities.

Cynkz looked to his side and noticed Orla's discomfort.

"Are you all right?" Cynkz asked.

Orla nodded and took in another soft breath.

"Are you sure you wish to continue? I may not always be able to look after you. Munderworld is—"

"I'll be fine," Orla said. "Let's just keep going."

"I guess heights just aren't your thing? Or was it the giant bird?" Fiddle asked.

"I said I'm fine. Let's go already."

They were close enough to the ground that Orla only needed to climb a few feet to reach the desert floor. The soft hiss of rolling sand proved to be the only real ambience available, other than the occasional taps of Orla's hands and feet as she lowered herself along the ends of the roots. Once at the bottom of the tree's structure, she placed herself on the sands below. Cynkz and Fiddle hovered to look out onto the desolate horizon.

"What's up with this place?" Fiddle asked.

"I feel as though I've asked myself that very same question with every realm we've visited thus far," Cynkz said.

"Haha! Very true."

They began to move forward, but Cynkz noticed Orla had gone quiet.

"Madam? Are you all right?" Cynkz said.

Orla looked at her feet, her brow pressed together into a confused expression.

"Orla?" Cynkz said.

Fiddle turned around to investigate. "Hey, what's wrong now?"

"I-I'm stuck!" Orla said.

Slowly she began to sink into the dark sand. Fiddle darted forward and around her, with his head in his hands.

"Orla! Cynkz, help me pull her out!" Fiddle said as he anxiously grabbed at her arm and began pulling up, to little effect.

Cynkz flew over and noticed how tightly the grains of sand were tugging at her skin. Several thin, bleeding red lines started to form along her calves and knees. Ripping her out would cause immense pain. It could possibly rip her legs from the rest of her body. He needed a better approach and settled on scooping her out.

The jester quickly burst into a cloud, and a massive orange, cartilaginous bill thrust from the smoke. The large bird opened its beak, revealing a peach-colored sack on its bottom that dug beneath the po woman, scooping her out, along with a bundle of dark sand with her. Cynkz fluttered his way to the roots before spitting out the contents of his beak, dropping the woman onto her side. As soon as she was safe, Cynkz reverted to his original form and landed on the roots. He gargled his own saliva, desperately trying to spit out whatever sand was left in his mouth, and Fiddle checked on Orla.

"Orla! Are you all right?" Fiddle said.

"Yeah, I'm all right. Thank you, Cynkz..."

Once he had dispersed the salty grains, Cynkz regained his composure and looked at Orla.

"Think nothing of it, madam," Cynkz said, "but your legs... How do they feel? What happened?"

Orla reached down, meekly wiping at the thin layer of dark particles speckling her lower legs. As she brushed off the matter, pieces of her skin went with it, leaving bleeding red spots dotted along the exposed skin. Orla tried, and failed, to hide her squeals.

Cynkz couldn't help but think about the weight of the new responsibility placed on him. He and Fiddle were more than capable of undergoing the stresses and dangers of Munderworld's oddities. It was easy to barrel through obstacles when only looking after yourself, a literal, high-flying, shapeshifting being. Even Fiddle was used to the odd scrape and altercation. Orla, on the other hand, was just a small, frail po. She projected a fierce air, but it was easy to tell, underneath it all, she was still a young girl, completely vulnerable to the elements surrounding her. A deep swelling pulled at Cynkz's heart. He knew the pain of failing to protect a dear friend and the current sting of uncertainty as to his own ability to prevent such a fate.

Even worse, he was exhausted from the constant flying, diving, and jumping into so many various forms. Cynkz had always been reserved and careful about his abilities, though recent predicaments had forced his hand numerous times, pushing him to take on larger and more demanding forms. His endurance was being tested in ways he had never imagined. The excitement of pushing himself to new heights was immediately weighed down with the possible consequences of getting careless, of making a mistake at a crucial moment.

"It looks like you've gotten most of the stuff off," Fiddle said. "Those scars'll heal up in no time. No need to worry!"

"Yeah..." Orla said under her breath, resting on an elbow as she leaned to the side.

"I can carry you forward," Cynkz said.

"You're willing to fly us around more?" Fiddle said.

"I was thinking of something more ... terrestrial."

"What'd you have in mind?"

Cynkz threw himself toward the sand. Just as he hit the ground, another burst of smoke erupted over him, and a new creature walked out: a quadruped possessing four hoofed feet, long, thin and bony legs, and a brown, stocky body bearing two distinctive humps protruding from its back. Its long, curved neck and pointed snout led its body like the head of a snake directing its slithering form. The tan-furred creature slunk to the edge of the root Orla was sitting on and placed the center of its dark humps in front of her.

"Ew, what is that supposed to be?" Fiddle said.

"It's a camel!" Orla said excitedly. "I remember seeing merchants from the east guiding them around when I was young. I always found them cute."

"It looks kinda gross," Fiddle said, crossing his arms and turning his shoulders away from the beast.

A wet snap cut the air, and a shining liquid glob flew at the imp. Fiddle caught wind of the projectile just in time to avoid a direct hit.

"Hey!" Fiddle shouted.

Orla's small shoulders and arms jittering from the uncontrollable spasms made from witnessing the comedy before her. She shuffled her body onto the camel, nestling between its humps.

"See? Told you it was gross," Fiddle said.

"I always thought they were fascinating," Orla said. "Peara, the po world, seemed to have a new animal or culture waiting around the corner. It was fun learning about them."

The camel stood, then began tramping forward. Orla wrapped her arms around the furry mound in front of her. Fiddle drifted to the side of the beast and looked at its small, beady brown eye.

"Hey, where are we going, anyway?" Fiddle said.

The camel began to chomp and adjust its mouth, shifting its lips up and down and to the side as if it were chewing on something.

"Woah! I'm not looking for any more of your spit—"

Cynkz finally opened his mouth and revealed the thread, a slim and white sliver of light wedged between the cracks in his tongue.

"Oh," Fiddle said. "It's still leading you around, huh?"

Cynkz closed his mouth and nodded.

"Where are you keeping it, anyway—You know what? Nevermind, I don't wanna know."

Orla laughed again. Fiddle drifted just enough so his face would be out of her view and gave a half-smile, trying to hide his boosted ego from entertaining their new friend.

"You two are so strange," Orla said.

"Eh, some say we're weird; others say we're funny. A few even think we're pests, scoundrels!" Fiddle said.

"Who would call you scoundrels, of all things?"

"Well!" Fiddle said. "I suppose we have time. I could tell you a few stories about our escapades up in Dulrot."

"That would be nice," Orla said as she gently rested her head on the soft mound of wool in her arms.

CHAPTER 14

DANCING SPECKS OF LIGHT WAVED ALONG THE horizon, forming a glittering line against the sky. The flat, black sky and the inexplicable, invisible light it cast upon the infinite expanse of ebony sands engulfed objects moving in the distance.

A small, tan mass could be seen walking peacefully along the sightline, bearing a faint glowing hue on its back, and another small red figure fluttering around them. The hiss of sands being dragged by weak winds carried far in all directions of the stark, barren wasteland, as well as the echoes of a few distant voices carrying conversation.

"So, about this 'quest' of yours," Orla said.

"What about it?" Fiddle asked.

"You two are going to all this trouble, but for what? To ask some king who may or may not still be with us questions?"

"It's mostly Cynkz who has questions; at least, I'd guess he does."

"Questions about what?"

"When we first got the hold of the thread, Cynkz took hold of it and was granted a bunch of weird visions."

"Visions?"

"Yeah, some random stuff from his time in the po world."

"You two think this king of yours may be able to shed some light on who, or what, Cynkz is?"

"Yeah. If anyone would know, the King would."

"Does this king have a name? Or is he so imposing that he 'shan't be named' out of fear and respect?"

"No, it's just that, I mean—"

"Hmm?"

"No one remembers what he looks like or what his name was. Some think the King selectively wiped everyone's memories after creating Munderworld. Even the old sentinels, his soldiers from the very beginning, can't remember a thing about him."

"And yet they serve him?"

"Yeah. I guess they have nothing better to do."

"Everything just gets more and more peculiar the deeper down the rabbit hole you go."

"Rabbit hole? What rabbits?"

"It's not meant to be literal; it's a figure of—"

Orla's head snapped around, her eyes focused on a single point in the distance. Fiddle looked puzzlingly at the woman.

"A figure of what?" Fiddle asked. "Hello! Orla! You all there?"

"Look, you little scoundrel," Orla said, as she lifted her thin wrist to point a finger.

Fiddle scoffed but followed the object of Orla's focus, as did Cynkz. Poking up from the horizon, a crude wooden stave could be seen leaning into the blank sky. Dull and tattered strips of cloth were wrapped under a large avian skull sitting atop the structure.

"It's one of those things!" Fiddle said.

"You've seen them before?" Orla asked.

"Yeah, we first saw them back in a huge swamp. They were one of the first things that stood out to us as soon as we left Dulrot, actually."

"Those are beacons," Orla said. "The maidens apparently use them to travel."

"You think if we follow them, we'll find one of the 'sisters'?"

"Maybe. If not, it could lead us to a way out of here."

"Seems good enough for me! What do you think, Cynkz?"

The humped beast immediately began shuffling toward the beacon.

"Seems like we're all on the same page," Fiddle said. "It'd be convenient if we could travel like the maidens do."

"Unfortunately, it's not that easy," Orla said.

"Why not?"

"You need a blessing from the great Sisters themselves, the ones in charge of their group, to be able to use the staves. Even then, who knows how they're supposed to be used?"

"Guess we'll just have to find out!"

"I suppose…"

The trio made their way next to the beacon, close enough to nearly touch the black and green moss covering the branch. Fiddle glanced at the beacon, something caught his attention.

"Hey look! Another one!" Fiddle said.

Another twisted branch sat on another hill. Before Cynkz could take a step forward, he listened to the sand. Much of it was moving, uneven rows of ebony grains flowing down the hill.

"It moves so easily, almost like water…" Orla noticed.

"It's gotta be the dirtiest water I've ever seen," Fiddle remarked.

Cynkz placed his weighty hoof into the ground and pushed himself forward. Down each hill they trekked before climbing up another and meeting the side of yet another beacon. At each beacon, the next was visible, making for easy markers in the otherwise barren realm. If not for the faint highlights of the sparkling sands and the occasional beacon sticking out of the top of each dune, Cynkz may have wandered in circles without being aware. They repeated this process in silence before a quick flash of light sparked at the corner of Fiddle's eye.

"Hey, did you guys—"

A flash of faded pink light popped in and out of view, deep in the horizon.

"There!" Orla snapped. "That must be a maiden! It has to be!"

Fiddle said, "Come on! Let's hurry up, Cynkz!"

The camel kicked his heels as hard as he could, propelling them forward. He ran across the smooth layers of sand, kicking up piles of grain and leaving soft hissing clouds as he ran. Fiddle stayed a bit ahead and high above, attempting to keep a proper sight line on the moving light.

The flashing light stopped and withdrew. As it faded, Fiddle could see the silhouette of a thin, hooded figure at its center. It looked as if the figure was kneeling. The imp quickly lowered himself to Cynkz's side.

"Cynkz, it looks like they're stopping for something. Let's see if we can approach them cautiously, surreptitious-like," Fiddle said.

The camel curled its flabby lip and nodded before slowing to a gentle trot. The harsh slapping of sand receded into soft scuffles, and the group made their way to the strange figure ahead.

The figure was merely a single wide dune away from the trio. It was reaching down into the sand without hesitation, their lissom digits cupping something. Cynkz stopped to watch what the hooded figure would do. Fiddle lowered himself and hid behind Orla, who hid behind the front hump on Cynkz's back. Faint murmurs came from the figure's direction, and after a moment of silence, it snapped its head up, the pointed tip of their layered, moss-green hood bouncing around as they moved.

Another moment of tense silence passed. The figure vanished into a flash of dull pink light.

"Aw, come on!" Fiddle yelled. "Just as it felt like we were getting somewhere."

Sobbing rose from the top of the dark sandy dune, catching the imp and the others off guard. They stared, motionless, trying to discern what was making the noise.

Orla and Fiddle shared a glance, and Fiddle looked at Cynkz, who kept his focus on the top of the hill. He crept forward and kept his head low. Orla shifted behind the hump to peek from the side, and Fiddle landed on the rear hump, peering over its top. The crying grew louder as they reached the edge of the hill.

Cynkz reached the top and noticed a small bump poking out of the sand. It was the face of an unfortunate, distressed po man! He was almost submerged by the sand, only the bare edge of his face remained above, thin streams of water running down the hills of his features as he cried out in agony.

Cynkz stepped toward the po and stopped, prompting Orla and Fiddle to reveal themselves.

"Are you … all right?" Orla asked hesitantly, knowing the answer but wanting to break the tense air.

"She's gone… She left me!" the man said.

"Who left you?" Fiddle asked. "You mean that weird cloaked person?"

"That was … a maiden of Elm…" the man said, gasping desperately between his words.

"A maiden?!" Orla said. "Why did she leave? Do you know where she went?"

"She's… I… I don't…" The man's breathing grew more and more weary. "Curse you! Curse you to the great tides of Saknii! You scared her away! You ruined my salvation!"

Fiddle twisted his brow. "What? We didn't do anything. We just—"

A quick, wet snap cut through the air, and a tiny glob of shining spittle hurled itself toward the imp. Fiddle narrowly dodged the missile.

"Hey! What's your problem?!" Fiddle said.

The man gritted his teeth as he twisted himself from side to side, completely immersing himself beneath the sand. A small bump of dark grains leveled themselves and rolled down the dune.

"Why is everyone spitting at me?!" Fiddle said, his tone rising to match his anger. "This place is boring and nasty and filled with boring and nasty people! What else can go wrong?"

A soft hiss began to rise from beneath Cynkz's feet. It was loud enough that Fiddle noticed it during his raving, and he looked over to the camel.

"Uh, Cynkz, your feet are sinking again," Fiddle said.

The brushing of sand grew louder and turned into a small rumbling. The entire face of the sand dune pulled down and away from them like a wave into the ocean.

Soon the dragging of sand grew loud enough to drown out the world around them, and in the distance the horizon lifted into the sky.

"It's a wave!" Fiddle shrieked. "A tidal wave of sand! We gotta get out of here—"

A series of yelps and howls rang from the distance, sharp, piercing calls high enough to break glass, even from miles away.

"Yip! Yip-Yip-Hee!"

"Hee-Yip! Hee-Yip-Yip!"

"Ya-ha-ha-ha!"

In the rising blanket of oppressive black sand, many small forms glided along the wave's surface. Countless faint hues faded in and out of sight as the wave rose, crowds of hapless po condemned to the whims of the desert. The twinkling auras pressed against the black wall reminded Cynkz of the starry night sky in Dulrot.

His attention was gripped by a row of smaller, fleshier forms sailing along the bottom edge of the incoming grainy surf; diminutive creatures with bright peachy skin, almost red and pink like flesh that had been ripped off. The creatures were riding the wave adeptly with their long, pointed feet curving into the sand. They were gangly, appearing malnourished as their ribs seemed to poke out of their boxy rib cages. Their limbs were long and thin, stretching out past their short bodies, and their hands consisted of three pointed digits that weaved strange motions in the air. These hand gestures were followed by the whipping of sand, as if telepathically shifting the landscape to their whims. Their bony shoulders connected to long and crooked necks, perpetually lurching as if after prey. Their eyes were tiny black beads embedded in fleshy pink craniums that fiercely reflected the light. Their faces consisted of lengthy snouts that reached out far past their heads and curled into bony, shovel-shaped tips. Their snouts parted into gnarled, crooked smiles that nearly wrapped around behind their eyes, and revealed shining yellow canines underneath. The creatures were loosely wrapped in tattered black and brown cloth that looked to be of the same material the po commonly wore; most likely they had been harvested from countless po to be used for their own purpose.

The sand-striding muns held a long stretch of rope in one of their hands. It reached into the sand in front of them. Attached to the reins, large white and yellow serpents bearing shovel-shaped heads and large spiked horns stuck out in the opposite direction of the scales.

They whipped their long bodies in a waving S-motion at blinding speed, creating ripples in the sand. The muns commanding them had no issue digging their pointed feet into these ripples, allowing them to glide effortlessly behind their serpentine steeds.

The sharp cackles and howls of the incoming muns cut into the ear like needles. Fiddle in particular seemed startled; everything from his eyes to his mouth and face and even his shoulders stretched back, as if some unseen force were tugging at his soul from behind, desperate to get him out of there.

"Let's go," Fiddle said. "Let's go, let's go, let's go!"

Fiddle darted toward the sky. Cynkz followed suit, kicking his hind legs into the air. Orla flew several feet ahead of a burst of colorless smoke. Cynkz, having returned to his original form, now bearing great black feathered wings, caught the woman in his arms before dashing into the sky behind Fiddle.

The trio flew higher and higher at frightening speed. Orla shut her eyes and clutched at the jester's collar, though Cynkz hardly noticed and kept his focus ahead.

They were above the great tidal wave as it peaked and its collected grains curled and flew back to the desert floor. The subsequent roar rattled the desert, forcing rows and rows of uneven waves to echo along its surface. The faint lights of the po trapped within scattered in all directions before being dragged back down into the depths. Cynkz and Fiddle paused to look down at the group of fleshy, scraggly muns circling beneath them. As the creatures weaved in and out, small circles began to form in the sand. The hiss of dragging sand swelled into a dozen rising twisters, each maelstrom a swirling mass of dark matter.

"What in Munder are they—"

A spike of glistening ebony shot past the imp before he could finish. Another one followed, this time aimed at Cynkz. He bowed backward and snapped his great dark wings. More dark projectiles whistled through the air, each one narrowly missing the jester as he bobbed and weaved in the air. Cynkz noticed the muns below were aiming for Orla.

Perhaps it was their occupation to ensure stray po are bound to the sands, Cynkz thought.

Fiddle noticed that the fleshy muns had their full attention on his companions. He gritted his teeth and flew down to the attackers. He inhaled as much as his little chest could take and blew out a great wave of fire. The muns screeched and wailed before scattering in every direction. The smell of singed cloth and flesh filled the otherwise sterile air.

Fiddle flew back up to Cynkz and noticed Orla still had her eyes tightly shut. Her grip shook against the jester's collar.

"Hey, I did it! You're safe now!" Fiddle said.

Slowly, Orla opened her eyes and loosened her grip. "We're awfully high, aren't we?!" Orla said.

"Pah! Not this again!" Fiddle said. "Are you afraid of heights?"

"A bit… Can we please go down?"

"I don't think that would be wise," Cynkz said.

"Why not?!" Fiddle said.

Cynkz motioned toward the ground in the distance. Fiddle and Orla saw the sand-striders forming a massive circle. Through their chanting and motions, the sand flattened, then sunk into a swirling vortex. The center of the whirlpool radiated an ominous hum as it began to suck in the air, acting as a massive, consuming vacuum. The conjured winds began pulling at the trio.

"Ah crud, we need to hurry!" Fiddle screamed.

"I have an idea," Cynkz said.

"What?"

"Catch!"

Cynkz immediately snapped his wings, heaving himself up. He used the momentum to toss Orla into Fiddle's arms. Fiddle struggled but was able to stabilize himself with the thin po woman in tow.

"Ack! Heavy!" Fiddle shrieked.

Orla gave Fiddle a sharp glare before wrapping her arms around his head, her legs dangling out to the side beyond the imp's grasp.

Cynkz dissolved into another massive cloud of colorless smoke.

Just as the sand muns continued their spell, the ground a violent maelstrom of spiked sand and sucking winds, a new mass wrapped around their formation. They whipped their heads to try and observe what was happening, but the entire whirlpool had been encircled by a gargantuan serpent.

A border made of countless rows of iridescent scales enclosed the muns within their own incantation. The serpent continued to coil its form around them, forcing them into the center of the whirlpool. Waves of dark sand followed the edges of the monstrous beast's form as it closed on top of the fleshy muns. A final, crushing snap stopped the action.

Once the echo of the serpent's action subsided, it loosened its form and a thin jester could be seen floating wearily above a flat expanse of deep rings formed in the sand.

Cynkz flew back up to his companions, the gasps of heavy breath keeping just ahead of him.

"Wow…" Orla whispered.

"Crazy, isn't it?!" Fiddle said, his voice as strained as his arms.

"I may be pushing myself to new limits, Fiddle," Cynkz said, his chest huffing in and out beneath the dark cloak draped over his shoulders.

"You're telling me!" Fiddle said. "I can't hold onto this anymore. Take her back!"

Cynkz drew in a deep breath and let out a faint, exasperated puff of air. Fiddle sputtered as he drew breaths in and out rapidly, ready to toss the "heavy" po woman back to his friend. Just as Fiddle was about to drop the woman, Cynkz darted forward to catch her hardly a foot below.

"I'd like to go down now!" Orla said, shaking from the commotion earlier or from Fiddle nearly dropping her. Cynkz smiled softly at the po woman and slowly began to drift toward the ground.

"Seems like you squashed those annoying muns! They were so loud and annoying," Fiddle said.

"We're safe for now, but what of the maiden?" Cynkz said. "Where do we go from here?"

"I saw weird pink flashes moving that way!" Fiddle said, pointing along a vague line of crude staves that stretched into the distance.

"I suppose we can always try again. We might even be able to get close enough to the maiden to speak with her this time. If she isn't already gone, that is."

"If we hurry, we might be able to tail her. Let's go!"

CHAPTER 15

PINK FLASHES MOVED ACROSS THE WAVES OF black sand. They moved and parted at each beacon before vanishing to the next. Eventually, the flashes stopped, and a thin figure bearing a pointed, moss-green cloak stepped into the open.

"Finally," the hooded figure said in a delicate voice, looking over their shoulder. "I hate working in this realm. It's either too quiet or too chaotic. There's no in between."

Her gaze found a great plateau in the distance.

"I should report back. Word is that damned minstrel is hovering about the realms. Thieving, lying bastard..."

The maiden stepped into another flash of pink light, continuing her path along the complicated line of crude staves sticking into the ground. Covering a significant distance, the blinking light reached the base of the plateau and disappeared into it. Another flash radiated from the flat top of the rocky structure, and the maiden stepped out into the open once again. The moss-green figure walked over to the edge of a large body of water at the mesa's center, stopping just shy of its rim and near another beacon. The maiden placed a delicate hand on top of the crow skull tied to the crown of the beacon. A short beam of intense pink light engulfed the pond. She released her hand and stepped into the water, her entire body turning parallel to the flat surface of water before her entire form was submerged. As soon as she was gone, the light faded, and the soft blue hue of the lake returned.

Three small dragonflies buzzed their way on top of the flat mesa and rested in a sparse patch of grass. Once they landed, a burst of colorless smoke shot up, revealing a jester, an imp, and a woman. Cynkz looked at his friends, both of whom were laying on the ground and breathing heavily. Fiddle picked himself up, patted his chest and drifted above Cynkz's head. Orla sat herself up and held a free hand to her chest, her head bobbing up and down slightly as she gasped for air.

"Sorry about that, madam," Cynkz said. "I wanted to ensure we remained undetected that time, to get a good look at the maiden as she traveled."

"I-I see..." Orla said.

"It's a bit of a pain, right?" Fiddle said.

"You weren't kidding," Orla said, her breathing softer and more steady as she regained composure. "It felt like a boulder was pressing down on my chest. Is *that* what you have to go through every time you shapeshift?"

"Indeed it is, but I've gotten used to it," Cynkz said.

Cynkz walked over to Orla and kneeled down, extending his long, pale hand to her. She looked at his hand, then at him before taking hold of it to be pulled up. She stared into his eyes for an uncomfortable amount of time. Cynkz stared back, though merely looked puzzled as he pressed his brow ever so slightly above his eyes. Orla, for some reason, could not remove her eyes from his, despite the discomfort.

"Just what are you, anyway?" Orla asked.

Cynkz's heavy brow recoiled, widening his eyes as he tried to think of a proper answer.

"I'm sorry," Orla said, breaking her gaze as she looked awkwardly to the ground.

"It's fine," Cynkz said. "I suppose I'm trying to find that answer myself. It's why I decided to go on this crazy journey to begin with."

Fiddle crossed his arms and pushed out his bottom lip, fidgeting about as his patience grew thin.

"If you two are done, let's keep going. We're making great progress!" Fiddle said.

"Agreed," Cynkz said, as he walked toward the beacon planted in the soil by the rim of the pond.

"What was that weird hooded lady talking about?" Fiddle asked.

"I'm not sure," Cynkz responded. "She mentioned something of a 'thieving minstrel.'"

"What's a minstrel?" Fiddle asked again.

"Essentially a musician, a bard, often employed to entertain royalty through song."

"So like a jester but less annoying?" Fiddle said, twirling around in the air and flashing a cheeky grin to his companion.

"Ha! In a sense, yes, I suppose," Cynkz said.

"We never had jesters where I lived," Orla said. "But I've heard stories."

"Oh?" Cynkz said, turning a curious look at the young woman. "What have you heard about them?"

"That they're pretty weird. Most were rejected members of their society, having to resort to crude humor and gross displays to entertain the nobility. Though I have heard a few were quite capable acting as political advisors and courtiers."

"That's about right," Cynkz said.

"Wait... were *you* a jester, back in the living world?" Orla asked, ending her statement with a slight turn of her head.

"I was, though I do not remember much of my working time, or how I happened to enter the profession."

"You sound educated, so I'd assume you were one of the smart ones."

"Perhaps, though I cannot say for sure—"

"Yeah, sometimes you're smart, and other times..." Fiddle said, shrugging his shoulders, a mischievous grin completely wrapping his features.

"You pick on your friend too much!" Orla said through a half-chuckle.

"Eh, he knows I'm just teasing," Fiddle remarked.

Cynkz shifted his focus to the beacon and the large body of flat, calm water. Despite the maiden altering the water to walk through, it seemed completely unperturbed. There was not a single ripple or wave in sight. Orla walked up to his side and looked down at her reflection in the water, her own eyes meeting that of the image in the pond.

"That weird flash of light..." Orla said.

"How did she manage it? Do you think she traveled to a new realm through here?" Fiddle asked.

"It's hard to say. I know that you cannot use the beacons without—"

A crash of water erupted from the center of the lake. Cynkz and Orla's stared wide-eyed at the center of the pond. A small red imp could be seen flying back out, coughing and wheezing.

"Eesh! I figured I would try just hopping in. There's nothing down there," Fiddle said, trailing water droplets on the rocky ground.

Orla laughed, then continued, "You can't use the beacons without the blessing of the sisters themselves. I know that much."

"I see..." Fiddle said.

"I doubt Fiddle nor I could make use of the beacons. They only recruit women, correct?" Cynkz said, looking at Orla.

"Yes, that is true," Orla said.

"Perhaps you could use the beacon? Maybe these 'sisters' would welcome, even guide, the hand of a possible new recruit?"

"Maybe, but I don't know how it would work, or how I could possibly—"

"Just grab the beacon and hope for the best!" Fiddle said. "That seems to be the best way to figure anything out, like when Cynkz first touched the thread and got those weird visions. I'm starting to feel left out; no visions or old ladies to guide me forward..."

"It's all right, my friend. In fact, it may be a blessing in disguise! One of us needs to remain sober if we wish to keep going," Cynkz said.

"Exactly! Though I wasn't 'all there' in the trippy place with that giant tree..."

"You were fine, for the most part."

"What happened there anyway? All I remember is the headache I had afterward."

"It's a funny story, but it'll have to wait for another time."

"Fine, fine."

Fiddle rested his hands on his hips and turned to Orla.

"Well? Think you could try it out?" Fiddle said.

“I suppose I could try. It’s not as if we have anything else to go off of,” Orla said.

“Take solace in the fact that we are here to support you,” Cynkz said. “If anything goes wrong, do not fear to release yourself from the beacon. We can always explore and find another way—”

“Thank you, but I think it’ll be fine,” Orla said.

Cynkz and Orla shared a soft smile before she stepped to the beacon. It was a surprisingly hefty looking instrument and stood a fair bit taller as she looked up to the animal skull tied to the branch’s top. She could see something within the dark sockets of the skull peering back at her. They were nothing more than grainy pockets of darkness, yet some invisible force compelled her to look on. As she reached ahead, she could feel the world receding into a darkness blanketing the realm. For a moment, nothing existed beyond her hand and the beacon. She could hear faint mumbling behind her, presumably Cynkz or Fiddle trying to speak with her, but she could not hear them in the void. Once her pale hand reached the textured surface of the stave, everything disappeared, and all that was left was the feeling of existing in nonexistence.

A speck of light emerged from the void. It was a star twinkling at the center of the blanket of darkness. Soon more and more specks materialized from the abyss, forming a beautiful night sky. As the stars withdrew farther into the sky, a vast landscape came into view and a sleek purple desert waved above the horizon, surrounded by nonsensically placed trees and rocks bordering its edges. The faint hue of countless po scattered across the land hid amongst the fauna.

The vision drew back and into the burning edges of the realm, where the harsh shift in light turned the world into a yellow haze. It overlooked an endless swamp of black muck. Streams of bleached vapors reached out from the dark mud, pulling the vision into the black sea. Once again, the world succumbed to absolute darkness before being split open, a gray tear opening the way to a vista revealing grinding stones and mountains.

A blue-gray haze colored the world, muting the life within it. Faint glowing orbs could be seen crawling in and out of the crevices between the mountains. The crumbling of rock and crashing of mountains drowned everything out. The vision pulled into one of the crevices, a large, violently shaped crack in one of the mountains that led to darkness, then faded into a soft blue light revealing rows and rows of squared stones leading to a strange, almost organic opening. The vision pulled into the strange opening, and the world crashed in like the jaws of a vicious predator.

Orla's eyes snapped open. Immediately she was overwhelmed by the crashing of new light bearing down on her senses, causing her to fall to her side. She could hear the faint voices from earlier, though now they were crisp and clear.

"Orla!" Cynkz cried out as he knelt down.

"What was that?!" Fiddle said. "You were holding onto that thing for minutes and didn't respond to anything. It was like you were asleep or something."

"The beacon… it showed… visions…" Orla said.

Fiddle said, "You two and your blasted 'visions.'"

"What did you see?" Cynkz asked.

"I think I saw the night sky you mentioned, in that place, Dulrot."

"Dulrot?!" Cynkz said, his features spreading apart, astonished at the woman's words. "What else did you see?"

"It wasn't for long, but I felt myself being dragged across Dulrot, and then into a black fire on the horizon that led me to a great swamp. The swamp reached out and grabbed me, and I was back in the stone region where we first met."

"Horgafell…" Fiddle said under his breath.

"Then I could feel myself being pulled deep into a cavern, with a strange blue light inside, before a great, abyssal jaw closed in on me, and I… I…"

"It's all right, Orla," Cynkz said.

"I never wanted to see that horrible place again…"

Fiddle drifted closer and began patting Orla's shoulder.

"You don't have to do it again if it was painful—"

"No!" Orla snapped. Fiddle recoiled in shock, flying back several feet as if anticipating a strike.

"I'm sorry, I just… Let me hold the beacon again. Something was pulling me through the realms. If I can harness it again, surely it will show us the way forward."

Cynkz and Fiddle looked at each other, then back to Orla.

"All right, then. Do what you feel you must," Cynkz said.

Orla picked herself up and stood before the beacon again. Before her fingers could reach the gnarled wooden surface of the staff, the world receded into darkness.

Once again the vision was enraptured in darkness, though the snap of stone jaws could be heard from behind. The darkness split open, revealing wild swirls of colors and vapors that blended with a sea of short trees. The wind carried her toward a massive tree, larger enough to split the sky. Countless po and walking mushrooms gathered below a giant, bowled flower at the tree's base. As the vision approached the tree, a great yellow mass of leather and mucous emerged and shot up into the sky. The new mass danced up and around the tree before disappearing into its rainbowed plumage.

The vision flew through the leaves of the great tree before succumbing to darkness. Faint lights glittered in the distant abyss, forming waving flat planes as they cut a flowing curve into the horizon. Orbs of light and glistening grains gathered together into massive waves as they crashed into the rising, rocky shores of plateaus. The violent happenings, from a distance at least, formed a tranquil ambience.

Orla remained motionless as her hand rested against the wooden stave. She resembled an immaculate marble statue. The soft brush of wind was near-indistinguishable from the soft breathing of her two companions. Cynkz and Fiddle stood in an awkward silence, unsure of what to do as they sheepishly fidgeted.

"You think she's all right?" Fiddle whispered into Cynkz's ear.

"I'm not sure," Cynkz whispered back. "Was I like this when I had my first vision in Dulrot?"

"Pfft," Fiddle scoffed.

"What?"

"You were worse."

"How so?"

"Your whole body was limp, and you kept mumbling nonsense in your sleep. It took everything I had to keep you from drifting off into the sun."

"I always figured I was a peaceful sleeper."

"Not that time!" Fiddle exclaimed. He threw his hands to his mouth to cover it, realizing his outburst.

"Honestly, my friend, I don't think we need to be so wary. She appears to be well-focused on her task."

"Thank goodness, all this being quiet-like is stressful."

"Much can be learned from listening rather than speaking, Fiddle."

"Eh, that's what you're here for."

A sharp, whimpering wail cut the air.

"Are you crying?" Fiddle said. "What's with the whimpering—"

"That was not me," Cynkz said, looking at the landscape and assuming an alert stance.

Fiddle drifted ahead. As he squinted, small fleshy blurs revealed themselves on the waving black horizon. Behind them, waves of ebony flowed, pushing them forward at blinding speed. More and more speeding blurs rose above the dunes, and an expansive wall of flat black grains carried dozens of howling surfers and their serpent mounts toward the plateau.

"Uh oh, we gotta go!" Fiddle said.

Fiddle darted toward Orla, fluttering back and forth as he desperately tried to move her away from the beacon.

"Come on! Wake up! Wake up! We gotta move!" Fiddle shouted as he strained himself.

"Sheesh, how'd she get so heavy all of a sudden? Some fierce hex or something must have taken hold of her. What do we do?!"

"We defend her, Fiddle. Her safety is our responsibility," Cynkz said.

"I mean, I guess, but—"

"Fiddle, you care about her too. You cannot fool me."

Fiddle sighed, throwing his shoulders in exasperation. "Fine, you're right! So what's the plan?"

"We keep them away from the plateau's edge."

"Sounds good! You gonna crush 'em again like before, or—"

"I'll fly out and distract them, try to smother, and deter them. I need you to stay near the cliff's edge and cover it with flame if anyone gets by me."

"Does fire work on them?"

"I suppose we'll just have to find out. But Fiddle..."

"Hmm?"

"Be very careful. Even as a scaled beast, I could feel the sand pulling greatly at my skin. Whatever you do, do not let the sands touch you or Orla."

"Don't worry about it! I got your back."

Cynkz nodded, then turned to face the desert. He ran to the cliff's edge. His footsteps left a trail of taps behind him before abruptly ending in a wind-breaking dive. He disappeared down the cliff and into a cloud of colorless smoke. emerging as an enormous, dark form. Two leathery spikes shot out like spears, cutting the air like claws against fur. Attached to each spike was a large, thick blanket of dark flesh that crashed against the wind, bending the element to its whim as it spread, propelling the rest of the beast's form through the sky with ease. Once the two webbed limbs stretched out, long enough to pierce the horizon, they snapped to the side, dispersing the smoke against the sand below. The black wings almost turned violet as it penetrated the thin layer of skin forming the creature's wings. Again the wings snapped, this time toward the ground, lifting the small, muscle-packed sphere of flesh and muscle connecting the two limbs together. The edges of the creature's head poked through, two large ears shot out like horns, and a third spike on the creature's face gave its head the appearance of a monstrous trident. The beast, a collection of spikes and flesh in the form of a terrifying bat-like entity, rose high into the abyss and flung itself toward its prey.

"That showoff," Fiddle said, grinning as he watched the jagged silhouette race into the distance.

The sand surfing muns poked their snouts up to look at the oncoming terror. They began to howl, commanding orders to one another. The group split into two, approximately twenty on each side, and rode off in different directions. Cynkz flung himself down with such speed that the wind surrounding him could be heard booming far off into the distance. He folded his wings and narrowly avoided contact with the ground. The pressure generated was enough to mimic the collision of a bomb, sending titanic waves of dark sand into the sky. It scooped up the group of fleshy muns and their serpentine mounts and sent them flying through the air.

The opposing muns swerved, cutting acute curves in the sand as they turned. They waved their gangly fingers and conjured up clumps of dark sand into dense spikes. Once angled toward the beast, they flung their limbs forward, shooting glistening black missiles at their target.

The harsh sound of their flight bounced off the inner walls of Cynkz's large ears, causing him to twitch. He torqued his wings at opposite angles, causing him to spin through the air. The flying spikes whisked past him as he evaded their onslaught.

The second group howled and split, darting off in all directions as they attempted to surround the flying beast. Cynkz snapped his wings, carving a steep path through the air and flying straight toward the sky. The sand-muns struggled to discern what the beast was doing as its dark body blended with the pitch black sky. For a moment, it appeared to stall in the air, its body forming a tight ball before whipping its limbs out again. From its center a piercing shriek barreled toward the muns. Before they could react, the waves blasted the ground at the center of their group. A deep pit carved a steep circle, and at its edges, a huge wave of sand shot up, carrying the muns with it. The deafening sound further debilitated the muns as they curled and withdrew from the impact. Small trails of deep red blood oozed out from every orifice, trailing behind them as they soared.

Fiddle waited and watched back on the plateau. More yowling could be heard in the distance—another group of sand-muns rose over the horizon, appearing to be similar in number to the first squad. Cynkz's jagged form violently snapped against the first group, showing that he was still preoccupied. Fiddle looked at Orla, who had not moved since the fighting began and drew in a deep breath, preparing himself for the oncoming assault.

As the new group neared the plateau, Fiddle flew to the cliff's edge and dropped to the ground. The hiss of sand being dragged and pushed grew louder before nearing the bottom of the rocky platform. Fiddle drew in a deep breath, puffing up his small chest as much as he could manage, and flung himself off the ledge, blowing a great wave of burning orange flames toward the ground. He exhaled so hard, and for so long, that he could scarcely see what he was aiming at. The heat produced caused even the imp to sweat and tear up, yet he continued, refusing to settle for anything less than a thorough job. He could hear the cries and screams of the sand muns. From the corner of his eyes, and between the tears blurring his vision, he could see charred bodies desperately crawling and scrambling away from the plateau. Eventually, his breath sputtered, and he finally stopped. Between the crackling of burnt sand and the handful of scorched creatures sitting motionless below, Fiddle was relieved at a job well done.

Or so he thought.

Panting and wheezing, Fiddle could hear a familiar howl off in the distance. Another wave of fleshy pink muns were making their way toward the plateau. Yet something was different; the other groups appeared more chaotic and freeform in their movement, as if they were improvising their tactics. Four sets of two muns rode toward the plateau. Each set worked tirelessly to whip up sand to their side, forming a sharp v-formation that expanded behind them. The bundles of sand that trailed behind them flew into the air and thickened, appearing like a stagnant mist. In the center of their formation, a new mun faded through, one totally unique in appearance, while commanding in its presence and inadvertently humorous in impression.

The new mun was several times larger than the little pink creatures before him. His body was round, a corpulent belly sticking out and guiding him as he surfed. His skin was a pale green, giving him an oddly ghastly and sickly complexion. His paunch led straight up to his chin, which receded below several layers of flab that grinded against the bottom jaw of his huge snout. His wide maw was open, cracking a crooked smile that revealed countless small yellow teeth that gleamed in the realm's invisible light. His eyes were, in contrast to the tiny black beads of his lessers, each a deep socket with milky, shining white orbs that shook as he bounced against the desert floor. He required four different serpents to pull him forward, each tied to a single leash that he held in a large and bony hand with lines of white hairs sticking out of its side. His free hand was perpetually raised, casting a swirling gesture that whipped up the mist into condensed vapor that moved at his command.

Fiddle looked closer at the sand the new muns were whipping and noticed their odd sheen, as if it were being wetted and hardened into a new substance. He drew in a deep breath and shouted to the horizon.

"Cynkz!" Fiddle's scream echoed into the distance, its waves reverberating against the air like loose boulders in the depths of a great cavern.

The bat-beast, still crashing up and down against the remaining muns from the first group, twitched his ear and looked to his friend. Immediately, the final group caught his eye, and he twisted his great, spiked wings to propel himself back to the plateau.

The pale green mun took notice and screeched to his followers, commanding them to turn toward the oncoming beast. Cynkz lowered, using the winds to drag huge waves of black sand toward the pale green mun.

Fiddle watched as two colossal streams of turning sand flew toward each other head on. Before the two forces could meet, the pale mun howled and laughed as he whipped up his bony hand, and with it, a sky-consuming blanket of wet, black mud curled overhead. The damp wall reached out and ahead like a hand reaching for its victim, the sand shining along its edges like dirtied fingernails.

Cynkz twisted the spiked ends of his wings, piercing a gaping hole through the mud wall. Another screech echoed from below, and countless hardened spikes shot up and grazed Cynkz's skin. Long red streaks dotted the surface of the bat-beast's leathery wings, leaving behind thin trails of blood. The beast's flight sputtered, and it limped through the air, barely making it to the plateau.

Burst into a massive cloud of colorless smoke, the jester landed on the surface of the flat mesa with a bone-cracking thump.

"Cynkz!" Fiddle screamed as he dashed over to his friend. "Are you all right?!"

"I'm… I'm fine," Cynkz said. He struggled to lift himself with arms, now covered in dozens of cuts and scars peaking from beneath his torn sleeves.

Fiddle held out his hands but stopped himself from instinctually touching his friend. He looked back at Orla before speaking to Cynkz: "Orla is still out like a light. What are we gonna do?"

The ground rumbled, the sand and pebbles on the stone surface shaking and rattling. Cynkz and Fiddle looked back to the edge of the plateau to see something wet and shining rising above the cliff. A colossal, undulating mass of black sand rose into the sky, vaguely taking the form of a crude beast stretching its ends like limbs over prey. Within its mass countless sands could be seen being wetted, and falling and rising, and repeating the process to grow its form. The hiss of falling sand succumbed to the harsh slap of wet muck being pressed against itself. Deep within the moving lump muffled screeches and howls could be heard, the cackling of violent creatures could be mistaken for the fake-beast's roar.

"We have to move!" Fiddle yelled. He began to pull at Orla's arm gripping the stave, but she would not budge. No matter how hard Fiddle tried to move her, she remained completely unfazed, lost in her visions.

Fiddle's breathing grew heavier and more desperate the longer he tried. "Dammit, dammit, dammit!" Fiddle said, his voice cracking, nearly tapering into a whimper as the shadow of the great sand form loomed overhead and reached for them.

Cynkz held his ground, his mind racing, desperately clawing for a solution like a hand grasping in the dark. As he stared at the new beast, he noticed something at its center. he round, pale green belly of the sand mun protruded ever so slightly from beneath the moist layer of the lumbering mass.

Spurred on by nothing but instinct, Cynkz pulled his shoulder back and his head forward. A huge white heron spread its wings as it emerged from the smoke, its beak held forward like a spear. A great orange tip pierced the pale green paunch at the center of the sand mass.

The sound of wet slapping sand stopped, and the air was filled with a blood curdling scream. The large sand mun's husky voice gave way to the wetted rattling of spit and blood as his body was forced through the wall of mud. Once he was firmly settled at the end of Cynkz's beak, snapped his bill open, matching the sound of dripping mud with torn flesh and bone.

The unnatural collection of mud and sand dispersed, revealing several pink bodies as they fell to the desert floor. Clumps of sand fell around the top of the plateau. Cynkz immediately realized the danger and turned around to check on Orla, who remained in her quiescent state. Barrels of wet black sand were flying at her. The huge crane turned its body as quickly as its lumbering form could and stretched out its left wing to shade the woman from the oncoming assault. As the sand hit the crane's wing, its entire body crumbled and fell to the ground. The bird burst into smoke, leaving only the jester lying at the center of a messy spread of black mud and grain.

Orla snapped out of her vision, releasing her grip on the beacon. Her senses slowly returned to her, and she could make out two red forms huddled against the floor. Something was wrong. Fiddle hunched over his friend and cried out to him. Cynkz appeared lifeless on the ground. She stumbled toward them, nearly tripping over her own feet.

She kneeled beside the imp and looked down at the jester, unable to parse the odd concoction of emotions swelling within her. As the sound of the crying imp faded into white noise, her vision blurred behind a rising wall of tears forming in her own eyes.

Chapter 16

The sharp cries of a small, wily imp echoed into the distance.

Orla could hardly muster the strength to speak, yet somehow managed to say purely out of desperation, "Fiddle, what happened? How long was I out?"

Fiddle continued to whimper and cry, ignoring the question. Orla did not hold it against him and placed a gentle hand on the imp's furry shoulder.

"You idiot…" Fiddle said as he finally calmed himself down to speak coherently.

"You idiot!" he yelled, slamming his tiny fist into the jester's torn and blackened shoulder.

"Ah! Ow!!" Cynkz said, his body jolting from the shock.

"Cynkz! You're alive!" Fiddle said.

Orla's eyes widened, the thin streams of tears nearly flung away by her shock.

Fiddle reached out to help his friend sit up.

"Fiddle, wait, I can manage on my own," Cynkz said in a tired hush.

The imp moved back a half step to give Cynkz room.

Once the jester was upright, he held his left arm, now covered in deep cuts and harsh black sand. Cynkz looked back to the horizon and watched as several small pink bodies fled into the distance.

"It seems we were successful in repelling our assailants," Cynkz said.

"Who cares about that!" Fiddle said. "Are you okay? Your arm looks…"

Cynkz looked down at his arm; it had been rendered to a sickly cylinder of shiny black grains and streaks of dried red blood that poked through the pale surface of his skin. He could barely move it, and his hand and fingers were completely stiff, as if wrapped in a cast of iron. The strangest thing of all was how heavy his arm felt. He was more than used to the strain of his abilities, most notably the increased weight of his ever-changing forms, yet something seemed to be pulling him down. He so rarely injured himself that the sight of his tainted arm seemed surreal, as if he could hardly accept the reality of his situation. Most worrying to him was that he mostly felt unworried, willing to move on and hope it could heal over time, as most things did in Munderworld if left alone.

Cynkz grew tired of pondering his own frailty and pulled his cloak over the mangled limb.

"I'll be fine," Cynkz said. "More importantly, are *you* all right, Orla?"

Her eyes remained fixed on Cynkz's concealed arm. After a moment, she noticed the jester's question and looked up to him, her face carrying the worried expression.

"I-I'm fine, really…" Orla said.

"Quite a bit occurred while you were in a trance. Were you able to learn anything?" Cynkz asked.

"Yes. I could feel the guiding hand of … something or someone. It guided my vision through the realms, though not in a way I knew possible. It was as if I was light phasing through the air."

"That's really weird," Fiddle said, "and sort of cryptic."

"Yeah, I… I can't really explain what I was feeling or what was happening."

"Is there a way forward for us?"

"Yes. I can activate the staff, and we can walk through the water like the maiden did."

"That's wonderful! Way to go, Orla!" Fiddle exclaimed.

"But ... I cannot guarantee where precisely we may end up. I can only guarantee a way forward. I do not have the slightest bit of control over this," Orla said.

"Well, we are not averse to taking risks, obviously," Cynkz said, resting his hand over his cloaked arm.

"That's what worries me," Orla said.

"I guess we didn't think this whole thing through, did we, Cynkz?" Fiddle said as he tried to smile through the heavy veil of his own concern.

Cynkz returned a warm smile back at his friend. "I suppose not, but Munderworld would be quite boring if we did nothing but sit around and pontificate our actions, would it not?"

"True! True, I suppose..."

"You two are just asking for punishment. Dulrot really must be a tranquil paradise if this is what you think of things," Orla said.

"We'll be fine!" Fiddle said. "We can take a beating. We've even taken a few beatings from sentinels! This is nothing."

"Actually, you're the only one who's been caught by a sentinel, if I recall," Cynkz said.

"And look how I turned out! Still fit as a..."

"Fit as a fiddle?"

"I can't believe I walked right into that..."

Orla laughed, just enough to force her hand to her face and her still wet eyes shut.

"You two buffoons are in way over your heads," Orla said.

"Well, we seemed to be doing all right so far," Fiddle said.

"It's only going to get harder from here," Orla said.

"How so? Were you able to peer into the happenings of the upcoming realms?" Cynkz asked.

"I did, sort of, but only as far as the next two. I think the Sisters of Elm are residing in the realm beyond the next," Orla said.

"We're getting close! I can feel it!" Fiddle said. "Maybe these creepy ladies can finally give us answers."

"If they'll have you," Orla said.

"They'll have to let us have an audience with them! We're basically handing them the best new recruit they could ask for!"

"Flattery is fine but ... just be careful about attempting to charm the Sisters if or when you meet them."

"Cynkz is good with the ladies! Actually, maybe not, I can't tell anymore," Fiddle said, crossing his arms and scratching at the tip of his tiny, pointed chin.

Cynkz patted himself down, wiping off stray bits of dark sand in the process.

"Let's go then," Cynkz said. "We haven't a moment to lose."

"But your arm…" Orla said, her worried expression returning as she looked to the jester's cloak.

"I'll be fine, Orla, really."

"If you say so…"

"Yeah, I'm sick of this place too," Fiddle said.

"All right then, follow me," Orla said.

The po woman picked herself up and walked over to the crude stave. She reached out her hand, stopping just before touching the beacon's surface.

"This should cause the water to light up. All you have to do is walk through it—"

"Can I dive in? There isn't much water in Dulrot, so I wanna make the most of a good swim!" Fiddle said, squirming as he drifted toward Orla and the edge of the lake.

"I insist that you *walk* through the portal. I do not know where exactly we will end up. You could end up diving into a rock wall, the mouth of a predator, or—"

"All right! I get your point. I'll be careful," Fiddle said.

"That goes for you too, Cynkz," Orla said, turning her head to look at the jester standing a ways from the lake's edge.

"No worries, madam. I shall heed your words," Cynkz said.

Orla nodded, her arm still stretched toward the staff. She drew in a weighty breath and pushed forward to place her hand against the splintered surface. The water began to glow, a bright pink burning into the black sky. A strange, deep hum could be heard pulsating at the edges of the pond. Orla released her hand from the stave and looked to her companions.

"I'll go first," Orla said. "Just follow my lead."

"Whatever you say, boss!" Fiddle said.

Orla stepped into the light, her body tipping over until it was nearly parallel to the water's flat surface. She disappeared completely into the light. Fiddle scurried to the water's edge before doing the same. Cynkz hesitated, looked back at the calm horizon, and moved to the light. As he stepped forward, he could feel the light wrapping around him, shifting his sense of direction with it. An overwhelming feeling of lightheadedness overtook him. He was completely awake and aware, yet moving into the light made him feel as if he were falling unconscious rather than falling into a portal. The radiance overtook him and he was gone, leaving behind nothing more than a fading pink hue that slowly dimmed as it receded into the dark sky.

CHAPTER 17

A SENSE OF WEIGHTLESSNESS OVERTOOK CYNKZ as the blinding light faded. The bright pink haze persisted, though its intensity shifted as the world below came into view. A sea of flushed mist coated the bottom of the world with tanned rocky spires stood out from the gaseous layer. Cynkz could feel his body being flung around, his flight disoriented by the instant switching of perspectives. He wanted nothing more than to land on solid ground, giving himself a moment to rest and wait for the nausea to subside.

The whipping of air met with a heavy, abrupt end as he landed on top of a mountainous spire. The impact of hitting solid ground and the instant stopping of his spinning came down upon his senses like a hammer bashing in his skull. The jester settled his senses, picked himself up, and realized he had crashed headfirst into an unforgiving crag.

At least, I didn't land on my arm, Cynkz thought.

He found himself in the middle of a wooded ravine, surrounded on all sides by steep rock walls and an odd assortment of sparse vegetation. Dark iridescent vines and stems reached out in every direction, loose ropes that connected the trees and plants together. Cynkz attempted to fly but struggled. His arm weighed him down significantly, enough that drifting about was a concerted effort. He noticed the spot in the ravine where he landed; a deep pit of dark cracks and fragmented stone sat where he impacted the ground. He almost smiled as he thought about what jokes Fiddle would make of his weight if he could see it.

Fiddle! Cynkz thought.

He drew in a heady breath and flew up to search for his lost companions. Once above the scant collection of trees, he looked out into the distance, a useful skill and favorite pastime of his in most other contexts.

The first detail to capture Cynkz's eye was the malicious fog that resided beneath the countless spires dotting the horizon. It was a flat, bright salmon-colored layer of gas that moved and expanded yet never rose upward. It almost crackled with an electrifying energy as it shifted around, giving the impression that there was no bottom to this world. The stone towers in the distance could be seen slowly rising in and out of the mist, a smooth rumbling of heavy material sending out a muffled echo through the pink fog. Many of the mountains were connected by long, thin branches that rose and sunk with them. They looked similar to crude, man-made bridges, though for what and for whom it was impossible to tell. The mist blurred the horizon, and from it, distant mountain ranges faded behind faint clouds of pink. Just above was the sky, a swirling, sickening mix of dull yellow and blue reflected the overwhelming pink smog.

Whereas Andion's swamp was at least ostensibly tranquil, Horgafell was blunt and unsubtle, and the drugged marsh of the swamp people was playful, and the sands of Saknii represented simple elegance, this realm was different. Everything blended together in harsh, unnatural ways leading to equally harsh, unnatural colors and reflections. The realm was coated in a soft malevolence; the impression that no one should be there, and those who were had only suffering to look forward to.

A rolling thunder echoed from below, and Cynkz looked down to see the platform underneath sink slowly into the mist. It seemed that there was no place for rest in this realm. Not that he wanted to waste any time; finding his companions was Cynkz's first and only priority.

He noticed a familiar white hue glowing from a spire. A group of po were nearby, probably hiding within similar ravines.

Perhaps they'd be willing to help, like Kadd and his group, Cynkz thought.

As Cynkz flew toward the pillar, his arm ached, and he looked at it once again, noticing just how tattered and shredded his sleeve was. He waved his hand across his black cloak. A small puff of colorless smoke fixed the rend, and he lengthened the cloak on his left side to cover and hide his injury more easily. The closer Cynkz was to the pillar, the more active he noticed the faint po lights became. The spire did not appear to be readying itself for descent. They were an odd collection of ragged men and women, appropriately disheveled and tattered.

Maybe I could lend a hand, offer them some reprieve, and they'll be willing to share information, Cynkz thought.

Once he was close enough, he could hear the po speaking to one another:

"It's another one!"

"Is he working with that bastard?"

"Not another mad minstrel!"

"We have nothing left… Why do your kind insist on tormenting us?"

Cynkz stopped and wondered what was going on. He remembered the maiden in the previous realm mentioning a dangerous minstrel. For some reason, the po were on edge at the mere sight of him. Most seemed charmed by his appearance, even saying he looked no different than a po in an odd outfit. It was not often po were so put off by him.

"Excuse me!" Cynkz called out.

"Stay back! We don't have anything for you! Just leave us be!" one of the po screamed back.

"I'm not here to harm you! I'm just looking for some information. I'm lost, you see—"

"Lies! All of your kind are liars! You'll get nothing from me!"

"I assure you, I'm not here to—"

Before Cynkz could finish his plea, the small bodies stranded on top of the pillar began to run and throw themselves off the edge. At first it was one couple, then nearly a dozen more followed their lead, before everything went quiet. Cynkz was frozen, unsure of what to make of the situation. His journey seemed to be going smoothly until now. Now, for whatever reason, everything was crashing down around him: his first true injury, the disappearance of his friends, and now he could not approach the po without them fleeing to their demise. As heavy as his arm felt, it compared little to the current weight on his conscience.

He tightened his lip and brow, drew in another tired breath and flew off, any way to get away from the current scene and his own troubled thoughts.

Yet even as drifted aimlessly, he could not help but think over everything he had recently learned.

Was it worth throwing away my otherwise peaceful time in Dulrot? Even then, what were Fiddle and I doing? We seemed to just cause trouble and could not even leave without being a nuisance, going so far as to possibly ruin a chance at salvation for that group of po following the apostle. My scheme put Fiddle in immediate danger, flung us into space, and dragged him all the way down here—and for what? Because I was bored and curious? Why did I embark on this journey, really? The vision in the thread could have been anything. Perhaps I was looking for an excuse to do something, anything, to leave and find new stimulation.

I've dragged Fiddle into numerous dangers, some of which I only escaped because of his doing. And Kadd, Harla, and the other po with them, I could not save them. I gave them a path forward, but to what? I lost them all in that wretched, drug-filled marsh. They had children with them, and yet I gave it so little thought. Why are children, of all people, trapped here, in such an awful place? Are mere children, po or not, meant to endure the suffering of Munderworld, and to find some way to move on and seek salvation? Is Dulrot the only realm to offer any chance of salvation? Just what is Munderworld? What is the purpose of this place?

And Orla… First impressions notwithstanding, she does not seem like one who deserves to be trapped down here, in any of these realms. My foolish adventure has dragged her into more danger. I could hardly protect her from measly muns and sand-muns without getting myself seriously injured. Now she's lost. For all I know, she and Fiddle could be lost somewhere in the pink fog below, writhing in perpetual agony…

Chapter 17

Even in my visions, I seemed to be coming into conflict with those around me in some way or causing some sort of trouble. Is that all I am? A troublemaker? A derelict? A bum? A scoundrel?

Cynkz had lost track of how long he drifted along the dull yellow sky, his long cloak fluttering behind, in his mind, probably gave any po who saw him the impression of a menacing tendril. He noticed more faint white lights scattering across the mountain tops, but was unmotivated, not wanting to attempt approaching them, lest he be greeted with gnashing and vitriol. He was desperate for a positive conversation, even if it was indirect.

Perhaps he could transform, disguise himself as something benign, or something that could sneak by and listen in. The more he thought of methods to sneak into a po's social circle, the more distasteful he grew with himself. *Such knavish, scoundrel tactics,* Cynkz thought in a half-hearted, half-joking manner.

A piercing scream caught his ear, and he turned his head to see what it came from. In another odd direction, Cynkz saw dozens of familiar po lights toppling over one another as they spilled off of a pillar in the distance. The movement was such that it seemed as though something was chasing them, perhaps some conscious danger was deliberately going after the poor po. Cynkz figured it wouldn't hurt to investigate and headed toward the commotion.

Cynkz was hesitant to do some sleuthing due in no small part to his injury and growing exhaustion. Still he pressed on. The shrill calls of the frightened po trailed off into the pink fog below, and what was left stood out to Cynkz. It was a gruff, husky voice that seemed to rattle from its own weight. He could not discern what exactly the new voice was saying, but the curiosity was overwhelming. He slowly drifted ahead, and a new figure came into view, floating in the air above the mountain.

As soon as the new figure was in view, the whites of their eyes expanded and greeted Cynkz' own gaze. For a moment, his heart stopped, both entities sharing the shock. The stranger was the first to soften their expression, and even smiled, before turning their body to fly toward Cynkz. As the stranger approached, they greeted Cynkz with the only charitable conversation he had received so far.

"Why hello there, my good sir!" the stranger said, their voice attempting to be warm beneath a heavy, throaty layer.

"Good day to you too, sir," Cynkz said back.

"Finally another polite soul has happened across this realm! As you have no doubt experienced, the po here do not make for good conversation."

"That is true, no doubt."

Cynkz looked the stranger over, needing more than a few moments to fully take in the details of their impression. The stranger appeared like a short man, an earthy-looking po with a significant paunch. His body was round, and his limbs appeared to be too thin and wiry for his mass. Despite this, he had the air of one who knew how to throw their weight around the way a soldier would. He wore an embellished, form-fitting coat with short coattails that split into two points behind him. Beneath was a tight blouse bearing a violet and emerald checker pattern. His trousers bore a pinstripe pattern and consisted of a dark purple shade. His shoes appeared to be a fine suede, a shining, ostentatious material that reflected the harsh pink light. Every part of his body was covered, save for his face. It was a round, almost swollen set of features that peered from behind a thin, scruffy veil of dark brown hair. His mustache and beard were a thick coat of fur that nearly concealed his expression, though for the time being, it was clear that he was attempting to smile. His eyes appeared too small for his face as they receded into dark sockets below his equally bushy brow. His pupils shined a deep brown, dark enough to reflect the pink light from below, just like his suede footwear.

"Ah! But where are my manners?" the stranger said. "I am Tall, Tall the Lutist!"

"A pleasure to make your acquaintance. I am Cynkz, the Jester."

"Oho! A jester? And from the sounds of it, an educated one. Were you an advisor of some sort back in the living world?"

"I believe I was a courtier, nothing so demanding as a personal advisor to any king."

"I see," Tall said as he tugged at the end of his meaty beard. "Still, a pleasant conversation in such a desolate place is priceless. What brings you here, dear jester?"

"In truth, I was beginning to wonder the same thing," Cynkz said as he lowered his eyes, making room for more melancholic thoughts.

"You're a curious one, a troubled one. I can tell."

"Is it obvious?"

"I'm afraid so. But as a jester, you perhaps know what it means to wear your heart on your sleeve, to have your emotions exposed to the world."

"Yes, you could say that."

"If it helps, I am looking for something myself!"

Cynkz' eyes perked up to look at the man before him. "May I ask what it is you're seeking?"

"My lute! I've lost it. Though I harbor no delusions of ever finding such a thing in a place like this."

"A lutist without his lute? That sounds like the beginning of a joke…"

"Ha! Ahahaha!"

Cynkz cracked a half-smile of his own.

"You truly are a jester! Say, how about we stick together for a while? Is there anything you'd like to know?"

"Actually, I came here with friends, though we've been separated."

"Ah, I see," Tall said, this time pulling at his beard more deliberately and vigorously than before. "I know some people who may be able to assist you."

Something stirred within Cynkz, though he could not pinpoint what the feeling was. He was injured, alone, and feeling down on himself. Yet something deeper clawed away at him, a sense of unease that raked at him like a bristly thorn bush being dragged across his skin. He had no other leads to go off of, and he figured he could play along with the stranger.

"All right then," Cynkz said. "I'm grateful for any assistance I can get."

"Splendid!" Tall exclaimed. "Follow me."

Tall excitedly flew ahead, nearly bouncing as he drifted through the air. Cynkz paused for a moment, then quieted his mind and followed him. He made sure to maintain a cautious distance behind his new guide.

A rolling, grumbling ambience filled the air. Between the rising and falling mountainous spires and the frizzling pop of the pink mist, the world gave the impression of diluted acid being constantly rubbed on one's skin. The atmosphere felt humid, thick with an invisible substance that threatened to suffocate anyone who breathed in too deeply. Flying through the air only exacerbated this feeling, though it was tame compared to the black swamp Cynkz and Fiddle faced early on. Yet that was not what he was worried about most.

Cynkz was not above leaving things to chance, to being grateful for coincidences and happenstance, yet the arrival and assistance of this stranger seemed almost too good to be true. This 'lutist,' Tall, who was anything but, was eerily quick to search for ways to help, to lead him forward in some way. Cynkz was no fool, and he knew that most were motivated by some form of personal gain. The question was: what exactly did Tall want?

The silence between the two as they flew across the crackling pink sea was palpable, perhaps thicker than the fog itself. Every spire and ravine they passed seemed another lost opportunity to strike up a question or begin a conversation. As Cynkz fretted over possible, seemingly benign ways to get the stranger talking, Tall cleared his throat and saved him the trouble.

"So," Tall said, through a husky cough, "what of these friends? It's uncommon for an odd group to work together and travel between realms."

"Our group is certainly odd, consisting of an imp, myself, and a young po woman—"

"Really?!" Tall nearly stalled himself in midair. "That truly is a motley group. What, pray tell, are you trying to accomplish? One would need to be seriously driven to willingly face Munderworld's dangers."

Cynkz paused, as he was torn between not wishing to divulge too much information but looking to gauge Tall's reaction. "The po woman wishes to become a maiden, to serve one of the great sisters, apparently."

"Ah, the Sisters of Elm. I suppose it's not too much of a coincidence. Theirs is one of the few myths that travel across the realms."

"A coincidence?"

"Yes, that is actually who I am leading you to. In all my time here, I have seen but one method forward."

Cynkz picked up his pace in anticipation.

"There is one spire that stands out from the rest," Tall explained. "It is much taller and larger than all the others, and rarely, if ever, descends into the fog below. It bears no vegetation but has a huge opening and a deep cave within its side. The cave is magically imbued and protects whatever is inside from the burning mist."

"How interesting!" Cynkz said. "But what of this magic? Is it the Sisters' doing?"

"You're a shrewd one, sir jester. Yes, they are the ones controlling the door into and out of this realm."

"Why do you stay here then? I doubt you merely hang around to provide good conversation and assistance to a strange passerby."

Tall turned to look Cynkz directly in his own black eyes.

"You truly think so little of my character? Am I so suspicious?"

Cynkz's brow flattened, his expression tightening along with his nerves. He refused to avert his gaze, though staring down the glint in Tall's eyes instilled the feeling of needles being driven into his spine. For a moment, he was unsure of what to do.

Tall glared at Cynkz, then relaxed his own stern expression, breaking into a hearty laugh.

"Haha! You'll have to excuse my teasing!" Tall said. "It's not often I have anyone to mess around with."

As the portly stranger turned to continue his flight forward, Cynkz relaxed his expression but not his apprehension. He waited for Tall to gain a bit of distance before following him.

"As to your question," Tall continued, "the same magic that protects whatever is inside the cave also keeps anyone from entering."

"I see. Why bring me to the magicked spire, then? I am just as ignorant about this barrier's properties as you are."

"I have a good feeling that you may be able to help me figure something out. You've made it this far, haven't you? Traversing the realms is no small feat, and you appear to have a talent for it!"

Again, Cynkz found himself caught in the midst of uncomfortable silence. This time, however, he did not have the comfort of counting passing spires. Tall seemed to be leading Cynkz out into no man's land. The expanse ahead became featureless, void of any distinct landmarks. Without the occasional pillar or the faded line of mountains carving a line on the horizon, it was near impossible to orient oneself. It was yet another overwhelming abyss, albeit a strange combination of rosy pinks receding into the murky yellows and pale blues swirling in the sky. Everything faded into the distant fog, and soon Cynkz found himself lost, entirely dependent on the guidance of the stranger.

A new feature began to peer through the distant mist. Most of the pillars were the size of a small mountain, something a po could walk across in a reasonable amount of time, but The new spire was several times larger than the others, and in the empty pink void, without any other points of reference or contrast, was an imposing structure. The way its form began to usurp everything in view reminded Cynkz of the great tree overlooking the fungal tribe. Oddest of all, its aura was a flat bright sheen that coated the entire structure with a shimmering blue layer. It was almost as painful to look at as it was unnatural.

Cynkz's focus was broken by the abrupt halting of Tall's flight. The corpulent gentleman sat himself upright, reached beneath his coat, and turned around to face the jester, bearing a sharp squint and a sneer.

"We're here," Tall said. "Look, I brought your little friend too! Say hi to him."

Tall held out a small, clear glass bottle between his finger and thumb. The bottle was oblong in shape, its rounded bottom clearly not made to be set on any sort of flat surface. Its top contained a small, tightly pressed cork that plugged its opening. An odd black mist rocked back and forth inside.

Cynkz, his anxiety briefly replaced with confusion, peered at the bottle, at first unsure of what to make of it. The longer he stared, the more he could make out patterns in the liquid's movements. Some of the shimmer reflecting off the bottle's edges swam past each other, forming a crude and simple face. The texture of the mist was reminiscent of the shaded form Fiddle took in Horgafell. Immediately, Cynkz's face stretched, his eyes widened, and his lips parted at the realization.

"Fiddle!"

CHAPTER 18

CYNKZ'S INITIAL SURPRISE TURNED TO ANGER as barked questions at Tall. "Just who are you, exactly? And how did you trap Fiddle? Explain yourself!"

The bottom of Tall's mustache pulled up into his beady eyes, vaguely showing a deep, sinister smile.

"Ahahahahaha! Fools! Fools everywhere!" Tall shouted.

Cynkz glared at the man, awaiting a proper answer.

"Those wretched hags have proven to be a significant roadblock. You think you're the only one to try and make their way through to the bottom of Munderworld?"

"It is a rare enough aspiration. I hadn't given it much thought."

"Of course not. But some of us have real ambitions and refuse to be cooped up in this sorry excuse for a world. It was easy enough, deceiving those along the way to get this far. The sentinels are dumb brutes, and the po make for easy fodder and tools, but the Sisters… They saw through my ruse and banished me before I could take full advantage of them."

"Advantage?" Cynkz said, his trailing voice accenting his befuddlement.

"The Sisters sit around, spying on the other realms, gleaning information and using those beneath them to fashion all sorts of trinkets. I presume you have seen the wooden staves they planted over several of the realms?"

"I have."

"They have made quite a few artifacts, such as this right here," Tall lifted the small bottle between his fingers and shook it around, causing the shadow inside it to bang against its edges.

Cynkz widened his stance, as if ready to leap forward and pounce. Tall smiled and raised his other hand to gesture dismissively toward the jester.

"Ah-ah! Don't try anything you'll regret. A mere slip of my grip and your friend takes a dip in the eternal smog below!"

"With a wit like that, you'd have made a notable jester—"

"I am no jester! I was a bard! A minstrel! And even a soldier back in the living world! I accomplished so much more than a measly clown ever could!"

"How did you trap Fiddle?"

"I met him a while ago. He's a mouthy one and wouldn't shut up about his 'friends' and 'his pal Cynkz.' It wasn't long before I was able to pry the story of your adventures through the realms and the thread."

"Fiddle, you fool…"

"He's no more a fool than you, Cynkz. You trusted me for this long, didn't you?"

"I suppose you're right. But what of the thread? What do you know about it?"

"About as much as you two do, which is enough for me,"Tall drew the bottle close to his face to leer into it.

"The thread," he continued, "is a piece of divinity itself. A sliver of power from a great apostle. If anything could be used to get ahead, to force entry into the maiden's realm, and curry favor with the greatest of kings—the Munder King himself—it is that thread."

"And what do you know about the Munder King? No one has seen or heard from him in ages."

"You believe that?"

Cynkz threw a squint at Tall. "What do you mean?"

"The Sisters know nearly as much as the Munder king himself. They have kept in contact with him! Though they are not so quick to divulge what their talks consist of."

"That's surprising. You seem like such a trustworthy, upstanding—"

"Do not toy with me!" Tall shouted. "You should be grateful I am telling you anything! I do enjoy a good conversation, that was the truth."

"Spit it out then, Tall. You just want the thread?"

"Yes. I'm feeling gracious and am willing to trade with you. Hand over the thread, and you get to have your friend back. Do we have a deal?"

His mind raced. Time, something that everyone in Munderworld lost value in, still proved to be of the utmost importance. It was rare to be pressed for urgency in Munderworld, yet here the jester stood, his own thoughts competing with one another to find an impossible solution to an impossible situation.

The one factor, an unknown, standing out in Cynkz's mind was that of the thread's effects upon contact. It seemed to have no effect on muns such as Fiddle, but a fellow po? It was possible, but it was also a long shot.

"Are you certain the thread will be the tool you need to move forward?" Cynkz said. "Both I and Fiddle have held the thread, and it is hardly noticeable in one's grip. It seems to have no outward properties or effects that one could use for anything productive."

"Hmph!" Tall scoffed, squinting his eyes as he swirled the bottle around in his hand. "I'll figure something out. Though that will no longer be any concern of yours. Hand over the thread. Now."

"Let's exchange at the same time. No funny business."

"Of course. No funny business."

Cynkz began to reach for the thread, but Tall interrupted him with another command.

"One more thing," Tall said. "Stop hiding your other arm. For all I know you could have a weapon or trick hiding beneath that cloak of yours. Let's see both hands."

Cynkz reluctantly adjusted his shoulder, pushing away the cloth to reveal a glistening black and blistered limb.

"The imp mentioned that his friend was injured trying to protect some wench. What did those muns in the desert do to cause that kind of damage?"

Cynkz merely tightened his lip and glared at Tall.

"Bah! It doesn't matter. A story for another time, perhaps! Haha!"

Cynkz reached beneath his cloak with his uninjured hand and pulled out the bright sliver of light. Strangely, it seemed to be pulling itself toward Tall, violently attempting to escape Cynkz's grip, as if it had a mind of its own.

"What a beautiful, lively piece that is. Look! It *wants* to be with me! Hahaha!" The gruff in Tall's voice lightened, assured of his victory.

Cynkz slowly drifted forward to the minstrel, and Tall did the same toward him. The feeling of unease swelled to unbearable levels. It was as if the jaws of a great beast were closing in around him, ready to clamp down on its prey at any moment. Cynkz did not like to fight but knew he had to be ready for anything. The crackling of the caustic fog, the rumbling of moving mountains, the faint hiss of the wind passing by—none of it existed. All that mattered was the bottle in Tall's hand and the thread pressed between Cynkz's fingers.

As Cynkz extended his hand, he realized something was off. His body was frozen! He could not move of his own free will. Some external force had its grips on him. Cynkz desperately squirmed as he tried to break free of whatever was holding him.

"You truly are a fool, just like your friend," Tall said. The husky minstrel pushed his other hand out from beneath his cloak, and revealed a small, crudely made bracelet, its material and texture similar to the wooden staves.

"I mentioned that I stole *multiple* trinkets from the maidens," Tall continued. "Did you wonder how I, a po, managed to fly about and move around as I do? These dark wooden beads are one of the many tools the maidens have fashioned. I can control and manipulate anything nearby with my mind, even an unsuspecting jester. You two are so foolish. You have no one to blame but yourselves for this."

Tall snatched the thread from Cynkz's grip. Before Cynkz could react, Tall tilted his other hand and listlessly dropped the bottle down toward the mist.

"Oops, I guess my grip slipped after all!" Tall exclaimed.

"Fiddle!" Cynkz screamed. He drew in a deep breath and twisted his body with all of his strength before bursting into a cloud of colorless smoke. A black serpent hurled itself down toward the bottle. Tall thrust his hand out and twisted the bracelet to attempt to catch Cynkz, but it had little effect.

"My, you are heavy," Tall said. "No matter. Go to your death, jester. The thread is mine!"

The thread was light, diaphanous, like a thin piece of silk that was hardly there. As Tall pressed the small sliver of light between his forefinger and thumb, a tingling sensation began to run through his body. Small crackles of electricity surged across his skin. Before the minstrel could react, a wide smile still spread across his face, the new sensation worming its way throughout his entire body before swelling at his head, filling his mind's eye with visions of the past.

Tall could see himself, sometime long ago, kneeling before a throne. His vision then from the perspective of the king who knighted him. His vision shifted to that of his fellow courtiers. As their perspective was now his, he could not see them, but felt their faces twisting and contorting in disgust and annoyance as they looked upon the braggart.

Everything flipped, and now he shared the perspective of a woman in bed. Her arms were tied and a thick, damp cloth was lodged into her mouth, making breathing difficult. He could feel her heart race as his own lumbering form made its way into the room. Tall blacked out just as his own body descended upon the woman.

Finally, the world shifted to a torn and bloody battlefield. He was on horseback, watching himself slaying countless soldiers under the banner of a long forgotten king. He could feel himself stride by, and a great, shining silver lance poked into view. He could feel its weight as he shifted the weapon down and toward the flailing minstrel, piercing his own bulky form.

A dark streak cut through the flat, pink mist. Cynkz threw himself down with all of his weight toward the small bottle as it rolled and hurtled toward the caustic fog below. The bottle was within eyesight. He burst into another cloud of his signature colorless smoke, returning to his original form. He instinctively reached out with his injured arm, and a great weight pulled him further and further into the abyss. As he stretched open his blackened, blistered fingers he could feel them singing by the corrosive mist. The jolt of pain shot through his body, overwhelming every sense in his body. He did not care and pressed on in spite of it. He gritted his teeth and forced himself through the upper layer of the mist before he was able to take hold of the bottle.

As soon as he felt the cool, smooth edge of the flask, he wrenched it toward his chest and grabbed the cork on top with his other hand. He ripped the bottle open, and the swirling black mass inside spilled out. The writhing shade collapsed in on itself and formed into a familiar husky red imp.

"Cynkz!" Fiddle screamed.

Cynkz twisted and stopped his descent into the fog. As he tried to thrust himself toward the sky, he felt noticeably lighter. He could no longer feel the sting of his injured arm.

Fiddle dashed toward him, his small red arms stretched out to the jester. Cynkz reached out and felt the rough, calloused hand of his friend gripping him, and the soft tug of the imp's weight as he desperately attempted to help pull his friend from the mist. Cynkz's mind was strangely calm, relieved to have his friend back with him. Cynkz twisted his body once more, flapping his long cloak, now burnt at its edges, like a mighty wing, finally propelling him up above.

The two saw the writing silhouette of a paunchy man as he flailed against the creamy pale yellows and blues in the sky. Tall screamed and thrashed his limbs. He was in such a violent state that he began to tear off his clothes and hair in a fit of madness.

Cynkz saw his opportunity. He transformed into a large black serpent and wrapped himself around the mad minstrel's legs. Pulling with his last bit of strength, he sent Tall hurtling toward the mist.

Fiddle flew past the minstrel on his way down and drew in a deep breath. A sharp, wet snap followed a burning expectorated mass of fire, and the imp released a messy ball of flame. It quickly expanded as it bolted toward the minstrel, and its loose form dispersed into wild shapes after hitting its target. Tall was reduced to an ashy shadow. His charred form stood out against the sickeningly bright pink fog below and the burning wet orange flame on top. His screams curled and rattled then faded into the crackles and hums of the natural forces engulfing him.

Cynkz felt a great sense of relief. Exhaustion overtook him, and the last thing he could remember was the pull of tiny hands struggling to guide him toward the blue mountain overlooking the confrontation.

CHAPTER 19

THE DARKNESS WAS LIKE A WARM BLANKET COMforting Cynkz's senses on a chill, late evening. Perhaps it was that he had pushed himself to lengths before unseen, or perhaps the injuries he had been ignoring caught up with him, but regardless, Cynkz was happy to have a moment of proper rest. The weight of one of his lost friends had been lifted off of his shoulders. He could hear the soft, distant hum of crackling fog, and the cool bristled texture of dry grass beneath him as he laid down. He drew in a breath, a most relaxing exertion, as if he were letting go of his worries, if only for a moment.

"I know you're awake!" Fiddle said.

"I figured," Cynkz said, his eyes still closed, preferring the blanket of darkness his shut lids provided.

"Somehow everything worked out, but..." Fiddle's words trailed off into nothing, the concern in his tone prompting Cynkz to open his eyes and return to the waking world.

"Fiddle? What's wrong?"

The jester attempted to lift himself up and was struck with the lack of support from the left side of his body. He stumbled slightly, jolting his senses. His eyes noticed the end of his long, tattered cloak stretching out beneath him. He followed the cloth up toward his legs, the previously shining crimson and purple material singed at its edges and seams, revealing the smallest bit of the bright pale skin underneath. His gaze moved further up to see similarly colored and textured clothing covering his waist and chest. The top half of his cloak, once draped neatly over his shoulders, was riddled with holes and tears, and equally scorched threads poking out in chaotic fashion. Beneath the ragged cloak barely covering his shoulder the tiniest bit of a charred lump sat where his arm once would have been. Cynkz knew the dampening effects of adrenaline, but the violent results of the previous danger still seemed surreal. For a moment, he could not believe it. His mind, perhaps in an attempt to make light of the situation, returned to his early words to Fiddle; the idea of an adventure without risk being nothing but. He could not help but chuckle faintly at the thought, a meek attempt to lighten the mood, as any good jester would do.

"Cynkz," Fiddle said, nearly whimpering beneath his breath. "I'm sorry..."

"It's... It's fine, Fiddle," Cynkz said, his voice as hushed as his friend's.

"It's not! What are you gonna do? You can't just walk off something like that!"

"Why not? It's my arm that's gone, not my leg."

"It's not a joke!" The imp's voice rattled the air, nearly shattering Cynkz's ears. "You could have died! No! You could have suffered a fate worse than death! All because I was stupid. I got caught by that bastard..."

"No, Fiddle. In truth, this is all my fault."

"What? How so?"

Cynkz pushed himself up from the ground with his good arm and leaned against a dark oak tree behind him. He drew in another breath as he looked up to the rustling, glittering leaves of the tree.

"I was the one who decided we should embark on this journey. I never considered the dangers we may face, and worse, I dragged you along thoughtlessly, exposing you to many horrible things. You nearly drowned in the chimera's swamp, were crushed in the mountains, and suffered under the sentinels in Horgafell."

"Cynkz..."

"The drugged marshland, the skin-tearing sands, and now this place… If it doesn't end, I led those poor po in Horgafell to perhaps a worse fate in the next realm and carelessly moved on despite Kadd's help. I should have gone back to look for Kadd and Harla and the other po, yet I was so focused on you. And Orla… she helped us get this far and for what? For all we know, she could be trapped on one of the many mountains, or worse, in the same caustic fog, sharing the same fate as Tall—"

"You can't blame yourself for everything," Fiddle said "There's only so much you can do. You can't save everyone, certainly not in a place as crazy as Munderworld. They ultimately chose their own fates and took their own risks. I *chose* to go with you on your adventure. Kadd and the others chose to help and travel along with us to the next realm. Orla chose to accompany us and face greater dangers in pursuit of her own goals. And you chose to help them."

"I suppose you're right…" Cynkz held his shoulder, staring at the place where his arm used to be.

"I guess it was only a matter of time before you finally got hurt a bit, huh?" Fiddle said. "Nobody down here has a perfect record, you know."

"That is true."

"So now what? Do you still want to go through with this? We don't know what we may find at the end of all this."

"It would be a terrible waste if we gave up now. However…"

"Hmm?" Fiddle looked at his friend, his face slightly twisted in confusion.

"The thread," Cynkz continued. "I lost it when I foolishly attempted to abide by that minstrel's bargain."

"Oh, you mean this thing?"

Fiddle held out a clenched fist and stretched open his red, bony fingers to reveal a thin sliver of light glittering at the center of his scratchy palm.

"The thread!" Cynkz exclaimed, eyes wide and his posture stretched. "But I gave it to Tall! How did you—"

"Eh, it was easy! Just as easy as the last time I snagged it!"

"Perhaps we can curry favor with the Sisters then, if they do reside in the next realm."

"Maybe they can help us find Orla? Or even rescue the other po as well?"

"We can only hope, dear friend."

Cynkz stood himself upright. Loose, burnt threads began to fly off of the seams of his attire and into the wind.

Fiddle waved at the dark threads floating by, attempting to keep them out of his beady eyes.

"You may want to clean up a bit. I don't think the Sisters will want to deal with such a messy looking bum," Fiddle said.

"True. Just a moment."

With a wave of his pale hand, the jester conjured a puff of colorless smoke across his body, and his outfit was made anew, though with a few notable changes. The crimson and violet harlequin pattern was now a single, dark sangria. His black cloak, once draped snuggly over both shoulders, was fitted into a half-cloak; a long, dark piece of cloth loosely fitting over his left shoulder, nearly reaching to the ground. The shining, velvet interior remained.

"Hey, you actually look a little cool now! Why didn't you dress yourself like that from the beginning?" Fiddle asked.

"Is clothing such an important matter in Munderworld?" Cynkz said as he gently brushed down the remaining few wrinkles in his cloak.

"I guess not."

Cynkz lifted himself up and began to drift into the air. Fiddle followed close behind him. The two flew some distance in front of the mountain. Up close, its blue aura was hardly noticeable, but from a distance, the mountain shimmered a cerulean reflection against the harsh light of the realm like ice in moonlight. Farther down the rocky mass was a huge opening, a cave embedded in the side of the structure. As Cynkz and Fiddle approached the mountain, the lighter its aura became, before completely receding into the air just as they reached the edge of the cavern's opening.

The two floating bodies receded into the shade of the dark cavern, and the ice-blue layer of light glimmered across the mountain's surface slowly descending into the crackling fumes below.

CHAPTER 20

"I HAVE TO ADMIT, DEAR FRIEND, I'M GROWING tired of my world being rendered to darkness," Cynkz said.

"Maybe if you didn't sleep all the time!" Fiddle responded.

Fiddle could sense Cynkz cracking a soft smile through the darkness or perhaps he was merely confident of his own charm.

The faint, salmon-colored reflections of the world outside had quickly faded to black, leaving the two in an uncomfortable damp and rocky void. The crackling hum of the fog had turned into great rumblings of stone and dirt grinding against itself as the entire structure continued its descent. The once shimmering layer of faint blue light coating the mountain's surface was no longer visible. There was little more for the two travelers to do other than sit and wait.

At least, that is what they would have done if the cavern could not be felt rotating. The cave's floor shifted slowly toward the side and became a wall. As the two hopped and skipped along the moving surfaces, what was once the floor became the ceiling, and circled back into another wall, returning as the floor. Any sense of direction or orientation was impossible in the meandering, spinning void.

"Wait a second, why are we walking? We could just float in the center of the room!" Fiddle shouted.

"You're walking?" Cynkz replied.

"Ha-ha-ha. I can hear your footsteps. Watch, I'm just gonna—"

The imp lifted himself into the void. The soft rustling of air was met with the harsh clap of a small skull colliding with a rocky surface.

"Ow! My head!" Fiddle screamed.

Cynkz cracked a soft smile, the curved press of thin lips holding in repressed laughter. Fiddle could sense this too, even as he slowly lowered himself back to what was currently the floor.

"Don't laugh! It was worth a shot."

"Of course, Fiddle."

The cavern's movement slowed to a halt, the opening's original ceiling resting firmly beneath the two occupants. A murky gray light rose over the cave's opening. Harsh edges of rocks and pebbles dripped into view, and the highlights of a certain jester and his scruffy, furred imp companion came forward, and the curtain of light encompassed the entire cavern. A great thud bellowed against the craggy surfaces within, and the cerulean barrier covering the mountain dissipated into the air. Cynkz was the first to step into the air. Fiddle followed closely, and the two were greeted with a new, nonsensical landscape.

The horizon seemed to nearly curl in on itself akin the page of a book turning beneath one another. There was no proper sky to speak of; the ground itself stretched into infinity in all directions. If the realm were not so large, it would give one the impression of being in a particularly spacious room. On the ground, countless trees and similar flora jutted from deep stone walls that wormed their way to form a complex maze. Deep crevices sprawled in thin lines along varying gray and brown walls like roots across the ground, many of which were obscured by the dark plumage of towering trees above. A general sweep of the realm overwhelmed the eye with exhaustive detail. It was visually tiring to try and make out anything in specific. There was one single element that helped to connect everything in a digestible way.

Stepping in and out of each of the maze's crevices were lumbering, painfully thin forms; spindly, tanned limbs reached into what would be considered the sky. They appeared as living tree branches that leisurely stepped in and out of the maze. These limbs, varying in number for each vessel, connected to a single body. It was a slightly thicker, equally tall carapace that undulated into a thin taper at its top.

As the trees moved, they tilted their world-spanning, willowy forms to the ground and revealed tiny black mandibles at their top. The mandibles bit down on whatever leaves were in range. Sometimes they would stretch up, nearly straightening their legs and their bodies before spewing out puffs of frizzling pink mist, similar to the fog from the previous realm. Their coughs seemed to trail off and dissipate, one of the few things one could use to orient a proper sense of direction. The giant bug-like entities would reach and stretch and walk across the curving landscape, pointing them in all directions as they moved.

"It looks like those bug-things are spitting out more of that pink mist," Fiddle said.

"Indeed," Cynkz said. "I'd rather keep our distance. I do not wish to find out if their excretions are as potent."

"This place is an absolute maze! We gotta be careful not to get lost."

"I fear we may already be lost, Fiddle. It could be some time before we make any progress."

"You know, we're always saying cool sounding stuff like 'time means nothing to us,,' but I'd be lying if I said I didn't get impatient."

"I know the feeling. But let us press on. There is no use sitting here talking about it."

"Ain't that the truth."

"Let's lay low for the time being. We do not know the parameters of these creatures. We should stay beneath the maze's cover for now."

"Aye-aye."

The two shifted downward and flew beneath the pillar that carried them. Cynkz turned a quick eye to the spire and noticed it was sitting out of the ground above, with no sign of having dug through anything. It was just as nonsensical as everything else in Munderworld, though it appeared decidedly neater than other elements, as if it had been specifically designed. *Just what sort of reach and power do the Sisters have to accomplish feats such as this?* Cynkz thought and turned his attention to the maze below.

Fiddle darted toward something ahead.

"Hey, Cynkz, check this out!"

Cynkz found another rough-hewn stave sticking from the ground. It possessed a number of dirtied cloth strips that hung low from the beacon's crown, indicating a lack of moving air. It reinforced an unsettling, stagnating feeling.

"You think these things could lead us to the Sisters?" Fiddle said. "Maybe we could harness it like Orla did?"

"I'm not in the mood to tempt more visions, Fiddle," Cynkz said.

"I don't blame you. Especially after how long Orla was trapped in her state when she touched one of these things—"

"Look at the ground." Cynkz pointed a long finger to the base of the beacon. "What do you suppose all those things are?"

A number of small, round beads were strewn about the dirt in haphazard patterns, dotting the soil with tiny gleams of dull light.

"Looks like someone was in a hurry," Fiddle said. "You think it was a maiden? Maybe she was running from something?"

"What would force a maiden to flee?"

"Well, the one maiden we saw didn't want to stick around for us or those sand muns."

"Very true, and I doubt this realm is any safer. If anyone was in a hurry…"

Cynkz noticed pressed strands of grass that formed around loose, svelte ovals that trailed off along the dirt path.

"Look, footprints," Cynkz said.

"The way the maiden moved, I figured they floated above the ground or something, or they just teleported everywhere," Fiddle said.

Cynkz looked up through the sparse gaps in the shaded treetops at the narrow, sharp carapaces cutting thin lines across the sky.

"I guess we have a good reason to remain on foot. Let's follow this trail."

Cynkz rested on the soil and began walking forward. Fiddle remained airborne, though followed closely behind his companion.

The occasional distant thumps of large, stemmed limbs hitting the ground blended with the rustling of leafy treetops being cut and nibbled on by the creatures. The clicks and chirps of unseen insects filled the air with an organic, invisible orchestra of infinite variety. It reminded Cynkz of the cooled, perpetual nights spent in Dulrot. Often, when he would perch somewhere to stargaze, nothing else accompanied him beyond soft winds and the occasional chitters and cheeps of unknown wildlife.

As they moved beneath the maze's shade, Cynkz had little to orient himself beyond the walls of trees and stone that guided them forward. Fiddle would hover above the towering tree line to ensure they were not walking in circles. Unfortunately, there were no distinct landmarks to guide them, and whatever trail the footsteps had started had disappeared. The duo were truly aimless. While not an entirely uncommon feeling, the potentially dangerous new environment, as well as Orla's unknown state, brought about the slow friction of anxiety. For once, getting ahead sooner, rather than later, was preferred.

Fiddle went up yet again, as he had nearly a dozen times since they began, yet came down quickly.

"Cynkz!" Fiddle said under a half-whisper, leaning in close to the jester's ear. "Up ahead, I saw a bunch of po lights under the trees."

"Hopefully, if there are po nearby, they're more talkative than those from the previous realm. Let's move quietly. See what's going on—"

A scream interrupted the jester's whisper, wrenching the duo's faces forward, wide eyes. After a tense pause, Cynkz pressed forward, shifting his weight from the tips of his toes toward his heels. Fiddle lowered below Cynkz's hat and stayed close behind.

The po's faint hues could be seen scattering away from them.

"Aw, come on!" Fiddle exclaimed. "We just wanna talk—"

A looming shade engulfed everything in sight, turning the otherwise clear scenery into a near-pitch black. The growing rumble of heavy material drowned all other sounds. The duo turned their heads to the sky to see what it was and were met with the oppressive tower of an insect's shell coming down on them. The wind breaking around the limb's monstrous form was enough to push the surrounding woods in wild directions.

Fiddle, nearly choking on a gasp, screamed out, "Ah! Move, move, move!"

The giant limb stopped just above the tree line. A thin seam began to part in the center of the tanned mass. It spread open, revealing two huge, black mandibles that clicked and clacked against the edges of the creature's carapace. Countless rows of teeth, glistening in what little light remained, highlighted a dripping liquid from their edges. The creature rattled its curved mandibles violently and emitted a loud, hissing noise, followed by the release of a great cloud of pink mist.

Cynkz was frozen and could do nothing but stare into the beast's maw. The world drowned out around him as he confronted the recent pains of the corrosive fog. Fiddle flew in, ramming his shoulder and head into Cynkz's shoulder, shouting at him. Cynkz broke from his stupor. Without a second thought, he recoiled into a burst of colorless smoke and emerged as a black falcon large enough to clamp down on Fiddle's arm and drag him out of the drowning mist. His great wings snapped back and forth, pushing away fumes and hurling them forward.

The two looked back to see the creature's face drowning in a cloud of pink smoke. It slowly shifted its head to one of the trees to gather some leaves between its mandibles and resumed eating.

The falcon released its grip on the imps arm and burst into a cloud of its own.

"That was close," Fiddle said.

"Yeah…"

"Are you all right, Cynkz?"

"I-I'll be fine. My nerves got the better of me is all."

Cynkz rolled his shoulders and drew in a quick breath before looking back to the winding forest.

"Did you see where the po went?" he said.

"Over there, it looks like they're gathering farther away," Fiddle said.

"Let's go back down so as to not draw the attention of these creatures."

"Agreed."

Once back down the two began their trek once more, ostensibly resuming almost as if nothing had happened.

The tranquility of the forest returned. The fluttering of papery leaves accented the wind, or what little wind existed, with a pleasant ambience. Small shimmers caught the edges of Fiddle's eye. Countless shining, waxy cuticles danced in the light as insects moved around in the dark. Many resumed their chirping. Despite the variety, they seemed to be working in rhythm with each other. It caused an uncanny effect from within the forest, confusing one's orientation. It was difficult to pinpoint where any particular sound was coming from, dulling what would otherwise be a useful method for marking progress through the chaotic woods.

The purpose of this soon became apparent as furred, tree dwelling rodents snuck across the branches. They moved deftly, hardly leaving a trace of their movement across the tree limbs. Small streaks of black and brown blurs danced above as they chased prey. One was successful, catching a large, horned critter between its tiny claws. It stopped to look around, then leaned in to nibble off parts of the insect's shell, then stopped again to look around anxiously. Fiddle stared, noticing the glint in its large eyes peering back at him. The two were locked in each other's gaze for just a bit too long to be considered comfortable. The rodent stuffed the insect in its pouch and scurried off.

Fiddle turned only to be met with an odd vine dangling in front of him. He nearly yelped.

"Ah! Well… it's just a stupid plant—"

A hiss interrupted the imp. Fiddle froze, his eyes pressed into a discerning squint as he stared at the vine hanging at an odd angle. He looked at it so hard that it almost appeared to hover toward him ever so slightly.

The dark vine lunged at the imp and opened at its end, revealing a set of jagged canines. Fiddle threw himself back with such force that he nearly lost balance. He was quick enough to duck and avoided the pouncing limb. The camouflaged serpent slowly closed its jaws and lowered back to its original position. Once Fiddle caught his breath, he turned to look for Cynkz, who had stopped to look back at him.

"Fiddle! Are you all right?" Cynkz said.

"Yeah, yeah I'm fine. You know, seeing you transform into snakes so often, I guess I forget how dangerous these things can be."

"Well, I'm glad you're all right. I suppose we need to be more careful—"

Just as Cynkz had turned to walk toward Fiddle, his foot pressed into a patch of particularly soft soil. He nearly fell into the dirt before catching himself. The wide edges of something sharp and uneven rose out of the ground with him, forming a barbed circle. Cynkz realized what was happening and thrust his body into another burst of colorless smoke that was immediately blown away by the snapping of a pair of massive, leathery jaws beneath him.

A small innocuous mosquito sat at the very tip of the snapping beast's mouth. It flew toward the imp, leaving the predator to slink back into the soil. The tiny insect went to Fiddle's side and burst into smoke, revealing the jester.

"Up above, down below, it seems like no matter where we go, there's danger," Fiddle said.

"Indeed. The one time I wish to exercise my legs I nearly end up losing them."

"Would you be willing to give up an arm and a leg for this adventure?"

"I'd rather not consider that option, my friend."

Murmurs echoed from behind a thick brush. Cynkz and Fiddle snapped their attention forward to listen.

"Do you think it's the po from earlier?" Fiddle asked.

"Mayhaps. Maybe we'll catch up to them this time," Cynkz said.

Cynkz crept forward. He pushed a small hole in the foliage with his hand. The two looked through to see a group of po, each carrying a number of crudely fashioned spears and clubs. They were slowly moving around a large, leafy bulb at the center of a small glade. The plant-like mass was half as tall as the towering oaks walling off the forest. A plume of shining azure and emerald slips of papery fronds stuck out from its top. Dark vines reached out from the strange plant and whipped around, forcing the po to duck and weave.

As the creature twisted and turned, Cynkz noticed something caught in one of its dark vines, Another po! It was wrapped by the plant's limb and was being thrashed around as the creature fought with the straggling po surrounding it.

One of the larger po, a tall man with ruffled blonde hair, stepped in front of the group and began waving his spear toward the plant. Two more po came forward to guard him, knocking away several flailing vines as they tried to close in. The remaining po sat back and began to conjure an incantation. They were too far away to hear clearly, though Cynkz was reminded of the po who worshiped Andion.

A writhing flame swelled between the po. Streams of orange fire swirled together into a massive ball of energy and flew toward the bulbous plant creature. The creature collapsed to dodge the attack, though several of the leaves on its top lit up. The plant immediately shot back up and stretched itself to the sky. It let loose a piercing wail that bounced off of the curved landscape. Even Cynkz and Fiddle needed to cover their ears, despite being a distance away from the commotion. Rows of ear-shattering cries echoed into the distance, stopping abruptly. A deep rumbling began to engulf the surrounding area, and a familiar looming shadow spread over the glade like a consuming layer of darkness.

The creature's black mandibles hung over the forest. All of the po froze, as did the bulbous creature. As the monstrous creature hissed and cracked its mandibles against the edges of its mouth, a faint salmon hue began to flow toward the forest floor. Cynkz leapt forward into colorless smoke, and from it emerged an immense black lizard. It ran in a circle around the glade, its mouth wide open as it picked up po along the way. Within seconds, every po was inside the lizard's pouch, and it darted off into the forest. Fiddle flew after him, leaving only the bulbous creature to stew in the overflow of pink fog. It melted into brown goo beneath the corrosive effects. All that was left was a gestating pile of rancid sludge, soon to be consumed by the towering insect.

A dark reptile scurried beneath a rocky nook within the maze. The lizard approached and stuck its head deep within the opening and released the contents of its pouch. A handful of faint, glowing bodies slid out onto the ground. Not much could be heard beyond the frantic coughing and slick movements of wet po as they struggled to reorient themselves.

"I apologize for the turbulent ride, my good fellows," Cynkz said. "It's not often I have to cart po around on such short notice."

The tall po from earlier stood up first, stumbling as he moved. Cynkz ran in and offered his hand.

"Who … are you?" asked the po.

"You can call me Cynkz. My friend should be here shortly."

"Cynkz! Sheesh, you move fast when you want to," Fiddle said as he burst through a nearby thicket.

"That's Fiddle."

"I'm… I'm Tagg. Thank you for getting us out of there."

"It's the least I can do."

Fiddle went to the jester's side and looked at Tagg, his face grimacing from the slimy liquid. "Who are you guys? What is this place?"

Tagg began to brush himself off and looked at the imp, his face pressed into a puzzled expression.

"I could ask you the same thing," Tagg said. "I've never seen a creature like you before."

"I'm just an imp, I suppose," Fiddle said.

"What an odd occurrence. What brings a jester and an imp to these forsaken woods?"

"In truth," Cynkz said, "we're trying to find the Sisters of Elm—"

"What?!" Tagg said, widening his eyes.

"What's wrong? Have you heard of them?" Fiddle asked the po.

"If you're talking about those damn maidens with the ominous cloaks, then yes, I know of them."

"Great!" Fiddle exclaimed. "Do you know how we could—"

"All I know is that they care *nothing* for us. They would rather keep to themselves and watch us rot," Tagg said.

Cynkz and Fiddle shared a confused look before turning back to the po.

"That's … quite odd," Cynkz said, "because the few things we have heard of the maidens is that they often go out of their way to help po. We witnessed one several realms back about to do just that."

"I wouldn't know anything about other realms, jester," Tagg said, averting his eyes from Cynkz's puzzled squint. "I'm sorry. You saved us, and I should be more grateful."

"No, it's all right," Cynkz said, lifting his hand to gesture calmly at the po. "Are the others all right?"

"Ah! Gara!" Tagg lifted his head, shock and concern filling his eyes. "She was the one being held by that monster!"

Tagg turned to the other po behind him and rushed to check on them. He ran over to the smallest one, a young girl with long, curled brown hair and dark skin. Another po woman stood and joined her group. Before long, they were huddled together, the collective intensity of their auras burned calmly in the shaded crevice. They looked at the jester and his imp friend.

Fiddle was reminded of the po he first helped in Horgafell, the feeling of pins and needles in the spine as a dozen eyes peered into him. Fiddle preferred to not maintain eye contact with those he did not know, but just as before, he steeled himself and remained firm. Cynkz, on the other hand, felt soothed, knowing that he had assisted more po and provided them with much needed safety and comfort. The warm feeling within quickly turned cold as he was also reminded of Orla, his imagination ran wild thinking of what tortures or dangers she may be enduring. The Sisters were their only hope of resolving the issue.

"Thank you again, strangers," Tagg said. "It means a lot to us, any kindness that is."

Cynkz stepped forward, his brow pressed into a look of determination, his thoughts still on Orla, "We desperately need to find the Sisters of Elm. If there is anything you can tell us, of where they may be..."

Tagg adopted a stern look, clearly finding the subject matter uncomfortable. He stood up and walked to the jester.

"Unfortunately, we do not know much," Tagg said. "Just that they do show up from time to time, and that they seem to care little for po struggling to protect ourselves in the wilds."

"Have any of you attempted to touch one of the staves?" Fiddle asked.

"I haven't," Tagg said, "but I have seen others try."

"What happened?"

"They ... went mad; at least, the men did. Every once in a while, a woman would touch one, go into a catatonic state, and then vanish, if they weren't eaten by something first."

"What's a catatonic?" Fiddle asked.

"Like a trance... Like what Orla underwent when she touched the stave on the plateau," Cynkz said.

"You've seen it too?" one of the po behind Tagg asked.

"Yes. We were traveling with a young woman who channeled a stave and helped us move forward. We have since been separated."

"That's amazing," the little po said.

"I want to find the Sisters so they can help us find her," Cynkz added.

"Well," Tagg replied, "it'd be nice if the maidens or these 'Sisters' or anyone were willing to—"

A bright, pink flash burned behind Cynkz. For a moment, the world around them turned salmon, then instantly returned to its original drab, woody colors. From behind a far off oak a pointed moss-green cloak stepped out and began to glide toward the group. Tagg became alert and stepped next to Cynkz. Cynkz widened his stance. Fiddle drifted up and back ever so slightly and noticed more green cloaks swarming toward them. Before the imp could call out to his companions, they were surrounded by the dark figures, each a lithe figure and holding their heads down, covering their faces with the shade of their hoods.

The first maiden walked toward the group, and the mass parted to allow her passage. The maiden stepped in front of Cynkz and spoke.

"You are Cynkz, correct?" the maiden said, a soft, yet sharp voice breaking from the shaded hood.

Cynkz drew in a deep breath, stood himself up straight and replied, "That I am. A pleasure to make your acquaintance, miss…?"

"You need not concern yourself with my name. Just know that I am here on behalf of the great Sisters of Elm."

Fiddle flew in front of Cynkz, his nerves giving way to anxiety. "The Sisters! So it's true then!" he said.

"I am sure all of you have heard many things about us," the maiden said. "We know that you are seeking something or are in need of something. We can help you."

"Why now?!" Tagg shouted. "You lot have done well to ignore us when we needed you before!"

"You'd have to ask the Sisters yourself, if they feel up to granting you an audience."

"That is precisely what we need," Cynkz asserted. "What must we do to be granted such a privilege?"

"Privilege?!" Tagg exclaimed, his lip curling in frustration.

"Hey! It's all right. Just let him work his charm," Fiddle whispered as he leaned toward the po man.

Tagg looked at the imp and calmed, relaxing his posture before looking forward to the hooded stranger.

The maiden continued, "You still have the bottle, correct?"

Cynkz looked at the maiden, surprised, then felt beneath his cloak to feel out the bottle. Its odd, oblong shape pressed into his chest.

"Yes, I do," Cynkz said.

"Good," the maiden replied. "As you may remember, the minstrel you encountered stole it from the Sisters. While we do not know what he did with the original contents, we ask that you refill it for us."

"I remember smelling something kind of funky when I was trapped in there," Fiddle said, rubbing a bony knuckle across the bottom of his chin.

"It was an enchanted venom."

"What?!" Fiddle's shriek was nearly as loud as the bulbous plant the po were fighting. Several of them looked around and to the sky, worried it would draw the attention of the giant walking creatures roaming the landscape.

"You needn't worry, little imp. It would have taken you already if it were to affect you."

"I mean, thanks, but I still feel a little concerned…"

"What is this venom?" Cynkz asked. "Where does it come from?"

"The venom is special, in that its effects persist through death and reformation. Unless properly diluted, it renders the victim to a paralytic state, still conscious but entirely unable to move or act of their own free will."

Fiddle rubbed the goosebumps on his arms and shoulders. "That sounds awful…"

"A particularly powerful and charming world serpent produces the toxin," the maiden continued. "She is at odds with the Sisters and will not give up more venom easily."

"How are we supposed to get more of the stuff?" Fiddle asked.

"That is for you to figure out. The most we can do is show you the way to her."

"I'm guessing this 'charming serpent' can communicate? Does she have a name?" Cynkz asked.

"Her name," the maiden said, "is Sulmara."

"A charming name for a charming personality, I'm sure," Cynkz added. "What did you mean when you called it a 'world serpent?'"

"Sulmara is of an ancient line of beasts that can travel between the realms," the maiden said, tilting her head just enough to reveal the tinted edges of her lips. They were thin and refined in their shape. Cynkz was, for some reason, reminded of the masked courtiers in his visions.

"I guess Kadd was right. If some creatures can force their way through the realms…"

"The Sisters know of your journey through the realms, Cynkz. Yet be warned: the serpent possesses a sharp tongue and a keen eye. She will attempt to deceive you, to play to your wants and desires. Hers is an eye that can peer into the many staves we have strewn about the realms. You must not fall to her temptations. Understand?"

Cynkz caught a fierce glint of the woman's eye beneath the shade of her cloak. They were not directly visible, but he could determine where her pupils were, and stared back into them.

"I understand," Cynkz said.

"Good. Also, you may wish to know that the serpent, Sulmara, is the most recent entity to have spoken with the Munder King. Keep that in mind."

Cynkz and Fiddle looked at one another in astonishment. The Munder King had nearly been reduced to myth. To speak with one who had, supposedly, been in contact with him, was too tempting a possibility to pass over.

The maiden titled her hood up even more, nearly revealing the whole of her face. She noticed their reaction, and continued:

"Yes, the Munder King is indeed alive and conscious. As much as the Sisters know of Munderworld, the king's throne, and his intentions, are a mystery to them. But he is still alive and well."

"I don't know if that's a good thing or bad thing for us," Fiddle said.

"Wait, I'd like to ask more questions," Cynkz said.

"There will be time for further inquiry once you have completed the task at hand." The maiden lowered her head again, the shaded veil concealing her face.

"What about the po? Is there anywhere safe for them to go?" Cynkz asked. Tagg perked up and glanced at the jester before looking back ahead to the maiden.

"We will look after them for the time being. But know that you are asking a lot of us and of the Sisters. We do not take kindly to having visitors forced upon us."

"Wait!" Tagg interrupted. "I'd like to accompany Cynkz, to help retrieve this venom."

"I have no issue with that, if the jester would have you, that is?"

Cynkz looked Tagg in his eyes, the hazel orbs reflecting intensely off of the gray light of the realm. After a stern stare, Cynkz pulled his lips into a warm smile before looking at the moss-green figure.

"Of course. The po we've had accompany us thus far seem to be quite helpful and good natured—"

"Good natured or self-interested?" the maiden said, cutting Cynkz off. "Remember that the po in Munderworld were put here for a reason, as were you."

Cynkz pressed his lips together and raised an eyebrow. He wondered what exactly she meant or what she may be reading into him.

"Hey, give him a break!" Fiddle exclaimed. "He's right, most of the po we've met seemed to be all right. Except for that one old lady who dared to call me scraggly…"

"If you two are done, we can ready a portal to the serpent's secret grotto deep in this realm," the maiden said.

"Of course. Let's go," Cynkz said.

The maiden turned to the group behind her. The row of moss-green cloaks parted before her and knelt. Several of the maidens quickly dug a shallow trench between them. Once finished, they reached beneath their cloaks and pulled out tiny flasks. They tipped them over to fill the trench with sparkling clear liquid. Despite the number of them, the nondescript flasks appeared far too small to be pouring out so much, yet the liquid filled the ditch. They returned the flasks to their cloaks and each held out their hands and began to chant. It was not until then that Cynkz noticed that every time po gathered together to chant an incantation, they resorted to speaking an indecipherable language. It felt oddly familiar to him, yet he could not understand a single word. He did not think much of it and put the thought to the back of his mind.

As their intonations grew, the liquid beneath their outstretched hands, possessing a wide variety of skin tones yet homogenized in grayness, brightened into a familiar pink light.

"I'm sure you two remember going through a portal just like this one?" the maiden said, turning to Cynkz and Fiddle. "You merely have to walk through it, just as you did before."

Fiddle looked at Cynkz, and Cynkz stepped forward to the edge of the new portal. He paused, looked around at the hooded figures around him, and drew in a deep breath. He stepped forward, just as he had before, into the shining pond. Fiddle flew forward and into the portal after him, and Tagg reluctantly followed.

In a flash, the three were gone.

CHAPTER 21

CYNKZ FOUND HIMSELF SHROUDED IN DARKness. A grainy moan emanated from deep within him, followed by the cackling chuckle of his imp friend. Tagg followed close behind, confused over their merriment.

In truth, Tagg was more focused on the texture of the ground. The sensation from the bottom of his calloused feet seemed far too soft. Soft soil often meant a trap of some sort, be it quicksand or an ambush predator setting up a strike. While Cynkz's footsteps could be heard carelessly pressing, and Fiddle preferred the air, Tagg traipsed carefully and quietly, to the point where he was nearly undetectable.

"Hey! Roll call!" Fiddle cried out.

"Here," Cynkz said.

Silence followed for a moment too long. Fiddle turned around, only to be met with darkness, yet he knew their new companion was there.

"Hey, Tagg! Roll call! Are you there?"

"I-I am here," Tagg said, tripping over his words as much as his feet.

"What's the matter?" Fiddle asked. "Afraid of the dark?"

"Ah, no. Well yes. But mostly it's the ground."

"What's wrong with it? Cynkz is anything weird about the ground?"

"It's a bit soft, I suppose," Cynkz replied.

"Precisely," Tagg asserted. "Soft ground often means an ambush. You two are certainly not built for survival."

"We've had a few run-ins with the wildlife," Fiddle said.

"True, I nearly stepped into what appeared to be a giant snapping turtle's jaws not long after we arrived," Cynkz said.

"So you two aren't completely hopeless, then," Tagg said.

"Apparently, we're just a couple of buffoons," Fiddle said.

"A duo of knaves," Cynkz said.

"Two unaware cuckoos!"

"Light-footed fools."

"Bumbling boobs!"

"Boobs? Really, Fiddle?"

"I mean… You know what I mean."

The two laughed, seeming at total peace with the dark, so much so that Tagg began to worry about his decision to join them on their venture. *I really should think my actions through more,* Tagg thought.

"Ah, I know what may help us," Cynkz said and reached into his cloak, pulling out the radiant thread. It pulled itself in a direction, away from the jester as he held it pressed between his fingers.

Tagg's eyes stretched wide as he stared at the heavenly filament. "What is *that?!*"

"It's just a thread," Fiddle replied.

"Only a thread?"

"Yeah, we stole it from an apostle—"

"What?! A celestial being! How?"

"Pfft, it's a long story."

"It must be quite the story, then."

"We nearly lost our lives getting it," Cynkz said as he guided the two.

"I figured a celestial being would not appreciate someone pilfering it," Tagg remarked.

Fiddle moved forward, keeping pace with the po. "I think it was angrier about the fact Cynkz shapeshifted into a fake apostle right in front of it—"

"You did *what?!* Actually, I don't wish to know any more about your dangerous games. Let's just keep going."

"As you wish, my good sir," Fiddle said, gesturing a curtsy in the dark.

Chapter 21

The group continued on led only by the shining sliver of light in Cynkz's hand. Eventually, a tiny speck of turquoise light at the center of the void could be seen ahead of them.

"Guess that's where we should head," Fiddle said.

"It seems odd that the maiden chose to drop us off in darkness, seemingly a fair distance away from where we need to be," Tagg said.

"Ugh," Cynkz replied in a huff.

"What's the matter, jester?"

"Cynkz is always complaining about having to 'wake up in darkness' or something. As if every chapter of his story began with it," Fiddle said.

"If you two are truly from the realms above… I supposed your story would have many chapters."

"You could say that. But what about you, po guy? What's your story?"

"I've been here for so long, it is hard to say," Tagg said, his voice quiet and soft as he thought back to his past. "I have seen many strange things and have fought against many wild monstrosities, all the while having to constantly look above to ensure those walking, towering creatures do not drown us in pink acid. The most I have been able to do is gather other po, to work together and keep each other's spirits up. Yet there are always casualties. A poison fruit, a lost leg, falling victim to the pink gasses of the large beasts. Sometimes, it's as simple as one losing sight of the group and wandering off in who knows what direction, never to be seen again."

"It's not too different from most of the other realms, you know," Fiddle said. "Almost every realm is beset with some kind of great peril."

"Almost?" Tagg looked in the imp's general direction, raising an eyebrow. Though it was completely dark, Fiddle could feel the po's incredulity through the void.

"Yeah, Dulrot ain't so bad as long as you don't get on the bad side of a wild mun or one of the sentinels."

"Dulrot? And what is a sentinel?"

"Dulrot is where we came from. It's the highest realm in Munderworld, and it's a pretty boring place. Sentinels are, well, they're these big, gangly stony muns that act like soldiers. They're either guarding something, or patrolling the realms, or being jerks, like in Horgafell…"

"I see. I suppose it is good that we do not have those to worry about here. They don't sound like anything I've seen in the wilds."

"Hopefully, we won't have to deal with them for the rest of our journey. Right, Cynkz?"

"Right, indeed," Cynkz said, several paces ahead and leading the way with nothing but the sounds of his heavy footsteps.

"Your friend doesn't talk so much, does he?" Tagg said.

"He talks enough."

"Fiddle does most of the talking when talking is not necessarily needed," Cynkz interjected.

"Hey! I mean, you're not wrong but still! There'd be an awful lot of dead air around here if I didn't say anything!"

"That is true," Cynkz said.

Tagg shook his head and smiled in the dark.

"You know, the maiden didn't tell what we were getting into," Fiddle said as he twiddled his thumbs.

"I tried to ask questions, but she seemed quick to push us forward," Cynkz added.

"Yeah… We have a bad habit of running into new situations."

"And yet we always find a way out, do we not?"

"True, but how far can luck, wit, and charm take us?"

"It will take us as far as it needs to."

"You seem quite self-assured," Tagg said.

"It never helps to be hesitant. Better to be decisive and get things done when you can."

"Aye, I can agree with that, jester."

"Does Cynkz really look like a jester?" Fiddle said. "He changed his garb not long ago."

"You know, I did not think much of it. A jester was the first thing that came to mind when I saw him."

"Hey Cynkz, maybe you should adopt a cowl! Or maybe a hood, like the maidens."

"I quite like my hat," Cynkz said.

"Why do you wear that thing? You have crazy long hair. Why not show it off?" Fiddle asked.

"Ah, it's not that important—"

"If I hadn't seen you without it, I'd think you were hiding a bald spot!" Fiddle said.

"Now *that* would be funny and worthy of a jester," Cynkz said.

"Are you dunderheads always so cheery?" Tagg asked.

"Dunderheads!" Fiddle exclaimed. "A couple of dunders in Munderland!"

"I have never, in all my time in Munder*world*, heard anyone refer to it as Munderland," Cynkz said.

"First time for everything," Fiddle said.

Tagg hurried forward and pointed ahead, his brawny limb barely lit by the faint blue lights in front of them. "It looks like we may be at the edge of a deep grotto. Watch your step."

Rows of small, glowing orbs dotted the ground, waving back and forth against the soft winds of the abyss. Together they formed a speckled layer that dipped far below and led the eye naturally to an opening revealing clear waters.

"Light! And clean water from the smell of it," Tagg said. "Could be as safe a place as any to get our bearings."

"Agreed. Let's hurry," Cynkz said.

The turquoise specks receded beneath a familiar gray light. A field of trim grass circled around a calm lake glistening brilliantly in the dull light. Running water trickled through the shade surrounding the grotto. At the center of the lake was a tree. It was a rather unassuming one, considering the great oaks that lined the wild maze in the rest of the realm, and certainly nothing compared to some of the timbers the other realms possessed. Yet there it stood, situated at the center of a sparkling grotto as if it knew it were in the center of a lavish painting. There were no animals, insects, or any other fauna to disturb the scenery. Despite the soothing tranquility of the place, the lack of living creatures gave an eerie, uncanny impression. Everything was too still, too calm, too peaceful to make sense.

"Something isn't right," Tagg muttered as he clenched his fists and straightened his shoulders.

"I agree," Cynkz said.

"Look there, beneath the tree," Fiddle exclaimed and pointed a bony finger at the sap.

Beneath the shade of the humble oak sat a crude stave. It appeared darker and older than any of the others Cynkz and Fiddle had seen. There were but a few bones and small animal skulls sitting on the ground around the stick and a single tattered rag wrapped around its top. The edges of the marker's near-black bark were splintered and covered in pallid moss, frayed collections of grayed whites and ashen greens mixing in with one another along the stave's surface.

"It's another one of those sticks the maidens love so much," Fiddle said.

"Perhaps it could be our way out of here," Cynkz said.

"We could always just fly out of here."

"We could, but where? The maidens seem to use the staves to watch and find what they need."

"You can fly too?" Tagg queried the jester.

"Yes," Cynkz replied.

"He can also shapeshift! Though you already saw that," Fiddle said.

"That I have," Tagg turned his head and looked at Cynkz. "Just what *are* you, then?"

"I believe I am a po, not unlike you. Or I think I am. My memory of who and what I was before the end of the po world is minimal and scattered."

"The po world? Peara? Peara ended?!"

"Apparently. Though I suppose many must have died long before it happened. It's not surprising that some may not have learned of its demise."

"H-how did Peara end? What happened?"

"I do not know, unfortunately. Perhaps the Sisters would be willing to share that information with us."

"Does the ground look weird to anyone else?" Fiddle asked as he scratched his head and gestured downward.

Indeed, the ground began to act strangely. Slow, deep waves of movement rolled beneath the grass, as if the world were an ocean without a shore to beat against. The soft, loose soil shifted around, though not enough to shake Cynkz or Tagg's footing. In fact, Cynkz seemed unmoved by the rising commotion, remaining nearly still in the ground. Tagg, on the other hand, was rocking back and forth as he tried to maintain his balance.

Cynkz jumped into the air and flew to Tagg's side, grabbing his arm. Fiddle noticed and assisted Cynkz. The trio fled high above the grotto and looked down to see a line of moving soil and grass, as if something were being dragged just beneath the surface. The once flat and tranquil surface of the lake was rippling, its undulating waves mimicking the rows of shifting soil surrounding it. The quiet air filled with the muffled, thundering hiss of dragging sand. Soon the moving lines tapered into the darkness, and all was silent and tense.

The faint clinking of layered scales echoed out from the darkness, followed by the smooth whisk of a sultry voice.

"It's been an age since I have had visitors… *Essssss.*"

Fiddle and Tagg stared into the dark, their pupils eclipsed by the surrounding white layer. As defensive as Cynkz remained, he could feel the prying eyes of something fierce looking into him.

The tips of lustrous ovals began to peer through the curtain of shadow. As the shade gave way like water, a prodigious form revealed itself. It had a large head, finely tapered at its tip though wide and rounded at its back. Its curves naturally led the eye toward two reflective beads peering calmly beneath angled, inviting eyelids. Shimmering scales of a pale coral hue shone against the dull light like a rainbow in the mist.

As the serpent moved, every color danced and sparkled, though the underlying pink tint remained constant. It was a heaving mass, a long rope of dense muscle that had been honed from eons of slithering about. Its body was well acquainted with combat, though one could only guess what that entailed. It was the sort of refined beauty known exclusively to the most successful of predators, the kind that lulled the observer beneath its spell, only for one to realize too late that it was trapped. Her eyes were larger than the visitors together, and her head nearly covered the opening of the grotto as it stood above them. She made little sound, the rustling of soil merely adding a soothing ambience to the air.

Cynkz could feel sweat accumulating on Tagg's arm. He could also see Fiddle from the corner of his eye, his mouth agape and eyes wider than he had ever seen them. Cynkz knew that if the beast wanted them dead, it would have acted before they could have reacted. If it went out of its way to speak to them, they may be safe for the time being.

The serpent smiled, or at least smiled as well as a scaly beast could manage. "You may rest upon my scales, little ones. *Essssss.* No need to strain yourselves in the air like that. Please, make yourselves at home. *Essssss.*"

Cynkz nodded at Fiddle. Fiddle finally snapped himself out of his stupor and looked back to Cynkz, though with a notable sense of worry weighing his brow.

The two set Tagg on top of the serpent's scales. When his feet touched down, he immediately recoiled. He drew in a deep breath and relaxed as best he could. Fiddle and Cynkz let go of the po, and Cynkz set himself down as well before looking up to the colossal viper. Fiddle fidgeted his tiny clawed fingers, wrestling with the idea of either running away or hiding behind Cynkz. It reminded him of the feeling of the po in the cave in Horgafell staring into him and the needles in his back as he grew anxious. He steeled himself, not wanting to screw anything up before starting a proper conversation.

Cynkz attempted to assert himself and establish something resembling equal conversational ground.

"I am Cynkz. And these two are my friends, Fiddle and Tagg. It is a pleasure to make your acquaintance, miss...?"

"Hmm, you do not need to be so formal!" the serpent said. "You may call me Sulmara."

"That's a beautiful name, fitting for such a lustrous serpent."

"I am flattered. And intrigued. *Essssss.*" The rumble of heavy mass moving through the air approached the trio as Sulmara lowered her head to them. "I have been watching you for some time, jester. Your shapeshifting ability is nothing short of extraordinary."

"Thank you. I too am flattered. Though, I must ask, how have you—"

"Through the staves the maidens use to move about and observe the realms. *Essssss.* I have long since learned how to manage them."

Cynkz lifted his hand to his chest, readying a gesture to accentuate his speech. "That is amazing. I have heard of your talents, though I did not know you could do that."

"I can do many things, but I cannot transform. How do you perform such immaculate mimicry, especially of serpentine forms? It is a thing to behold. *Essssss.*"

"To be quite honest, it is a mystery to me. Adopting your form is as natural to me as breathing, Sulmara."

"Ooh, a mystery. *Essssss.*" Sulmara leaned in farther, her head turned to the side to bring her head uncomfortably close to Cynkz. Cynkz remained steady and focused on his reflection beaming from her eye. "You are a curious one, jesssssster. You possess the sharp eyes of a brilliant viper and can easily see the beauty we hold beyond our intimidating fangs and scales."

Fiddle drifted forward, replacing his fidgeting motions with hung arms. "Sheesh, you two should just date already."

Sulmara immediately whipped her head, the force of her motion rippling throughout the length of her form. Tagg was, for a moment, frightened beyond belief, his knees jerking up to ready a fruitless escape. Cynkz remained still, though inside he was screaming. The shock of the possible implication his mouthy friend brought forward turned every emotion within him upside down.

"A shapeshifter could… *Essssss.* No, *would* make for a good mate. *Essssss.*"

Cynkz glared at his companion. Fiddle chuckled worriedly and shrugged, pulling back into himself as he drifted nonchalantly behind Tagg.

What have I gotten myself into…? Tagg thought.

"I know of your struggle, *essssss.* I know what you've lost, *essssss.* Your goal is so simple. I could easily take you to the bottom of Munderworld. I could take you to the king himself. *Essssss.*"

"For free?!" Fiddle blurted before his mind could catch up.

"Nothing is free, little shadow. *Essssss.* I am not in the business of carting around fools. It would only be me, and Cynkz, together. *Essssss.*"

Cynkz looked at what constituted the ground beneath him; his own warped reflection within the shining scales beneath his feet. "I'd have to abandon my friends and the po. I'd also have to throw away any hope of working with the maidens or the Sisters… On Orla and Kadd…"

"Yessssss."

Tagg stepped forward, resting his calloused hand on the jester's bony shoulder, and whispered, "Do not listen to her! Remember the maiden's words. The serpent is clearly lying. Whatever it is you're seeking, whatever it is you're working toward, you've already given so much to get this far. Could you turn your back on everyone? I know you're a good—"

Cynkz placed his hand on Tagg's, then stepped away from the po's grip.

"So, what will it be, handsome? *Essssss.*"

"In truth, my love—"

"Ooh! Oh my…"

"I think your offer is a most welcome one. To have the warmth of another, our slithering forms wrapped around one another in endless ecstasy, scales sliding upon scales, the rhythm of friction taking our experience to unforeseen heights…"

Sulmara weaved her way back and forth above the jester. Her lashes fluttered like the wings of a black dove ready to embrace its kin.

"Oh! A poet too?" Sulmara said. "A sweet serenade for me? *Essssss.* Please, you're too much!"

"Cynkz…" Fiddle drifted forward, his brow pushing tight lines into his forehead. A small tear brewed at the corner of his eye. "You can't be serious… I know you'd never—"

Cynkz shared a fierce glare from the corner of his eye. It was the pained expression of a man filled with regret and shame for doing what he felt must be done at the expense of what he wants to do. Fiddle's face softened into one of mourning before he looked away and flew to Tagg's side.

"Too much?" Cynkz said, turning his attention back to the great serpent. "We have yet to even begin, my love!"

"Yessssss! Transform! Now! Become a divine, serpentine body! So much ecstasy yet to be experienced!" Sulmara's voice boomed through the grotto, the piercing hiss of her tongue filling the air like sand in a great dune.

"Just a moment, Sulmara." Cynkz pulled the small bottle from his cloak and held it in front of him. "The least we could do is give the others a little something, a farewell gift to those who brought us together."

"Ah, the venom. Essssss." Sulmara lifted her head and looked at the jester, the slight pressing and pulling of the scaly muscles on her face revealing underlying ruminations. "Very well. A parting gift, then. Hold it close and I will give you what you seek. *Essssss.*"

Sulmara turned her head sideways. Cynkz pulled out the cork from the bottle's top with his teeth and held it forward, motioning toward the serpent. Sulmara leaned in, then quickly snapped open her massive jaw, revealing a most beautiful, shining piece of curved bone. It pulled through a fleshy membrane at the top of her mouth, sweeping back into a long, elegant curve. The force of her mouth snarling open pressed a great wind along the scaled surface of her body, nearly pushing Tagg and Fiddle off balance. The serpent flexed the membrane holding her tooth, and from a canal at the fang's tip, a single drop of radiant venom dripped down.

Cynkz caught the liquid inside the bottle and quickly closed it, paying extra care as he pressed the cork. Sulmara pulled her head back and relaxed her jaw. Cynkz held the bottle up to the light, swirling around the pale, lavender liquid before carelessly tossing it to Fiddle and Tagg. Fiddle was quick enough to dash forward and catch it. He turned his concerned face back to his friend.

"Now, *essssss,*" Sulmara said as she eyed the jester up and down. "Transform! Assume your girthiest, shiniest form for me!"

"As you wish..."

Cynkz leaped forward into a burst of ashen smoke. From within the cloud another serpent emerged, its body growing longer than what should be possible. An immense, sky-consuming reptile with a pure black body covered in shining, iridescent scales coiled before settling itself before Sulmara. The clicking of thousands of large, hard scales pressing against each other filled the air.

Sulmara looked down at the new viper, turning her head slightly in a puzzled, almost playful manner.

"Cynkz... This form is impressive, but... *essssss*... This form is too small for me."

The new serpent exploded into gray smoke, and the jester nearly fell back down to the ground.

"Ah, my apologies," Cynkz said. "Please, let me try once more."

"Of course. *Essssss.*"

Tagg and Fiddle looked at each other from the corner of their eyes, signaling a shared befuddlement over the situation.

Cynkz drew in a deep breath and leapt forward again. An even greater burst of colorless smoke erupted. Another ropey mass of black scales and muscle swam forth through the air and across Sulmara's all-consuming form before settling. It was perhaps the largest form Cynkz had ever assumed; it stretched from the beginning to end of the grotto, disappearing into the shade to emerge somewhere else. In any other context, it could easily be assumed to be infinite in length.

Sulmara looked down, the look of disappointment forcing harsh angles into her otherwise limited facial expression.

"My love, Cynkz, I don't think is going to work."

Cynkz coiled back, falling into a cloud of smoke before settling down on Sulmara's scales again in his mun form.

"I-I can... Just give me one more chance..."

Sulmara looked at the jester expectantly.

Cynkz gathered himself one final time and puffed his chest out as he filled his lungs to their limit. He threw himself forward into a final burst of smoke and came forth in a form beyond anything he had ever managed.

The smokey cloud persisted, almost thick and stable, as one would expect of a portal. A slithering form rushed out from within, innumerable small ovals packed tightly against one another flew across, their sheen dancing wildly in the light as they passed. The new creature's body quickly filled the grotto, piling layers onto itself the way water would in a cavern. Even Sulmara shifted her own body to make room for the jester's transformation. Tagg nearly fell back into one of Sulmara's crevices, saved only by Fiddle who grabbed his hand and pulled him into open space.

Cynkz's transformation finished its unveiling and seemed to cover every inch of all that lay beneath the top light shining through the opening above the grotto. Its peculiarities became apparent; it appeared stretched, as if one had taken a snake in both hands and pulled them apart to artificially lengthen its body. Its body seemed far too thin, giving it a weak and sickly impression. Its head was diamond-shaped, a dark visage pulling forth into a fine and delicate point. Its eyes, unlike the usual round and shining beads, were angular and sharp. Oddly set scalene shapes housed a glossy, pitch-black layer consumed whatever light hit its surface. If one did not know any better, they would mistake the creature for some sort of alien, or a child's illustration brought to life.

Sulmara's eyes sat wide and blank at the strange, emaciated creature looking at her. She could feel the sting of pins and needles in her back, wanting to reel back and get away from the unseemly trespasser, if there was anywhere to run to in such a cozy space. She flicked her forked tongue several times as she pondered just what to make of the situation.

The unnatural abomination began to shake. It caved in on itself into a familiar cloud of gray smoke that filled the grotto. Cynkz fell to the ground and was caught by the serpent's sliding body.

Fiddle dashed to his friend's side. Tagg climbed up the scaly mound and followed suit.

"Cynkz! Are you… Are you all right?" Fiddle said.

Cynkz moaned, barely able to move.

"I don't think this is going to work… *Essssss.*"

"No, please," Cynkz exclaimed, desperately pushing to sit up.

"It's all right, Cynkz," Sulmara said, in a drained, tired voice beneath her breath.

"I can try again! It just takes a bit of time to—"

"No, Cynkz. I've seen enough. *Essssss.* I thank you for trying, for giving me a bit of hope and excitement. You three may leave. *Essssssssssss…*"

Sulmara began to slither in a wide circle around the grotto. As her lustrous body receded into the shade, a moving row of soil rolled beneath the grass. The great serpent's hissing faded into nothing, and the grotto was still and tranquil once more.

Cynkz looked on for a moment to see if Sulmara was gone. He picked himself up, brushed off his cloak and quietly made his way to the beacon beneath the undisturbed tree. Fiddle and Tagg shared a look of confusion before following him. Fiddle, without hesitation or complaint, grabbed Tagg's hands and carried him over the lake before dropping him off next to Cynkz.

"We could probably use this stave to get out of here," Cynkz said. "I've a feeling the maiden figured we would try channeling it to teleport at their behest once we completed our task."

Fiddle fists clenched. He said through gritted teeth, "You sound so sure. But Cynkz, what in Munder was all that earlier—"

Before the imp could finish, Cynkz reached out and touched the stave. The entire tree was engulfed in a great pink flash of light. As the radiance receded back to the soft greens and blues of the grotto, the three vanished without a trace.

CHAPTER 22

IN A DEEP RECESS OF THE MAZED WOODS, A BRIGHT flash coated the shaded, murky oaks with a rose-colored flash. Three confused souls tried to orient themselves in a new environment. The trio found themselves sitting in front of a deep burrow, a round and angled hole that disappeared into darkness. The distant thumps and crashes of the towering insects could be heard, though the sky was completely shaded by a dense thicket of overlapping leaves and branches.

"Cynkz! I need to know!" Fiddle screamed.

"Quiet down, Fiddle," Cynkz said, "or you'll attract those big creatures."

"I don't care! Why would you even consider throwing all of us away like garbage? Even me! I've stuck with you through thick and thin! And for what?!"

Cynkz looked at the imp, the edge of his lips twitched as he tried, and failed, to hold in his laughter.

"What's so funny, you lowdown, dirty, knavish—"

"It seems I've improved a great deal since we first left Dulrot."

"What?"

"It feels as though it were yesterday that dear old Rackel was criticizing my acting ability…"

Fiddle looked on, at first dumbfounded, before sinking his head into his hands. "You've gotta be kidding me."

Cynkz finally cracked and laughed more heartily than he had ever done on their journey. Tagg nearly tripped over himself as he stumbled toward the jester.

"So… all of that was an act?" Tagg said and fidgeted with his hands. "The looks, the calls of love, even the transformations?"

Fiddle smiled and laughed.

"What made you think Sulmara would go along with all of that?"

Cynkz calmed himself and merely shrugged, his bony shoulders pointing up at a similar angle to his wry grin.

"In truth, I didn't. It came naturally to me."

"Yeah, 'as naturally as adopting your form, sweet Sulmara.'" Fiddle waved his arms, his intonation pitched comically high as he mocked the jester's mannerisms.

"I'm sorry, Fiddle, I am. But I needed the act to be convincing."

"Yeah, yeah, yeah. It's fine. I guess I'll call us even for the times I picked on ya before."

"I take back what I said earlier," Tagg said. "You two have *no* survival prowess."

The three exchanged looks and broke out in laughter.

A glowing orb bobbed its way toward the group from deep within the burrow. Cynkz was the first to notice, then Fiddle and Tagg looked into the hole and waited, their breath bated and hearts stopped. Fiddle appeared more curious than anything, having to stop himself from diving into the burrow to see what exactly was approaching them.

The taps of small footsteps became clear, and a short, old woman holding a lantern on the end of a dark stave came out of the dark.

"You young things seem to be in good spirits," the old woman said. "I suppose that means you were successful?"

"Are you one of the maidens?" Fiddle asked.

"Oh heavens, no," the old woman, barely waist high and appearing more like a bundle of wrapped and tattered cloth, gestured her free hand as if to dismiss the imp's assumption. "I only help out where I'm needed. Come with me and I'll take you to see the others."

"The others?" Tagg perked up. "The other po? Are they safe?"

"Yes, yes. They are fine."

Tagg breathed a sigh of relief. His shoulders relaxed and fell, as if the weight of the world had been lifted from them.

"And you, mister jester," the old woman pointed a long, bony finger at Cynkz. "The Sisters want to see you personally."

"Ooh, we get a special audience with the legendary Sisters of Elm, finally," Fiddle said.

"Just the jester, but I suppose you can come too." The old woman turned, the lantern rocking back and forth against the hard wood of her staff as she moved.

"You 'suppose?!'" Fiddle exclaimed, "I'm as awesome as Cynkz, you know! I'm always helping!"

"Yes, yes, I'm sure you do, little one," the old woman said, dismissively waving her hand.

"It's all right, Fiddle. You have my appreciation, if nothing else," Cynkz said, before walking forward.

"And mine too, little imp!" Tagg said, barely able to keep himself from skipping into the burrow after the old woman.

"At least *someone* appreciates me," Fiddle mumbled, and he too flew into the dark hole.

The intrepid visitors moved down into the tunnel, guided by the bobbing orb of light. A soft wind echoed throughout the burrow, filling the darkness with a dim whistling sound that was broken by the constant tips and taps of feet pressing against an unusually smooth surface. Tagg thought harder ground should be more reassuring, yet he was as worried as ever. He could not get his thoughts off of his friends.

Fiddle, likewise, had grown impatient with all of the walking and flew past Cynkz to get beside the old woman leading them forward. He looked down his pointed nose at the woman, as if trying to be taken seriously.

"Hey, old lady! Where are we—"

"Hush! We're almost there," the old woman said. "I swear, why is it always the little ones that make the most noise?"

Fiddle flattened his brow and grit his teeth, though he knew better than to garner the ire of the one leading them through such a dark and cramped environment. Figuring it would be wiser to save his words for later, he receded to Cynkz's side, reserving his frustrations to bouts of clenched fists and loud huffs.

A familiar blue sheen emanated from the end of the tunnel. It bore the same, almost crystalline edge as the aura on the mountain that led Cynkz and Fiddle to the realm. As they approached, its luster faded, as if it were a door slowly opening for them. The old woman's short silhouette broke the layer of light as she made her way to the entrance's ledge. She turned around and smiled, holding out her free hand.

"Welcome to our humble little home. Don't mind the mess."

The sight that greeted the travelers was as impressive as it was dizzying. The sheer drop in height was enough to make the palms of anyone not blessed with the gift of flight with a warm blanket of sweat. Dozens of thin, makeshift bridges and walkways cut across the soft green light, a crisscrossing of hard dark lines against the flat hue. Many ledges consisted of irregular combinations of rock and wood leading to countless cozy-looking structures. Hooded figures, some bearing loose bundles of rags and others the familiar moss-green hoods, walked across the many paths. Some were empty handed but most carried baubles and trinkets, piles of loose cloth, and pots filled with steaming liquids of odd colors.

At the center, an immense pillar was carved out of the ground. It appeared to operate as the central structure for the establishment. The top blended into the hard rock ceiling and the bottom reached endlessly into the depths of the pit beyond whatever light was visible from their perch.

"This way, young ones," the old woman gestured from the side of a winding ledge. As the group followed the precipitous pathway downward, the old woman addressed her followers.

"You may ask questions now," she said.

"Finally!" Fiddle said, expressing his frustration with a toss of his hands. "Where are we? Who are you? Where are the other po? Why did you guys have us get this weird venom? Also what are—"

"Enough!" the old woman shouted. "Pah! Nevermind. I'll just have the Sisters explain."

Tagg stepped forward. "Are the others all right? I'd like to see them again."

"Of course," she said. "Where do you think I'm taking you?"

"Oh thank you! Thank you so much—"

"We're here."

They stood before a large shack built into the underground rock wall. Moving shadows crossed the light pouring out from the many gaps in the structure's wall. Muffled voices could be heard overlapping one another in hectic conversation. Tagg immediately perked up as he recognized some of the voices. He hurried through the cracked door, and a dozen eyes were set upon him; mostly the po he had traveled with initially, as well as a few maidens in their signature robes, the hoods pulled back revealing soft, pale faces and long dry hair.

"Tagg's back!"

Gara, the smallest of the po, ran up to Tagg and hugged him around his waist. The others got up and joined in. Tagg's eyes began to water, and he shut them tight in a vain attempt to hold in the tears.

"Y-you're all right, all of you! Thank the Creator!"

Cynkz paused. His relief at their reunion was quickly beset with curiosity at the po's words.

The Creator? I remember the sentinels speaking about such a thing in Dulrot. I wonder... Cynkz's thoughts trailed off into wordless ruminations.

"Let's move along, Mister Jester. It would be unwise to keep the Sisters waiting."

The old woman began walking ahead once again, knowing, if not outright expecting, Cynkz and Fiddle to follow her posthaste.

The old woman made her way across a wooden bridge, the light taps of her small feet forcing small creaks as she navigated the splintered crossing. Fiddle flew ahead without a second thought. Cynkz, on the other hand, looked down and watched his steps carefully, placing the balls of his feet with trepidation. Everything appeared stable, and he relaxed his leg.

A loud snap pierced the air and echoed through the cavern. Cynkz immediately stopped, and as he darted his eyes around, he could see the many faces of the maidens, as well as Fiddle and the old woman, staring at him. Cynkz slowly pulled his foot back and rolled his shoulders to regain his composure.

"My apologies, madam," Cynkz said. "I figured I would enjoy a walk, but I suppose I should fly to avoid damaging your property further."

The old woman looked at the broken strip of wood. "Just what have you been eating, boy? That wood comes from the finest oak in the realm. Not even the heaviest critters could break it if they tried."

"I've always wondered that too!" Fiddle exclaimed. "It's so weird, right? Good thing he can fly."

"Yes, that is convenient," she said. "When you're ready, let's continue."

Cynkz bowed and lifted himself into the air, this time following close behind Fiddle. Cynkz lowered his head just enough to cover the stares of the many maidens on the walkways above.

They found themselves below the shanty town.

"This isn't a trap, right?" Fiddle asked.

"If it was, you two would already be in it, wouldn't you?" the old woman responded.

"I guess so…"

Cynkz drifted forward. "If I may be so bold, ma'am?"

"Oh, please, call me Krulgilliard! We reserve the title of ma'am for the elderly and the Sisters."

"Ah, of course. Miss Krulgilliard. I—"

"Please, please, just Krulgilliard. Miss Krulgill was my mother."

"Krulgilliard, do you think the Sisters could help us find specific po? We lost good friends on the way to your realm."

"I believe so. If anyone knows anything around here, it is the Sisters."

"They must be quite something. Po and mun alike have spoken about them in many of the other realms," Fiddle said.

"That makes sense. When Yla was still around, the Sisters were quite productive."

"Yla?" Cynkz raised a sharp brow.

"Yla was one of the five Sisters. But she was a feisty one. She always wanted to explore. Whatever territory they scouted for themselves, it was never enough for her. Perhaps that was her undoing…"

"Her undoing?" Fiddle said. "What happened?"

"If the Sisters are so inclined, I'm sure they'll tell you about it."

The old woman stopped at a seemingly random spot in the middle of the dark park, far below the shifting green lights.

"We're here," she said.

"Where's here?" Fiddle asked as he looked around.

"Just over there, in the ground, is the door to the great Sisters of Elm. They don't get out much."

The old woman tapped the ground in front of her with the bottom of her staff. A deep, booming echo rang out, and the thin seam of a large doorway revealed itself in the dirt.

The old woman turned to Cynkz and gestured for him to come forward. Cynkz landed on the ground and walked to her and bent over slightly so she could reach him. The old woman dusted off his hat and straightened his collar.

"Now be polite. Be honest. Do these two things and you'll have nothing to worry about," she said.

"Thank you, Krulgilliard," Cynkz said.

"And you, little imp. Watch that mouth of yours. I suggest you let your friend do the talking."

"But I… All right, all right," Fiddle said, crossing his arms as he turned in the air.

"You two have walked through our portals before, so you know the drill. I'll close the door behind you to give you some privacy."

The creaking of a pair of red oak doors stopped with a thud, loud enough to shake the dirt. The old woman stepped back and gestured toward Cynkz and Fiddle.

"It was so nice to meet you," Krulgilliard said with a soft smile. "Be sure to come visit me once in a while, you hear?"

Cynkz smiled and nodded his head. As he walked toward the opening and his body angled parallel to the floor, Fiddle flew behind him, waving at the old woman. Krulgilliard tapped the ground once more with her staff, and the great red oaks slowly creaked shut.

CHAPTER 23

A SHRILL VOICE CALLED FORTH FROM THE DARK. "Come into the light, ye weary travelers. We have much to discuss."

Fiddle leaned in toward Cynkz's ear. "I really, *really* hope this isn't another trap."

A beam of harsh light illuminated a spot in the void. Cynkz walked forward and stood at its center. He felt as if he had been centered on a target, bordered by the larger ring of near-blinding white light. Fiddle entered and had to cover his beady eyes with hands. His reddish skin and fur almost looked pink beneath the spotlight.

The bitter voice returned. "Ah, 'tis a rare occasion, for we do not receive many guests. Thou art honored, I am sure."

"It is a pleasure to finally meet you," Cynkz said, his sharp eyes unhindered as his pointed cap shaded them. "I have heard so much about you all."

"Indeed. Ours is a name that holdeth a great weight. But alas, where art thine manners? I shan't forgo a proper introduction."

"I am Cynkz. And this here," Cynkz extended a gesture toward his companion, "is my greatest friend, Fiddle."

"A pleasure."

A slight creaking of wood emitted from the void, and a craggy, sunken face emerged from beneath the dark shade above Cynkz.

"I am the first, Foa Hime Ilde."

Another scrape of old wood shot out from behind Cynkz and Fiddle. They turned around to be greeted with another, equally weathered face.

"I am the second, Lea Bruk Ilde."

From the side, another face broke through the curtain of light.

"I am the third, Tia Voge Ilde."

Finally, from the opposite site, the last face emerged from the void.

"And I am the fourth, and final, Una Jaiy Ilde."

Together the faces breathed in unison and spoke together.

"We are the Sisters of Elm, travelers of the realms. The all-knowing, all-seeking eyes of the dark, advisors to the King of Munder himself."

Foa looked down and smiled. "Welcome, then, little travelers! Welcome to true darkness!"

The faces smiled and laughed together, their cackles synced perfectly. Their piercing howls cut the air around Cynkz and Fiddle like the sharp wings of a horde of insects, somehow moving around them yet still, unmoving and all-consuming.

Foa stopped abruptly, and the others followed her lead. "What is it that you seek, young Cynkz?"

"I need to—"

"What kind of circus is this?!" Fiddle nearly pushed Cynkz to the side as he moved forward. "What's with all this nonsense? Look, if I give you the—"

"Hush, little one!" Foa screamed, her voice booming in a wave that could crumple the straightest of spines.

"Let the cute one talk!" Una said.

Tia leaned over slightly, the sunken shades around her eyes squinting toward her sister. "Una, you did *not* just ruin our little play?"

"What?" Una said, her voice considerably lighter in both tone and pitch. "I'm just being honest. It's not often we get a good looking man in our quarters."

"Why do you always have to stand out, Una?" Lea said, the wrinkles at the side of her mouth pressing deeper lines into her face. "Just once it'd be nice to have our fun go unhindered."

"I don't know why you hags feel the need to gang up on me. I'm just—"

"Enough!"

Foa's scream shook the room, and everyone was quiet. She took in a deep, weighted breath and sighed.

"My good sir, do you have the venom, perchance?"

"Yep! It's right here." Fiddle pulled the small bottle from beneath a loose fold of furred skin. "You guys wouldn't believe what we had to do in order to—"

"Wait… Where did you just pull that from?" Tia said, her voice soft and tainted with disbelief.

"It's a pocket of skin. I can hold all sorts of stuff on account of how stretchy I am!" Fiddle said, thumbing his skin like the collar of a finely tailored suit.

"That is … *disgusting!*" Tia's face nearly fell back into the darkness and was accompanied by the scrapes and squeals of strained wood.

"That is, indeed, quite the sight," Una said. "Foa, you have the net, correct? I don't wanna touch that thing."

Foa released the most strained, exasperated groan Cynkz had ever heard in his life. It was the type of release one saved for the private company of a vexing family member, the kind one would normally refrain from expressing in public out of sheer courtesy. The clinks and clanks of hardwood and slippery instruments being rummaged through sent muffled scuffs of sound through the air. The heaving of a small body could be heard pulling against wood furniture before her face returned to the light.

"Here," Foa said, "place it inside the net—*carefully*—if you will."

A crooked branch consisting of the same dark and crude wood as the staves, poked through the wall of light, revealing a weaving of stained string around its end. Fiddle readied the bottle in his hand, the lavender concoction swirling around as he fluttered forth, and dropped it into the net.

"Finally!" Foa shrieked and yanked the net into the dark. "All right ladies, let's hang up the cloak and dagger. It was fun while it lasted."

A gangly, thin hand stretched from beneath Foa and snapped its fingers. The harsh spotlight ceased, and everything was pitch black. The moving of wooden stools and shuffling of small bodies could be heard as they scurried across the dark room. Fiddle huddled close to Cynkz and gripped his cloak. Cynkz merely raised an eyebrow and tried to pinpoint the intentions of the bodies moving in the void.

A faint warmth could be felt not far off in the distance, and a small flame lifted toward a lamp. Once inside, the fire revealed the true nature of the room in which they stood.

It was an exceptionally tall space; high enough that it was difficult to discern the distance of the hanging lamps and baubles strung to the rocky ceiling. Five tall stools stood in a circle around Cynkz and Fiddle and were high enough Cynkz would not have been able to reach the seat with his hands if he stood on his toes. There were several low tables and lower stools strewn about their edges. Countless papers and clothes of all colors were laid in messy order. Many wooden beads and carvings glittered in the warm light, dotting the room with small specks, not unlike stars in the empty night sky. In the corners of the room, a number of finely crafted tools and instruments were carelessly placed against the wall the way one would stash a broomstick or shovel. A number of carved open doorways decorated the walls on the far side of the room, though it was too dark to reasonably see what was inside of them.

The old women, with their short, hunched bodies and dangling, loose cloth wrapping, scuttled back and forth across the room as they lit torches and cleaned a space at one of the tables. It would have been difficult to tell the Sisters apart from one another, if not from their hair and their voices. Foa at least seemed to stand up just a bit straighter than the others, asserting her position above them.

Foa held the net with the bottle as she carefully placed its contents on the cleared surface.

"I can't believe it actually worked," Lea said, her loose, grayed dreads swaying listlessly in the air as she moved.

"I don't know why we take such gambles," Una said, her near-white strands clumped together in a bouncing bun.

"Even now we are risking a lot. The last time we had a guest it was that damn minstrel who nearly killed us and stole who-knows what," Tia said through a curtain of short, straight hair that pooled at the tip of her shoulders.

"True, but we persisted, just as we always have. And now look—we have a new and capable friend to help us," Foa said as she set down the net on the tabletop and adjusted her white, braided ponytail.

Cynkz noticed how her braid nearly touched the floor, reminding him of his own lengthy strands.

Fiddle looked at Cynkz, confused and unsure.

Cynkz took in a breath and walked over to the woman at the table. When he was but a few steps away, Foa turned, and her sisters did the same.

"Thank you, Cynkz. You've done quite a lot for us, and we are forever grateful, truly we are."

"I do not believe I've done all *that* much, to be quite honest," Cynkz said.

"No, you have. We first saw you and your companion flying above Andion's swamp. We figured you would have perished in Horgafell, but no, you persisted and went out of your way to help both your friend and the po in that drug-filled marsh. Even better, you went out of your way to protect young Orla, and led her directly to us—"

"You know of Orla?!" Cynkz's shock pulled him toward Foa.

"Why yes," Foa said. "We brought her here not long after you used that portal in the dark desert of Saknii."

"She was safe all this time? That's… quite the relief…"

"Wow, guess you guys ain't so bad after all," Fiddle said.

"Do not praise us just yet. For it was us who led you to the mountains of Hemin, where the corrosive mist lay."

"And Tall?" Cynkz said, looking at Foa with sharp eyes.

"Yes, we led you to Tall. We did not necessarily mean for you, or Fiddle, to get hurt. But we did not know how else to deal with him. We were able to repel him and locked him out of our realm, but he had stolen quite a few things from us. So long as he remained free, he was a threat."

"I see…"

"Well, he's a threat no more!" Fiddle said, thumbing the skin around his neck again like an exquisite coat. "Cynkz pulled him into the mist, and I toasted him."

"And our belongings," Foa said.

"Oh… Whoops." Fiddle drifted back several feet in shame.

"It is all right. It was unfair of us to burden you with our problems. But you managed to retrieve one artifact—the bottle." Foa looked back at the small, shining container as it sat on its side, the bobbing venom glistening in the torchlight.

"It must be a special bottle if it was able to pull me in and trap me like it did,' Fiddle said. "It's not often I'm forced to turn into shadow."

"It's a rare skill, one that only *his* children possess—"

"Whose children?"

"The Munder King. His children are born of shadow and carry darkness with them much like their father."

"What?!" Fiddle shrieked, nearly falling over himself in the air as he reeled back. "There's more of us? I have siblings?!"

"Yes. though most have been lost to time, fallen victim to one poor fate or another, perhaps all trapped in the farthest corners of Munderworld."

"Why doesn't the Munder King do something? He could go and find them and—"

"The king does not care for much, least of all his bastard spawn."

"Oh…" Fiddle lowered himself to the floor and sat, slouched over.

Cynkz knelt down and placed a soft hand on Fiddle's back.

"Fiddle, I'm sorry, friend," he said.

"It's all right, I guess," Fiddle said. "Who needs him anyway? Not like he ever did nothin' for me, anyhow."

"You know what this means, right?"

"Huh?" Fiddle looked up at Cynkz, his cheek pressed up toward his eye as he raised his furry brow.

"You're a prince! Son of the dark king himself! A prince of Munderworld!"

Fiddle gasped, his beady eyes nearly popping from their sockets.

"Oh my! I'm royalty, baby! Ha!"

A new voice called out from one of the adjacent dark rooms. "Sounds like you two are just as troublesome as ever."

Cynkz and Fiddle perked up, their eyes pulling their faces in anticipation. The hue of a frail young po woman walked out from the edge of a dark doorway.

"Orla!" Fiddle sprung up and flung himself to the po woman. The two shared a tight hug.

"It's good to see you as well, Fiddle," Orla patted the imp's back and looked at Cynkz.

"I like the new look, Cynkz," Orla said.

"I figured it was time for a change," Cynkz said. "I see you're finally a true maiden now, judging by your new cloak."

"Well, I still have a lot to learn. I can't teleport or anything yet."

"She shows great promise," Foa said. "She can withstand nearly all of our magics with little issue."

"She's a natural. I knew it," Fiddle said.

"Your arm," Orla said as she walked over to Cynkz, reaching for a hand that was no longer there. "Did you ever get it healed?"

Cynkz quickly stepped back a half foot and turned his shoulder away. Orla stopped, then looked back up to Cynkz's face, her own features weighed down with concern.

"It... Oh, I see... I'm sorry, Cynkz," Orla said.

"It's nothing, truly. I have adjusted to it quite well. I still have my good hand, at least." Cynkz's eyes nearly closed as he smiled warmly at Orla.

The young po woman's heavy expression lightened, and she returned the smile.

"That's good. Thank you, again, for everything. You didn't have to save me. Especially after our first encounter, you'd have been right to leave me to suffer in Horgafell."

"I had to help you. It was the right thing to do. And look at how productive and fortuitous a decision it turned out to be! You helped us escape Saknii, and now you're on your way to becoming a true maiden of Elm. I could not have asked for a better outcome."

Orla reached out and took Cynkz's good hand. She wrapped it with her own, her eyes focused downward as she tried to hide the oncoming tears.

"You remember when I asked you what you were? And how you didn't know how to respond? I think I know the answer."

"And what would that answer be, Orla?"

Orla looked up into Cynkz's sharp eyes, her own bright pupils piercing his. "You're a good person."

Cynkz held contact, though his pale face began to redden. He wondered if she could feel his palm growing warm from a slight sweat. Orla merely smiled and held on.

"Hey! No hogging him all to yourself, rookie!" Una hobbled forward, placing her own wrinkled hand on top of theirs.

Orla looked surprised for a moment, then lifted one of her hands to cover her mouth as she laughed. Una joined her, then caught a glimpse of Cynkz smiling at the both of them. Una's dark cheeks began to warm, and she immediately let go to hide her own flushed reaction.

"I have to agree with Orla," Lea said. "The new colors and cloak make you look more interesting and mysterious."

"Ah, thank you, truly, but such flattery is not necessary." Cynkz turned his head to look at Lea, his genial expression focused solely on her. Lea was caught off guard, and her own cheeks began to warm. She too had to turn away to hide.

Tia rested a bony elbow on the table, nestled between a number of small beads and arcane trinkets. "Pah! You children are so emotional."

Tia waved her hand in disdain, accidentally knocking a large, dark wooden bead off the table. It rolled several feet toward Cynkz, who, without hesitation, picked it up and walked it over to Tia. The jester knelt down and held the item out to the old woman.

"My apologies, Tia," Cynkz said, the sharp glint of his black pupils reflecting the warm, dancing fire in the torches surrounding the room. "Here you go, madame."

Tia stared for a moment too long before sheepishly taking the item from his hand. Before she could say thank you, she noticed the tingling sensation of her fingertips touching his hand as she grabbed the bead. Her cheeks tightened and began to glow before hid her face.

"If you ladies don't behave, I'm kicking all of you out!" Foa's voice was stern, hitting the air like a judge's gavel.

"You just want him all to yourself!" Una replied.

"Ugh, you fools. We should be discussing our next action," Foa said.

"I agree," Cynkz said. "I still wish to continue forward, to the Munder King himself."

"Me too!" Fiddle said. "I'd like to give my pops a few words."

"Hmm…" Foa raised a thin finger to her small, rounded chin. She looked at Cynkz, then Fiddle, and rubbed her chin several times more.

"What's wrong?" Fiddle asked.

"I do not think you two are quite ready yet, if you'll ever be."

"What?! But we've come so far!"

"I know, and your progress is nothing short of commendable, however..."

"What lies ahead for us, ma'am?" Cynkz asked.

"You are very, *very* close to the end of Munderworld. But... What lies ahead is beyond even our watchful eye."

"We have overcome many dangers already."

"You have, but what remains is dark and treacherous. If you made it to the king himself, who is to say he will not obliterate you? Cast you to the abyss to be torn apart by the infinite chasm that is his throne?"

"What else can we do? We're past the point of no return," Fiddle asked.

"With our guidance, and a little elbow grease, we could guide you back to Dulrot—"

"No!" Cynkz said, his voice rising. "I must continue! I need to learn of my past, of the regret weighing me down, of what I was and who I am!"

"I believe Orla's assessment is adequate, Cynkz. You are good, and have done good things, and will continue to do more. What more could you want?"

"I want the truth. I want to know why I am here and what lies beyond."

The room grew quiet. Everyone looked at each other. Fiddle drifted to Orla's side as he fidgeted with his hands, now close to his chest. Foa glared deeply into Cynkz's sharp eyes, now pressed into a fierce squint. They could have sliced stone and cut a sentinel in two.

"What will it take to convince you we are ready to move ahead?" Cynkz asked.

"You could stay with us, aid us in attending to our duties, and maybe if I see it fit—"

"That is not good enough I'm afraid, madame."

"My word is not good enough for you? My offer is not good enough for you?" Foa grabbed her staff and stood up as straight as she could manage, never breaking her gaze from Cynkz. "Tell me then, Cynkz, what would be good enough for you?"

"May we have a moment alone?"

"What?!" Fiddle shrieked.

"Cynkz, what are you planning?" Orla asked.

"Hey, why should she get to hog him all to herself?!" Una shouted.

"Enough," Foa said. "All of you, go wait outside."

"But why—"

Foa lifted her staff and slammed its bottom against the ground. A strange aura stretched out from the top of the rugged crook and wrapped the entire room in strings of thick, lime-green light. Everyone, other than Foa and Cynkz, were slowly lifted above the ground and clumped together into a loose mass of bodies. They were thrust through the giant red oak doors and thrown outside, leaving nothing but the booming thud of the doors shutting.

Cynkz took a deep breath before contemplating his next move.

Here we go... Cynkz thought.

CHAPTER 24

"JUST WHAT DO YOU THINK YOU CAN ACCOMplish, young jester?" Foa said, having yet to remove her gaze from Cynkz.

Cynkz turned around and looked at the old woman sitting several feet before him. Both of her small, thin hands clasped the lengthy staff as she peaked around her grip with a curious look.

"Krulgilliard, the old woman who escorted us through your village, she mentioned someone named Yla."

"Ah, of course she would." Foa pulled her staff close to her chest as she shook her head. "Gossip travels around here pretty quickly, as you could no doubt surmise on your own."

"Who was she?"

"There were five Sisters long ago. Yla Fron Ilde, she was never satisfied. I always warned her that Munderworld requires caution, but she never listened to anyone, not even her big sister. She loved to move about. I used to joke that she always remained the youngest of us because she got so much exercise from all her traveling."

"What happened to her?"

"She insisted on venturing down into Munderworld. It was eons ago, though to us it still feels as though it were yesterday. I see the same intense light in your eyes as hers."

"Is the path ahead that perilous?"

"Perhaps. We maintained contact with her for a short while when she left. She managed to reach the ends of the great caves of Ihl, though as soon as she went beyond the screaming walls, she vanished into nothing. It was as if something had gotten a hold of her, gripped by the darkness itself, from which nothing can escape, not even light."

"The caves of Ihl? Screaming walls?"

"Hmph, I've already said too much." Foa straightened her back and hobbled toward Cynkz, wagging a gangly finger at him.

"I know your type, jester!" Foa's voice began to rise, an authoritative weight bearing down around her. "You curious souls are never satisfied! You can never be grateful for what you have! Your selfish wants and insatiable appetite for novelty brings you to throw away the love of the people around you! And for what?!"

Foa rested her flailing arm and pulled it back to her staff. She took a deep breath to calm herself before continuing.

"It is never worth it. Few things remain constant in Munderworld. The love of the family and friends around you is one of them. You would do well to hold on to that, Cynkz. Not just for your sake, but for the sake of those you grow close to, your friends, the po you help along the way, all of them. Even now, you're trying to drag your closest friend, Fiddle, into greater danger. Is your curiosity worth potentially losing your dearest companion?"

Cynkz closed his eyes and lowered his head, thinking back on his past experiences, and how much had changed in such a short amount of time.

"Fiddle told me something important, after we dealt with Tall," Cynkz opened his eyes and looked at Foa, his sharp features softened. "He told me that I should not feel bad for what I have done, and that I cannot bear the weight of everyone's decisions, no matter where they may lead. Fiddle told me, above all else, he *chose* to accompany me on this journey, to help me see it through. That Orla *chose* to accompany us into the black desert and beyond. That Kadd, and the po we helped in Horgafell *chose* to take the risk of leaving that place for a new, unknown realm. Ultimately, we each choose what we do, and who we are. As do the ones we love. Whatever the consequences may be, the least we can do is respect that."

Foa remained still, her face pulled wide in astonishment. For a moment she was speechless, at a complete loss for words. Her eyes began to slightly twitch, as if she were looking for a rebuke. Her cheeks began to tighten into knots beneath her eyes as they sparkled from a wet layer forming underneath them. Foa released a hand from her staff to lower her head into its palm.

"Yla…" she whispered, "I'm so sorry…"

She wiped several tears along the back of her hand before gripping her staff. She drew in a breath, then looked into Cynkz's eyes.

"In truth, we are supposed to help the po. I'm sure you've heard stories of us uplifting po to Dulrot, giving them a chance at salvation. Sometimes, we recruit fledgling women to join us here, those whom we believe may be capable of being saved."

"Not everyone looks favorably upon you, unfortunately."

"No, whatever ire some may feel for us is deserved. After Yla disappeared, we… Well, we became complacent. We ventured out less and less. In fact, none of us, the Sisters, have left this cobbled hole of a village in eons. We used to go out and regularly assist po. But, with the end of Peara, the po world, and our sister's disappearance, we just… I don't know how to explain. It was hard for us."

Cynkz offered a warm smile and stepped forward. He knelt down and placed a soft hand on Foa's shoulder, squeezing it gently. "It's all right, Foa. There's no need to blame yourself," Cynkz said.

"Lately, it seems you've been doing our job better than we have, Cynkz." Foa reached up and placed her hand on top of Cynkz's.

"I think you can do much better than I ever could. But I'm always willing to lend a hand, or simply an ear, wherever it is needed."

Foa's eyes began to overflow with sparkling liquid. Her lids and cheeks began to twitch as she tried desperately to hold in her tears. It was too much, and before her face could be seen twisting into—what she believed at least—a discomfiting display, she threw herself into Cynkz's chest and wrapped her frail arms around him as best as she could. Her staff fell to the ground and bounced lightly. Cynkz placed his hand on her back and felt the slight spasms as she sobbed.

Foa eventually took in a deep, satisfying inhale and rested herself for a moment.

"All right…" Foa whispered.

"Hmm?" Cynkz raised an eyebrow and turned his head.

"I'll let you two through to the next realm, but on one, actually," Foa lifted her head and released her grip of the jester. "I'll let you through on *two* conditions."

"Name your price, madame!"

"First, I want you to try your best to find Yla. If, by some miracle, you can find her, and she is fine, please tell her that we love her and we miss her. I do not know what her plans are, or if she would want to come back, but she will always have a home here."

"Of course," Cynkz said. "I was sort of planning on doing that anyway—"

"Second!" Foa held up two bony fingers.

Cynkz froze, wondering what she had in store for him.

Foa gestured for Cynkz to come in close. He obliged the old woman's command, and she leaned into his ear and whispered. As she relayed her information, a cheerful grin stretched his face, a thin barrier that was hardly enough to hold in a laugh. Cynkz waited for her to finish then leaned back and stood.

"Ah, my good maiden, I'll do you one even better," Cynkz said with a bow.

Cynkz stepped several paces back, and with a flick of his arm from beneath his cloak, a burst of pale smoke engulfed the room. As the cloud dispersed, two new forms emerged from its shadows. Cynkz had taken on the style of a dandy. He maintained his black and velvet half-cloak, draped exquisitely over his left side, yet he wore a puffed blouse, its white ruffles peeking out from beneath a fitted black vest. At the bottom of the vest's split, he wore a glistening gold belt that hugged his waist tightly and led to a pair of slim, gray trousers that billowed and narrowed toward the knees. The legs of his pants were tucked into a pair of shining black boots that tapered in perfect alignment with the rest of his outfit. The rim and soles of his shoes matched the material of his golden belt. His trusted, pointed hat was gone, revealing copious amounts of shining, pitch black hair that was pulled apart to the sides and tied back together at the back to form his long braid. As he looked down to his mistress, the pointed hairs of his goatee blended in with the few hairs on his chest poking through the top of his parted shirt.

Foa revealed herself from the fog in a new form, standing nearly as tall as Cynkz. Her skin was vibrant and supple as it tightly hugged her frame. Her face was smooth, free from the lines of worry and stress that naturally weighed down one's expression as they aged. Her own long braid remained, though it was a bright and shining dark blonde that nearly turned white against the light. A pair of bright, shining hazel eyes sat atop two rosy red cheeks framing succulent, glistening lips. Her shoulders tapered elegantly toward a slender frame dressed in a fitted, elaborate dress with colors that matched the gentleman's attire. Her gown bore rows of white ruffles that puffed out from beneath tight gold seams framed by a velvet corset. At her thin waist, layers of lustrous material billowed into a pleasing bell shape that draped her hips and spread along the floor.

Foa looked down at her dress, then her hands; what were once gangly, wrinkled appendages were delicate, pointed digits. Her first thought was of how they might feel plucking across fine strings of a harp or running through the shining strands of a gentleman's coiffed hair.

Foa smiled. As she tried to step forward, she felt the cool sensation of a pair of heels. She stumbled and began to fall, only for Cynkz to swoop in and catch her. She stared into the jester's eyes, each pupil a round, black disc that danced against the remaining faint fumes of colorless smoke.

Foa slowly pulled herself up, taking hold of Cynkz's hand and wrapping her other one around his side. Cynkz thought of the courtiers and nobles in his visions. He did not know specific dances, and instead mimicked the movements he witnessed many of them doing. All that he needed to do was lead his partner, and she would follow, allowing for the soft rhythm of two bodies moving in perfect synchronicity. There was no need for music, save for the song of two souls sharing a moment in time that was their own.

Cynkz never removed his eyes from hers as they swayed back and forth. As they were lost in each other's gaze, they moved without regard to their surroundings, narrowly avoiding crude furniture and loose baubles and trinkets that littered the ground. Foa, normally uptight about her novelties, ignored them even as the tips of her pointed heels brushed tools that were swept away beneath the swings and thrusts of her dress.

Eventually, the two accidentally circled their way into a wall. As Foa's back was pressed against the hard, stony surface, Cynkz continued forward. His hand slipped from hers and placed itself at the tip of her chin. Even as he cradled the lower contour of her face, his gaze never left hers. The two stared for what seemed too long, yet they could not stop. The edges of their finely featured faces were highlighted by the soft, orange glow of the dancing fires that lit the room. The wet layer of their eyes glittered like dim stars; powerful sources of warmth and light that were both too far away to comprehend, and yet could be felt as if right next to each other.

Cynkz slowly leaned in, his mind clear and his thoughts, for once, quieted. Foa's heart began to race, the world around them rendered to silence, save for the faint thrusts of breath working up from her bosom and her increasingly beating heart. Just as the heat from Cynkz's lips could be felt on hers, she turned her head away and placed a light finger on his mouth.

"That'll do, jester," Foa whispered, her voice polished and smooth as a finely tuned string of a harp.

Cynkz smiled and pulled himself back. Foa reached for a trinket that lay on a stand next to them. It was a silver ring, its edges forming a braided pattern that flowed into a perfect circle. Foa held the ring up to Cynkz, offering it to him.

"Take this. It will allow us to watch you and communicate with you as you travel. If you ever see Yla, she will recognize the pattern," Foa said.

"It's beautiful, Foa. Thank you," Cynkz said. He took hold of the ring between his forefinger and thumb, and turned it to observe its sparkling, silvery edge as it danced in the light.

"No. Thank you, Cynkz. You've helped to brighten up this old woman's day in an unforgettable way."

"Time doesn't mean much in Munderworld. You know that. In the grand scheme of things, you will be forever young, my dear."

Foa smiled and turned away, her cheeks turning into a fierce vermilion shade.

She walked over to her staff, still laying on the ground, and picked it up. She was nearly as tall as the instrument, caught off guard enough that she needed to eye it up and down to get a proper handling. She turned to one of the dark openings at the far side of the room and waved the pole toward it. A familiar, crystalline sheen of white and blue light emitted from the dark hole before evaporating. Foa took a final look at the jester.

"Through this door you will find the caves of Ihl. It is dark, but all you need to do is follow its path and you will find yourself surrounded by the screaming walls."

"You said Yla made her way through the caverns, correct? Is there anything I need to know will help me and Fiddle?"

"Yes, there is one bit of advice I can give. Do not follow the light. It is a trap."

"A trap?"

"Munderworld, at its heart, is a world of darkness. It is the creation of a supreme, dark being, the Munder King. His throne lies within the void, where nothing, not even light, can escape. What you may see in the caves of Ihl will be there to ensnare you, to capture you within its walls, like so many of the poor souls."

"I understand."

"I know you will be successful, Cynkz. You have the same look in your eyes as she did. She was a smart and crafty one, just like you."

"I do hope I can live up to her accomplishments, someday."

"I'm sure she'll tell you all about what she's done when you meet her."

Foa walked up to Cynkz and held his hand, their thin, light fingers draped over one another effortlessly.

"Please," Foa whispered. "I know that this illusion cannot last forever. Even now I can feel the weight of its effects bearing down on me. Please, hold it for as long as you can, and go. I'll be sure to point Fiddle in your direction shortly."

"Thank you again, Foa. And be sure to tell Orla—"

"Ah, don't worry. I'll be light on the details. Especially with Una and that mouth of hers, the last thing I need is her gossiping and anger riling up the entire colony."

He smiled warmly and slowly began to back toward the opening. As his hand slipped from hers, he noticed a thin, watery layer forming around her eyes, the lights within them glittering.

Cynkz turned and descended into the darkness, leaving behind a signature puff of colorless smoke behind him.

CHAPTER 25

THE WARM GLOW OF THE TORCHES SOON FADED beneath a heavy blanket of shadow. It was easy enough for Cynkz to feel his way through the tunnel, though nothing could be seen, not by a normal eye. The harsh, unfeeling rock of the walls and floor slid past and an eerie chill ran through him, like wind through a forest, working its way across every bit of exposed skin. A muffled howling could be heard coming from further within. Again, Cynkz thought it might just be wind, but he remembered Foa's words: *the screaming walls.* It was then he recognized precisely what he was hearing—the pained moans and cries of po!

His mind felt disorganized, his thoughts and feelings reaching in every direction as he tried to make sense of it. Where precisely was he in relation to the world behind him? What of the impression the Sisters left on him, and what would Orla do now that she was on her way to becoming a full maiden? Would Sulmara have kept her word if he had truly decided to stay by her side? And what of Foa and their interaction? What did she really think of him? And what of her warning? Why would he need to avoid the light?

As his mind pondered every possible question and possibility, he realized something that should not have evaded him for so long: *Where is Fiddle?*

"Cynkz!" A sharp voice rang from behind, deep in the dark.

Cynkz put his mind at ease and waited for his companion.

"Fiddle! I'm a bit farther down!" he called out.

"You don't have to yell. I'm here," Fiddle said, sitting in the air in front of Cynkz.

"Ah, you'll have to excuse me. It is too dark to see much of anything, and I underestimated how fast you are."

"I can see a fair bit in here, actually." Fiddle gestured around him, his confident flailing invisible to Cynkz in the dark.

"I suppose a being born of shadow would have that advantage," Cynkz said.

"I always figured you liked the dark as well?"

"Only when it is beneath a star-filled sky, I'm afraid."

"Can't you turn into something that has night vision? Like a bug or wild cat or something?"

"I do not like to transform in enclosed spaces. At least, not into beasts."

"Don't tell me you're claustrophobic, Cynkz!"

"When you spend so much time as free as a bird in the night sky, anything smaller feels like a cage."

"That's awfully poetic sounding and kind of a bummer."

"My apologies, Fiddle. You'll have to excuse my melancholy. A lot is on my mind at the moment."

"Yeah, Foa kind of pushed you forward without letting you say goodbye to everyone else. What happened, anyway? I saw a bunch of your weird, gray smoke coating the floor as I left."

"Oh, that. Well…"

Fiddle swatted at Cynkz' shoulder. "Eh, you can tell me another time. Let's get through this already."

Cynkz smiled and placed his hand back on the cave wall before continuing.

"Fiddle, what do you see, exactly? Is there anything strange about this cave?"

"Sort of," Fiddle said, twisting his head to peer through the dark. "The walls look like a soft stone, and the formations are smooth and swirling around each other like waves."

"I figured as much while running my hand along the walls. Can you see anything up ahead?"

Fiddle squinted. "Yeah, it looks like a ledge coming up. Do you hear that? Is that wind? I know caves can be creepy, but this is a bit much."

"Foa mentioned 'screaming walls' and to be wary of the light."

"What a kooky old hag. Why is it that not a single thing can make sense? I miss Dulrot and even Rackel."

"Me too, Fiddle."

The sounds of Cynkz's hand and feet brushing across the rocky surface began to recede beneath the cries of the cavern. He gripped the wall tighter as he moved, and at one point, seemed to grab hold of a particularly soft bit of wall that moaned softly in his ear. Repulsed, Cynkz recoiled his hand back to his chest and stared into the dark.

"What was that?! Fiddle, can you see what I just grabbed?"

"It… It's a po!"

"What?"

"It's a po, trapped in the wall! Eugh, there's so many of them in the walls and the floor. The whole place is made of them."

Cynkz focused and could sense tiny movements around him. Beneath his feet, he could feel the writhing of tightly packed bodies as they twitched and pushed against one another. Their cries were muffled, e weak, yet piercing. Each foot felt as though it were atop the beating heart of something near dead yet forced to cling painfully to life.

Just ahead was the ledge Fiddle mentioned. The dark edge formed a thin line where light peeked from below.

"Watch it, just ahead the floor drops off," Fiddle said.

"I can see it," Cynkz replied. "Barely."

Cynkz approached the ledge timorously, his hand close to his side, and hadn't much to guide him beyond the writhing hard floor and the soft hue. Cynkz walked up to the ledge and stood, squinting his eyes into sharper shapes as he attempted to parse the landscape ahead.

Countless moaning souls formed the dark rocky layers of the walls. Each one was pressed against another, their bodies forced to twist and turn as they helplessly writhed. The collective wails of the damned echoed throughout the chamber, their hisses and squeals trailing into the dark recesses of numerous tunnel entrances scattered throughout the room. At the bottom of the room was a thin, transparent layer of pale liquid. A musky, pungent vapor rose from its surface, some mixture of saliva, dirt, and blood. Small bubbles of air from the open mouths beneath could be seen tearing through to the top. The cavern was humid, the air itself thick and viscous, as though the room had been drowned in an invisible fog. Worse still, the vapors of exasperated breaths could be felt crawling back and forth across the skin. They were the final, desperate reaching of weak limbs grasping for something, anything, that may offer a release.

Cynkz could not help but grimace at the sight, his nostrils flaring and his lip curling. Mud and sand and tar were easy things to deal with. The sweat of the damned, the tears of the hopeless, the crying of the helpless, the gurgling of stale blood; these were beyond him. It took everything to refrain from throwing up, the thought of his regurgitation only falling onto the face of whatever hapless po may be trapped beneath him too much to handle.

Fiddle pinched his nostrils together and attempted to cover his ears. He switched his arms back and forth as he tried to put up a barrier along his orifices before noticing Cynkz's expression.

"Let's hurry up, Cynkz. I can't stand this place," Fiddle said.

"You and I both, friend."

Some of the po were dying but not in the normal way. Upon death, a po soul would disperse and slowly reform over time somewhere random. Within the cavern, however, the soul would merely leave its current spot and swim through the air to another open crevice within a nearby wall or rock. Their body would reform quickly, just for them to be forced to endure more torture.

"How in Munder are we meant to get through this place?" Fiddle asked.

"Foa mentioned that their long lost sister, Yla, made it through here, so not all hope is lost," Cynkz said.

"What? Really?! Did she say how she did it?"

"Unfortunately, no—"

"Of course."

Cynkz at the silvery ring on his middle finger. He lightly dragged his thumb along the bottom edge, spinning it around the base of his digit, noting how the braided pattern glistened brilliantly in what little light remained in the dark cavern.

"She said that Yla, upon reaching the end of the cavern, was taken by something. It was as if darkness itself had gripped her and pulled her into the abyss," Cynkz said.

"Well, whatever it was, it's gotta be better than this. Let's hurry," Fiddle said.

"Agreed."

Cynkz began drifting forward toward the open tunnels. Fiddle followed closely behind. The trapped po seemed to scream louder as they flew about. What once was a series of strained drawls turned into a cacophony of guttural wheezes, pained whines, and phlegm-soaked coughs. Every harsh sound was amplified by the viscous liquid below.

"Ack! I can't take this anymore!" Fiddle threw his tiny hands down as he turned and screamed, "Will you all *shut up!!*"

The final snap of the imp's shriek bounced off of every surface and crashed through the dark openings leading out of the cavern. The wails ceased, and all was still. Before Fiddle could finish a confident smirk, the po worked themselves up again and continued their symphony.

Cynkz had to restrain himself, this time from laughing. The light revealed a number of harsh lines being pressed together on the imp's face as he grumbled.

Fiddle tugged lightly at Cynkz's cloak.

"Cynkz," Fiddle whimpered. "You got any way of helping me out here?"

"I have an idea, old friend," Cynkz said through a smile and threw his arm to the side, dragging his cloak into a puff of colorless smoke. The dark, velvet-laced veil stretched around Cynkz, forming a black, oblong barrier around him. The center of the new shape parted, revealing the jester's pale face as he looked out.

"We can travel in this protective barrier. It should help to dampen the noise," Cynkz said.

Without a second thought, Fiddle dove inside and rested at the bottom of the parted cloth. Cynkz tightened the cape around them slightly before continuing forward into the darkest tunnel nearby.

Cynkz figured Fiddle would be his eyes and help guide him through the darkness. Yet no matter how far they traveled, or how much they tried, they couldn't escape the faint light. It seemed as if the end of every tunnel possessed an ominous radiance.

"We've been traveling for some time," Cynkz said.

"Yeah," Fiddle said. "Yet no matter what, it feels like the light is following us."

"Fiddle, can you retrieve the thread from my coat? Hold it out and see if it's able to lead us."

"No problem, cap'n!"

The imp threw a sloppy salute and dove further into Cynkz's cloak. After some violent rummaging about, Fiddle popped out, the thread at the end of his outstretched arm. The two continued, yet noticed something odd; every time there were multiple tunnels to choose from, the thread chose the path with the most light. Cynkz ignored it for a while until they reached another large and empty chamber.

"The thread has been more than helpful, but I feel compelled to heed Foa's advice," Cynkz said.

"I agree," Fiddle said. The imp quickly dove back into the cloak and returned the thread into a pocket in Cynkz coat.

"All these tunnels look the same. Are we lost?" Fiddle asked.

"Well," Cynkz said, inhaling an exasperated breath that pushed the edges of his cloaked barrier like a balloon, "We've been consistently moving downward. I'd imagine that is the way ahead. Though who really knows in a place such as this."

"Is it just me, or is the light getting stronger as we move farther?"

"Hmmm…"

"Cynkz?"

Cynkz nearly closed his eyes as he squinted, attempting to focus his senses on a bright hue emitting from within one of the tunnels. Nearly a minute of silence passed, or at least what could be considered silence among the screaming walls of Ihl. The stagnant light began to bounce, as if something were walking toward them.

Cynkz's eyes widened, yet another sound forced his brow into a pressed line; the distressed tinge of hard nails dragging along the tender stone walls flowed out from within.

"We need to go, *now!*" Cynkz quickly turned and dashed through one of the darker tunnels on the opposite side of the cavern. Despite picking up speed, the entity could be heard clawing and stomping forward vigorously. It was heavy, as with each thunderous step contained a dozen trapped po crying out in agony beneath its heels.

The duo made their way as quickly as they could manage. Rows of waving, screaming walls turned into dark blurs as they flew by. The po appeared to grow more agitated as they descended into the dark caves. It was not long before Cynkz, shrouded in his dampening cloak, could hardly tolerate the noise.

The damp winds rushing past their faces abruptly stopped as they came to a dead-end, the first one of its kind. The menacing scratching and ever-growing light continued toward them. With no other choice, Cynkz turned around to face their pursuer.

The two were greeted by an impossibly harsh light that nearly blinded them. Even when they closed their eyes and turned their heads, the burning glow penetrated their clenched lids. Every single po making up the surrounding walls screamed ferociously, their ghastly shrieks pitched high enough to crack glass. Once the cries reached their apex, a new voice barreled through the chaos.

"All of you! Quiet!"

Immediately, everything went silent. Cynkz and Fiddle had little else other than the ringing in their ears and the fading of intense, white light as their senses adjusted to the new calm. A small form began to come into view as the two looked ahead.

A diminutive, yet lanky body stood before them, blocking off their retreat. He wore the most exquisite black cloth that appeared a deep azure shade against the pure white light. The cloth draped elegantly around his body into a loose cloak and hood. His skin appeared stony, tightly held against packed musculature, and was a faded blue-grey hue. Within his blocky grip was a tall staff that stretched far above the figure and opened at its top into a large, golden ring holding an impossibly bright orb suspended at its center. His face possessed refined features, flat, beady eyes sitting behind an elongated snout and lips curled up and then down toward its rear.

Fiddle's face stretched wide, his mouth agape, and his eyes two open orbs that nearly popped out of their sockets. "What?! You mean it was just a tiny sentinel this whole time?!"

"Tiny?" he said. "You dare to mock me, imp?"

Cynkz noticed an opportunity for discussion and began to work his charm.

"Excuse my friend, good sir," Cynkz said, attempting to gesture a curtsy within his cloak. "We are mere travelers trying to find our way through—"

"Find your way through? *To where?*" The sentinel's voice became heavy, as if pressing down with authority. "This is *my* realm, and I guard all that is here. Normally, it is the occasional po that is sent here for punishment. Who exactly are you two?"

"I am Cynkz, and this here is—"

"I ain't telling you a damn thing, you runt!" Fiddle waved his arm and wagged his finger at the sentinel, expressing total disregard for Cynkz's attempt at polite conversation. "What's a sentinel doing down here, anyway?"

The sentinel's staff began to rattle within his shaking grip. His other hand clenched into a fist so tightly, it sounded similar to stone being crunched against stone.

"How *dare* you! I am the leader of all sentinels! I am the progenitor of all who guard Munderworld! I am Lord Topphil, and you *will* respect my title!"

"Strange, we've heard that Horgafell was the originating point of the sentinels," Cynkz said.

"Hmph," Topphil scoffed. "The higher up in Munderworld you go, the more distorted the truth becomes. Information turns to myth and loose tales as it is passed around."

"That's neat, but what do you want?" Fiddle said. "We'd like to move on and get out of here."

Toppling grimaced, his lip curled into a fierce snarl that laced his words with a bitter hiss. "I would *never* be so negligent as to let two strangers escape *my* realm. Imagine if you went on to bother Eshra'Tel? Imagine if, by some miracle, you made it to the Munder King himself? What an embarrassment that would be for me."

"Who? What are you talking about? Fiddle asked. "Are all you sentinels just here to keep people from bothering the Munder King's nap?"

"That mouth of yours..." Topphil drew in a deep breath before continuing. "You two will be thanking me soon enough. You buffoons would never make it past Eshra'Tel."

"Who is Eshra'Tel? I have heard the name before," Cynkz said.

"It matters not. Consider yourselves fortunate that you will not be meeting him," Topphil said.

Fiddle gripped the edges of Cynkz's cloak and nearly threw at the sentinel in frustration. "You little rat! What's stopping us from—"

Topphil lifted his staff, its top edge gleaming with light, and tossed it to his opposite hand. He tilted his head back and widened his jaws as far as they could manage. His roar was deep, its effects like a boulder dropping through the body, shaking everything to its core. It rang out in waves, and each gesticulation shook the world around them. As the walls cracked, pale po bodies began to spill out in a sea of rendered, damned souls overflowing the tunnels.

Cynkz and Fiddle attempted to pull into the cloak for protection, but it was too late. Within seconds, the two were entirely covered by a writhing mass of squirming bodies, dirt, and rock. Topphil ceased his call to observe the destruction he had wrought. Something felt off to him, however. Normally, when po were released from the wall they instantly melded into the first solid object or surface they came across. Here, they maintained the form of a massive, pulsating mound.

As the sentinel stepped forward, a growing rumble started beneath his stony soles. The heap of living, twisting, glowing carcasses shook violently and erupted in a burst of colorless smoke. As the po were dispersed, a giant horned beetle shot forth.

Topphil remained undeterred. "Hmph, a measly beast will not be able to stop me."

The arthropod shoved its massive horn past Topphil, who narrowly escaped its point. The beetle could hardly fit inside the tunnel, and as it barreled forward, its bulbous shell forced Topphil into a nearby wall, stunning him long enough for the creature to dart away. Fiddle poked his head from just beneath one of the insect's wings and looked back at the sentinel.

"Ha! See ya, chump!" Fiddle could not resist the urge to taunt, despite knowing Cynkz often preferred for him to be respectful.

The two return to a large cavern. In front of them sat pathways of darkness leading to cramped chasms.

"Which way do we go?" Fiddle said beneath a worried breath.

Topphil's call echoed behind them, shooting through the open spaces and into the dark passages ahead. The rumbling of heavy steps followed. Cynkz slowly stepped to the center of the chamber, his large, bristled limbs sinking deep into the stale liquid pooled beneath them.

From each tunnel entrance new creatures emerged. They were pale dirt and liquid-stained worms. Their heads, bulbous and smooth, first came into sight. These heads possessed countless frills, darker shades of violet lined by lighter hues of fleshy pinks and whites. There were no eyes, at least none that could be seen. Their bodies were long and serpentine, yet muscular and fibrous; each movement was violent yet controlled as it swayed its midsection back and forth to propel itself forward. Their limbs were short stumps that flailed efficiently against the cavern walls, guiding their bodies the way one would see a fish swim through water. Worst of all, their skin shone brilliantly, their movements creating blinding streaks of light as they moved. Despite their appearance and movement, they were completely silent, swift and adept as a hawk that lay in wait in the treetops, or a snake waiting along a string of grass before pouncing onto its prey.

As the slithering wyrms flowed around the cave, surrounding the two with a menacing light, Cynkz, without a second thought, pulled toward the center of the chamber and began to burrow into the ground. It was surprisingly easy for him in beetle form to break through the tender rows of po bodies embedded in the ground. Mere moments was all it took for him to be completely submerged, and waves of stale liquid and twisted po souls were thrown in every direction as he thrashed about.

Just as the trailing sound of crushed dirt and soft bodies began to taper, the wyrms locked their sights on the new hole. Topphil arrived in time to witness their action. A great burst of wet orange flame shot out from the hole, a stream of spitfire that billowed out and dispersed along the cavern's ceiling. Frightening shrieks echoed from the burrow, along with the stench of burnt flesh and steam.

"That smell," Topphil said beneath his breath. "That imp's capable of spitting out quite a flame, I'll admit."

Topphil pulled his staff close to his chest and leapt upward. He flew into the hole, his angle precise, like a missile seeking its target. He called out again, and the faint hue of more wyrms came into view.

Fiddle turned his head in response to the sentinel's call. The gleaming, piercing light of the Topphil's staff could be seen flying toward them at troubling speed. Rows of packed bodies revealed themselves as the contours of their writhing forms and were highlighted by the dashing beam.

Cynkz continued digging as fast as he could, pushing through the tight space, leaving Fiddle to defend the rear. Fiddle drew in another, deeper breath and blew forth. The dark burrow was illuminated by the burning amber of a raging dense ball of flame that filled the tunnel's confines. The confined space amplified everything inside and focused the barreling fireball into a searing missile that charred the po-filled walls. The burning flame was torn apart and dispersed as Topphil emerged from it, effortlessly waving the fire to his side. Topphil pulled his arms close to his body, turning his body into a zipping spear.

Fiddle took in another breath and reared his shoulders back in preparation for another attack. Before he could finish his inhale, the sentinel's granite feet impacted the rear of the beetle's black shell. Everything shook and rattled against the ribbed mass of bodies crumbling around them. Small flames seeped from the corners of Fiddle's mouth. He felt the cold grip of stone fingers wrapping around his neck.

The sentinel's fingers began to close, collapsing the imp's throat.

Fiddle, with trails of wet flame and blood spewing from his mouth, pulled back as hard as he could and retreated into shadow. The sentinel's staff was still emitting intense light, turning the tunnel white. Fiddle had been reduced to a small, slithering black shape that shot around the air.

Topphil watched as the menacing little shade flew around and back, straight for his beady eyes. He began to reach and claw at his own eyes, desperately trying to pull the biting, dark veil form his face. Topphil lifted himself up as he flailed, banging his limbs and driving jagged lines through the walls with his staff. As the tunnel began to crumble, the beetle carrying the fighters finally had enough room to easily shift around.

Cynkz turned to face the threat, and the diminutive sentinel, in desperation, lifted the gleaming end of his weapon and channeled its energy. The world around them was consumed by the radiance of a white-hot glow. Fiddle's shadow retreated, lifting from the sentinel's face and writhing in the open, burning air. Cynkz, seeing an opportunity, burst into colorless smoke, reverting back to his original form to leap forward and take hold Fiddle.

His cloak followed his arm and stretched around him before bursting into pale smoke. From the cloud, a perfect, dark obsidian orb filled the edges of the tunnel. Its black, curved edges pressed violently into the surrounding walls, breaking the walls like splinters from a tree. The menacing orb continuously expanded with no regard for its surroundings, grinding the sentinel's entire body into the wall with its insurmountable weight. The gleaming staff snapped in two. Countless formless po bodies were thrown around, their screams accenting every bit of open air with woe and agony.

Topphil summoned every bit of strength his small body could muster and pushed the turbulent sphere back enough to inhale. He let loose a piercing roar that rippled throughout the nooks and crevices. An aural quake of destruction tore the world apart. It was such that it even shook Cynkz out of his shapeshifting, leaving him and Fiddle to fall into the open, endless darkness below.

The sentinel realized his mistake. As he tried to dive toward his opponents, the soft pull of small hands and fingers wrapping around his arms. He looked up only to realize that the sea of po, once restrained by the walls of the caves of Ihl, had been loosened by his scream, and were piling into a sinister mass of vengeful spirits. Topphil struggled and screamed, his deafening roars turned into whimpers that trailed into the abyss. The messy heap of bodies gestated as they pulled in and out, their collective strength consuming the sentinel entirely.

Cynkz and Fiddle, along with a number of loose po, continued falling down into the abyss. They struggled against the open air, only to realize an invisible force dense beyond words drew them down. The straggling bodies began to spread in all directions. The jester and the imp reached helplessly out to one another in the void. Cynkz could have sworn he saw Fiddle's lips moving, perhaps screaming out to him, but nothing came out. All was torn apart, and nothing was left beyond the infinite curtain of the void.

CHAPTER 26

ALL WAS DARK. NOTHING COULD BE SEEN OR heard, only felt.

Cynkz felt something dragging him along the blanket of the void. A deep, suffocating sense of dread filled him. His heart felt like an impenetrable piece of diamond, his stomach like a rock that had been dropped carelessly into a lake. His limbs were lifeless, heavy and motionless, whatever flow of blood or life that normally carried them was gone. Something was looking at him, and its hate was so potent it could be felt penetrating the abyss.

A thin sliver of light parted the darkness. It appeared to curve toward and away from his view, as if it were following the contours of an orb. The light continued to spread into an impossibly long and rounded diamond into the shape of a predator's vertical pupil. Its edges began to burn into the darkness, withering away into a dark shape that peered directly into his soul.

Cynkz's mind was as empty as the barren void that consumed his senses. All that seemed to remain of him was that which could be felt, and all he could feel was a thick, potent miasma more akin to a storm of raging emotions; anger, hatred, resentment, bitterness, spite, and many more that could hardly be described. None were comfortable.

As the rounded eye came into focus, it looked upon him, and its words echoed forth.

You... heavy... the thread! Mine!

Its words could not be heard. They were felt as frightening, malicious strings of energy that forced their way between the walls of his heart. They struck the edges of his soul with such force that he felt he may break at any moment.

He instinctively tried to pull himself in, to cover himself with his own body, but nothing was there. He was forced to confront the entity in his most vulnerable state. He was not even permitted the comfort of covering his eyes.

The voice struck out again, this time focusing its anger on a single point like the tip of a spear:

The thread! The power of the cosmos! Give it... to me!

Cynkz fell into the eye of the abyss. The curved edges revealed yet another writhing mass of lights. Infinite po souls were being dragged around an unseeable sphere like loose threads along a streaming river. Their cries were quieter and calmer than the ones from the caves above. Perhaps they were a soft admission of their fate. Whatever bodily autonomy they may have been granted was ripped away from them. There was nothing left for them but to go with the flow of madness and despair.

Cynkz could feel the invasive squirming of invisible fingers worming their way across his body. They were like rows and rows of frigid pokes and pulls and stabs that held him in place as they worked toward his center.

Still, his mind remained empty. Only the feeling of death, hopelessness, and the void remained.

As the ghostly fingers worked their way to his core, a familiar sliver of light presented itself before him; it was the thread in all its beauty. Its elegant curve and the endless bits of stardust that flowed from its center was a soothing contrast to the harsh canvas before him.

The eye screamed, its voice rippling through everything, rattling the rivers of souls like bark in a tree struck by lightning.

The thread! Heavy... Dense...

The weight of Omun, and God, the Creator...

Power... Freedom...

Mine!

Cynkz could see it so clearly he believed it was an illusion. Yet he felt compelled to reach out to it, just as he had many times before. There was no arm to lift, no hand to grab, no fingers to touch, yet he felt a deep compulsion pulling his arm to the thread.

The moment it was in his ethereal grasp, the voice screamed again, crying out desperately to him.

Noooooooo!

You cannot … deny me! Think of what we could do… What we could accomplish!

The realms… The world… The stars…

They could be…

Ours!

The soft shard of light began to pull, lightly as a feather, so light that if one were not looking at it they would not know it was happening. It as it pulsed between his fingers, and he could feel himself—his core, his essence, his soul—being dragged gently away from the menacing eye.

The eye screamed, the dark edges of the pupil brightening with a burning, white fury. The streams of po were forced toward Cynkz like spectral daggers. Somehow they could not reach him. Countless faint hues compressed together, stretching out to take hold of whatever they could, and yet they could not. He was beyond them.

The voice screamed and wailed. It helplessly cried and gnashed against the dark, its rage nearly bursting through the veil of abyss.

Cynkz' s mind was clear, and all that he felt was the warmth of the sliver of light pressed gingerly between his fingers. A great weight had been lifted from his shoulders as he was pulled out of view of the baleful presence above. Soon, his pale hand came into view, along with the shining edge of his dark cloak being dragged further into the darkness.

The thread slipped through his fingers and receded into the shade below. Despite this, he felt at ease and continued his quiet descent. He dared not look up, however, afraid that the eye may still be peering into him from a world away.

He also noticed that he could not fly upward. Some insurmountable force had its hold on him. There was nothing left to do but continue his way and confront whatever may lie at the bottom of the world, in that pitiful pit of darkness beneath it all.

Cynkz was not sure how long he had been falling nor did he care. Everything was peaceful, and the weight of all that had come before was, for a time, gone. Perhaps he had merely been drifting through a dark ocean. Perhaps he had truly died. Maybe it was truly the end.

Until a new voice called out to him, one that could be heard in earnest.

"Welcome to my home, Cynkz. I've been waiting for you for some time."

Chapter 27

Cynkz whipped his head around. For a moment, he was afraid it was the eye calling to him again, perhaps trying to trick him. The new voice was different. It spoke normally, or at least as normally as a booming call through an infinite blanket of darkness could be. It did not wrack its way through his core. It seemed almost reasonable, as if it merely wanted to be heard.

"Below you, jester!"

With no proper frame of reference, Cynkz struggled to orient himself in any particular way. Yet, he instinctively felt the piercing gaze of something great beneath him. He turned to look and was greeted with nothing but emptiness. Then, the shade began to flow away like water, and an incomprehensible form slowly revealed itself.

First were its wings. They were world-consuming blankets of some strange, otherworldly, almost leathery material that shaped themselves like moth wings. They shot out into infinity, whatever horizon the abyss concealed was not beyond its reach. A thin, bony frame held them together, not dissimilar to the pointed limbs on a bat, their knife-like tips grand enough to pierce the realms. They were a deep violet—so dark they nearly blended in with the void. They came out in many layers, in perfect symmetry on either side, at least four or five sets all originating from a single point.

Next was its body. A heaving, impossibly dense mass of muscle and skin formed a shape vaguely reminiscent of a man's torso. Its chest was a burnt, reddish hue, perhaps closer in color to Fiddle's coarse fur and skin. It was impossible to see where, or how, the many wings connected to it. Two humanoid arms reached out from the chest, their length not proportional to the anatomy. Each hand pressed with the force of storms, winds that could topple any tree in Munderworld with little effort. Each finger could have been a limb in its own right, thick and muscular at their base yet coming to fine, blackened points. Each nail was a pitch black curve of plate that could have plucked the smallest of creatures from the craftiest of hiding spots. Looking at them, it was difficult to discern where exactly their points ended.

Finally, there was the head. It was disproportionate to the rest of its form. His face resembled that of a male po, his features so refined that he could be mistaken for a marble statue of old. The bridge of his nose was straight as a stone column and came to a fine point. His lips were thin and reflected a fleshy, amber color against the light. They were pressed into a flat line, each edge ending beneath the middle point of his eyes. The lips were cut with such precision that one would almost expect a clear, noble vibrato to leave them. A dark, silky flame grew out infinitely from the top of his skull, sinking into the surrounding abyss, perhaps even feeding it.

His eyes were of particular note. They were surprisingly large, deep black orbs. They had no whites and were dark and consuming as the void around them. Their topmost layer reflected the light, and at the center were rich, lavender pupils that could be seen peering out into the world. Their sockets seemed massive, yet he kept his expression pulled into a hard squint. It was as though the weight of infinite lifetimes weighed heavy on him, and he looked into the world with an uncanny, reserved sorrow. They were the eyes of someone who had many regrets and was not inclined to make more.

His elaborate, otherworldly detail reminded Cynkz of the apostle, if only for a moment. Cynkz could not help but stare. Those extra seconds forced to look at the almighty presence seemed to, for once, have the opposite effect of that of a jester; it didn't charm as much as it instilled him with awe and fear.

The entity noticed and broke the silence once more.

"Jester... Cynkz... What brings you here? Don't tell me you came all this way to look dumbfounded at your king?"

Cynkz shook himself out of his stupor, gathering whatever nerve he had left and gestured a slight curtsy in the air.

"I presume you are the legendary Munder King?" Cynkz said. "You'll have to excuse my discourtesy, your highness. I would bow properly before you, if I were not, at the moment, aimlessly floating in the abyss."

The King laughed, his cackle like a storm blowing through a dark, withered forest. It would have been endearing if it were not so terribly forceful. Cynkz looked up through the blasting winds to notice the King's face. When he smiled, he did not put his entire face into the action. Again, some deep sense of sorrow appeared to be restraining him. Being a jester, and a courtier, and a shapeshifter, Cynkz was no stranger to the masks people wore. It was a small relief that even one as powerful and menacing as the King of Darkness would be as vulnerable to this principle as any other.

"You are a funny one, jester," the king said. "I have been watching you for some time, since before you got hold of the thread. I never would have guessed that the thread would have spurred you on such a journey."

The King rested his world-spanning arms to his sides, and leaned forward, his black and lavender eyes pressing themselves into the sharp slits. Cynkz felt the impulse to back away, to turn and hide, yet he remained. He knew there was nowhere he could possibly go, and kings often enjoyed a proper showing of confidence and reverence. He stayed his ground and met the King, eye-to-eye.

"The question remains. Why did you come here?"

Cynkz drew in a small breath in an attempt to hide the nervous clearing of his throat. "I have many reasons for coming here; to see if the rumors were true, that our King still lived. To ask about the thread, and the visions it has granted me, seemingly at random throughout my journey. To inquire as to my origins, and why I can hardly remember who or what I was in the po world, save for the odd vision and a poem that has stayed with me since the beginning."

"Maybe these visions are odd dreams of yours? Muns and po still dream, even in Munderworld."

"That is another rumor I have heard, your highness: that you can influence people's memories and dreams. If I may be so bold—"

"Ah, yes, I can. Dreams, thoughts, memories, these things are not so separate from the waking world, not as much as we'd like them to be."

"My visions, are they perhaps *your* doing?"

"Ha!"

Another thunderous, void-shattering bellow exploded from the King's chest. It took quite a bit of effort for Cynkz to remain still, to not be blown away.

"No, Cynkz. To tamper with such fundamental and ethereal matters is too much work to do often. I am not interested in such things," the King said.

"What of Horgafell, the giant?" Cynkz asked. His heart's pace was picking up, a part of him wanting to test how many questions he could get away with.

"The giant ... Horgafell was but a nuisance. Overall, he was not important, but I needed him subdued in some manner. Much like Eshra'Tel."

The King lifted his left arm and pointed a shining black claw to the eye above. Cynkz hesitated, not wanting to risk being caught in the menacing orb's gaze. Though if the Munder King, of all beings, wanted to show him something, he had better oblige.

Cynkz looked up, and what he saw sparked something—perhaps wonder, perhaps awe, perhaps merely a sheer sense of something overwhelming. The great, shining black orb reflected all of the light above it, and cast the image of Munderworld across the entire abyss. Cynkz could see everything; the dark and rolling sands of Saknii, countless fungal tribals as they traipsed across the drugged marsh, the clashing mountains of Horgafell, even the placid plains and wandering po of Dulrot.

The image shifted as Cynkz moved his eyes, allowing him to hone his sights onto specific things within each realm. He turned his gaze to the maze-like forest beneath the corrosive fog in the mountains. It was surprisingly easy to find the Sisters, who were huddled together around some arcane object, listening in. Orla was there, standing behind them, just as attentive as the other women. Cynkz's focus was brought back to the magnificent, terrifying eye, its burning pupil spinning as it threw its burning edges across the darkness around it.

"How is this possible?" Cynkz asked. "It's amazing."

"Eshra'Tel, my old confidante, was once a supremely powerful Omun, like I was. When he and I, and several others, were banished, cast out of Omundisia, the land of the Creator and Omun. He insisted we focus our effort and energy toward escape and amassing another rebellion. I simply refused. In truth, we were given a world of our own to play with as we saw fit. Not necessarily the worst of punishments. I did not have the passion to go gallivanting across the higher realms and through the cosmos only to fight another losing battle. He would not shut up about it, however. Tensions grew and our differences escalated to conflict. If Munderworld was to have any sort of stability, I needed to incapacitate him."

"What is he now? I could see the massive eye 'hear' him screaming at me and felt countless cold hands and fingers trying to pry my soul apart."

"I destroyed his physical body. All that remains is one of his eyes. The rest of him, his bodily essence, remains twisted and contorted by his eye. It can pull in helpless souls and other things, but not much else. Though you already know that."

"Why keep his eye?"

"I use it as a lens, to easily watch and observe the realms."

"Why would you need that? Couldn't you go and watch over the realms yourself?"

"No… I cannot."

The king leaned back into a mournful sigh, the mild gasp of his lamentation filling the air with an oddly warm and comforting breeze.

"When I was banished, I was completely stripped of my status as a being of light. This dark pit you see," the king said, motioning his giant hand, "I am bound to it. My body is one with the darkness, an ever-growing miasma continuing to pull me in and consume me. I can sense and influence Munderworld, but I cannot physically see it. In fact, I cannot look up to stars anymore, perhaps a final twisting of the knife for my punishment."

Cynkz took notice that all of the images produced across the veil looked down on the realms of Munderworld. Not a single piece of the great projected tapestry showed the sky.

"That is … saddening, to say the least," Cynkz murmured beneath his breath.

"Yes," the King said. "I am not allowed to look back to my brothers in the cosmos. All I have is this pit, and Munderworld."

"I'm sorry."

"For what?"

"All this time you must have seen me looking up to the stars, mumbling that silly poem to myself. It must have been like a mockery of your punishment."

"Not really, Cynkz. I could catch glimpses of the stars reflecting from your own dark eyes. It was not much, but it was something. You spent so much time stargazing that I was able to get a good look of the night sky through you. In a sense, I should be thanking you."

"That is quite the honor, your highness."

"Do you know how you were able to make it through Eshra'Tel?"

"Not really, no." Cynkz looked down at his hand, his eyes looking past it as he was lost in the feelings and emotions he felt through the experience. "I just … felt the thread. It pulled me down and away. I couldn't think or move or do anything, really. I just followed the thread."

"Here, take another look at it. You may notice something."

The King took his hand and gently grabbed something out of the abyss. He slowly lowered his heaving limb and opened his palm. The tiny sliver of sparkling light quietly drifted toward Cynkz, who reached out and took hold of it.

Cynkz held it up and began to twist and turn it. The top end of the thread, as he turned it away, seemed to recede into darkness. Part of the filament was tainted, ever so slightly, by a murky, looming shadow. It maintained its form, its bright hue fading into a splinter of the void.

The light and dark highlights shone brilliantly off Cynkz's dark eyes. He spun the thread between his fingers before turning his attention back to the Munder King.

"How long has this been here?" Cynkz asked.

"Since the beginning," the King replied. "Every light has its shadow and vice versa. Not even the apostles, or the Omun, are beyond their own shades."

"This was your doing?"

"Yes."

"The instances where I felt the thread pulling me toward something, it was you?"

"Correct."

"Even during the times it seemed to purposefully lead me to more danger?"

"I wanted to see if you were capable. I wanted to keep things fun."

"It seems many of those who help us always do so with something in mind for themselves."

"Ah, my naive young jester. Such is the way of—"

"Wait!" Cynkz's head shot up, his eyes framing a stunned expression. "Fiddle! Where is he?! Is he all right? The last time I saw him was before we fell into the eye."

"Hmmm…"

"W-what's wrong? Is he—"

"Your friend is fine. I can see him now, spinning around in circles in the storm of chaos within Eshra'Tel."

"Can you save him? Please, I beg you—"

"Cynkz, you do not need to grovel. I'll pull him down in just a moment."

"Is something the matter, your highness?"

The king leaned his monstrous form to one side before reaching up with one of his hands to scratch at his chin. It sounded as if a tree were being dragged through a meadow, and its echo shot far into the abyss. Every minute action demanded the world's attention.

"I was merely hoping for a few more moments of peace before bringing him here," the King said.

"He can be a bit mouthy. I'm sure you witnessed him back in the caves."

"It is not that. In fact, I found his exchange with that boisterous runt of a sentinel amusing. I know he is going to have a never ending stream of questions waiting for me."

"I could ask him to remain still if you wish—"

"No, no. It is fine. Considering what I have put you through, and the entertainment you have brought me, the least I can do is listen to a few questions."

The dark deity reached toward the eye. As he stretched his limb, it seemed to disappear into the horizon, merging with the eye's refracted light. He dragged a long, jagged finger down with a string of waving shadow stuck to his nail's tip. The writhing shade pulled itself off of the black claw. It spun around wildly before collapsing into an infinitely small point and exploding into the imp's familiar form.

"Fiddle!" Cynkz exclaimed. "You're all right!"

Just as he dove in to give his friend a hug, the imp's body began to convulse.

"Fiddle? Fiddle, are you—"

"Ack!"

The imp assumed a fetal position, holding himself as he coughed violently, drifting aimlessly to the jester's side.

The King assumed a more proper, upright position. "Give him a moment. He'll be fine."

"I suppose he was exposed to Eshra'Tel for significantly longer than I was," Cynkz said.

"You two are quite brave. Few are foolish enough to tempt the wrath of an apostle, a lesser Omun."

"If I had known any better, I may not have gone through with it."

"Heh, fools. I suppose it is the way of the universe that a king should be accosted by his fools."

Cynkz pulled his shoulders back into a soft shrug and smiled. "In truth, I'm surprised that our antics even worked."

"I have never seen an Omun, apostle or not, 'miss' its target. You two were spared, though for what, I do not know."

The King rubbed the tip of his chin again. His eyes squinted fiercely, his gaze unfocused as he was lost in thought.

"Perhaps it was a means of allowing you your visions?" the King said. "I have looked sparsely at your visions, in fact. They are so scattered and disconnected that I cannot make sense of them."

"I see…" Cynkz looked to his feet, his shoulders slumped and his face adopting a veneer of stoic dejection. "Even the poem? No insight as to its origins? Or if the woman I first saw in the vision was of any import?"

"The poem. I have heard you recite it to yourself many times. How did it go again?"

Cynkz drew in a breath and relaxed before answering. "Every star, near and far, waits for us to just reach out and accept them."

"A beautiful verse, from a time long before most po could even fathom existed." The King focused his gaze back to the jester. "All I know, Cynkz, is that you and I have an odd commonality. It appears we are attracted to a particular type of woman."

"That's an odd thing for two as different as you and I to share," Cynkz said.

"For all I know, we may share a number of things in common, jester," the King said.

Cynkz stared at the imp, still spinning and coughing from the shock of his previous trauma. Fiddle appeared to be settling himself in the air, no longer convulsing involuntarily.

"What exactly happened to Tall?" Cynkz turned around to look back at the King. "When Fiddle held the thread, he said he could not feel it. If he could not visually see it in his grasp, he would not know it was there. Yet when the minstrel took it—"

"Ahahaha! The minstrel! His memories! It was so easy!" The king's voice boomed, stirring up great, warm winds that, while pleasant against his skin, nearly blew Cynkz away. Fiddle, still vulnerable, rolled multiple tree lengths toward the abyss before stopping.

"I figured I would mimic the thread's abilities." The King began to smile, a tiny smirk on such a large face impossible to not notice. "I 'coaxed' the thread, pushing it to remind him of his biggest regrets and sins. It was fun to dig through his mind, forcing him to witness a small handful of his atrocities from the perspective of his victims."

"How creatively vicious, your highness," Cynkz said.

"Come now, do not pretend you are above a little fun, a little charm and deceit to get what you need. Sulmara was lying, by the way. She has not seen me since I eradicated her vermin siblings."

"Why did you—"

"For the same reason I subdued the giant Horgafell. I do not want pests upending the terrain of my beautiful creation. Munderworld is all I have now, remember?"

"That makes sense, I suppose. Sulmara did not seem to be an agreeable personality."

"So you played it smart and ruined her expectations, leaving her defeated and dejected."

"She seems strong. She'll be fine."

"How deliciously vicious, jester."

Cynkz glanced away, unsure of what to make of the conversation. Should he be proud? Upset at his deception? If others are often misleading him, was it wrong to return the favor? Can one rise above such things, and do better? Was it worth doing better if it put oneself at further risk? Or risk the well-being of others? Cynkz sought answers but seemed to be coming up with more questions.

"I cannot give you all of the answers you seek," the King said. "I could, in truth, only give you scattered pieces of information and history. There are other places you should seek if you want to truly learn more about yourself, about the po, and their world, Peara."

"What happened to Peara?" Cynkz almost stopped himself, feeling a bit presumptuous to ask more questions despite the King's recent words. "Why did it end so abruptly?"

The King's face softened. He turned his head so as to look his nose down at the jester. He stared for what felt like a moment too long before turning his sharp, dark eyes toward the endless images of Munderworld dancing across the darkness.

"It was my fault," the King uttered. It was a whisper that bellowed out into the abyss like soft thunder.

"What?"

"The Creator—the supreme being, the embodiment of all light, all that is, and ever will be—has His plans laid out strictly for creation. And yet I did something that broke His precious 'timeline,' something that was never supposed to happen. It was, in the grand scheme, a small action, perhaps a most insignificant one, and yet it was one completely of my own free will. One that, in His view, had ramifications that reached farther than I could ever hope to see. My actions angered The Creator, shook Him to His core. Perhaps it was a threat to all causality. Who knows? What I do know is that despite the pain, the shame, the remorse, the destruction it wrought, I would do it again, with nary a second thought."

"If I may be so bold, your highness—"

The King quickly raised his hand, gesturing for Cynkz to stop and listen. "You may have heard along your travels, that I was once an Omun. I was, in fact, the most powerful of all Omun. I worked directly below the Creator, a privilege no others were permitted as no other was powerful enough to handle. Omun have an immense responsibility. They are essentially caretakers of the universe, working to ensure the Creator's plan goes smoothly. Omun are forbidden from getting directly involved with any under their protection, however. It is the most difficult part of the job. Least of all, an Omun isn't allowed to get intimate with a mere po. Who knows what kind of monstrosity would come out of that relationship?"

"Wait, so you—"

"That is enough, Cynkz. Perhaps if you are fated to learn more, you will find answers in the final land of po."

"The 'final land'? What is that?"

"The great city of Potarium. It's an endless land, set ashore a boundless, dark ocean. Its expanse is the one thing connecting our world, the world of the dead, of Munderworld, to the rest of creation."

"Why haven't you—"

Before Cynkz could process his building frustration from being interrupted consecutive times, Fiddle burst forth between Cynkz and the King. Whether his continued spasms were from excitement or trauma was anyone's guess.

"Father!" Fiddle cried out. "Is it true? Are you my dad?!"

The king rested onto his side and began to massage the bridge of his nose, with long, clawed fingers.

"My word, here we go…"

"So it's true! You're my dad! I'm the prince of darkness! Muahahaha! I wanna rub this in Rackel's face! Just you wait—"

The King flicked his hand out toward the two visitors, the bitter tinge of vexation accenting his snappy movements. "You're called Fiddle, correct?"

"Why yes! Yes, I am," Fiddle said, thumbing the loose skin on his collar like the top of a finely spruced blouse.

"Who gave you that name?" the King asked. "I do not recall giving any of my offspring names after I came down here."

"I'm … not sure, really. It just sort of stuck over time. I've had it since before I met Cynkz."

"I see…"

"You know, a lot of people say that in Munderworld." Fiddle postured upright, mimicking his father's more noble, thoughtful stature. "'I see… Hmm, hmmmm…'"

"Hehe, you're a lively one, at least." The king rested his arm at his side as he looked at the imp, amused. "The fact that you were able to make it here proves you're at least capable. More so than any of your siblings."

"That's right! I have brothers and sisters, huh?"

"Hundreds," the King said.

Fiddle leaned toward Cynkz and playfully elbowed the jester's side. "Sheesh, guess there isn't much else for a king to do here than 'get busy,' huh?"

"I have traveled across the cosmos, battled through the heavens, and have created a world of my own that hardly needs my help to continue its existence. I've had my fun, with mun and po alike. I have done enough, or so I thought. In truth, I wanted to be left alone, to relax and slumber for the rest of eternity if fate would allow it."

Fiddle sat and stared, doe-eyed at his father. The King returned the look with a raised brow and a curled lip, curious of the imp's thoughts.

"Man," Fiddle said. "All this time I was so excited to meet you, but you're basically a sleepy old man—"

The King clasped his hands into tight fists, producing a force so explosive the dark, invisible walls of the abyss shook. It took everything within Cynkz to maintain his ground. Fiddle could only grab on to his cloak to keep from being flung into the far reaches of the void.

"You will respect your father, imp! With a mere thought I could wipe you from existence, erase the memories of everyone you love, and you would be gone! Forever!"

Cynkz sat in his braced stance, a single bead of sweat barreling down the side of his face. Fiddle was neatly tucked behind him, shivering against his back.

The King let the tense air sit for a moment before smiling, relaxing his posture to chuckle to himself. Cynkz loosened his own stance, and Fiddle conjured up the courage to peek from behind the jester's shoulder.

"You'll have to excuse me. I get carried away sometimes," the King said. "It is quite reassuring to know my children are capable or have the potential to be."

"S-so where are they, then?" Fiddle asked.

"I'm sure most of them are still alive, doing their best to eke out some sort of existence at the far reaches of the many realms." The

King wagged his finger across the tip of his chin, as if the thought of his children's well-being were an extraneous afterthought.

"We have to help them!" Fiddle exclaimed.

"Why?" the King asked. "What do you plan to do? Create a mun-filled court? Establish a high council of imps?"

Fiddle's eyes widened, cradled by the wildest grin Cynkz had ever seen.

"That would be amazing! Think of the possibilities!" Fiddle threw his arms about, gesturing his imaginings with reckless abandon.

"You really should be careful what you say around Fiddle," Cynkz said. "He is easily inspired."

The King rested his head upon his hand and sighed.

"I suppose it would be beneficial to allow others access to my throne, to re-establish communication with those of import. It may prove necessary for what lies ahead."

Cynkz and Fiddle shared a confused look.

"What do you mean?" Fiddle asked.

"No one in Munderworld is permitted access to the higher realms without my blessing, save the apostles who come and go as they please, and whomever they decide to 'save.'"

"What of Yla?" Cynkz asked.

"The ring," the King said, casually pointing toward the jester. "Hold it out for me, if you will."

Cynkz reluctantly stretched out his arm and opened his palm, revealing the shining, braided ring. The king carefully lowered the long, black nail on his foremost finger and gently tapped the silvery band with the tip. Several echoes rolled out from the ring, layering over one another, each voice a familiar sound.

"That sounds like the Sisters!" Cynkz exclaimed.

The voices responded, each excited sound nearly tripping over the one next to it.

"Cynkz! Is that you? We can hear you!"

"Hey handsome, how are you?"

"Una, for the love of all that is—"

"You're gonna scare them off if you all don't shut it."

"Orla's here too. Say hello to Cynkz and the Munder King."

"H-how are you? Cynkz, Fiddle, are you all right?"

Fiddle grew excited and nearly jumped into Cynkz's open palm.

"Orla! Old ladies!" Fiddle was screaming at the ring, causing Cynkz to pull away a hair. "We told you we could make it, didn't we?"

"Silence!" the King's voice boomed. "You sibling, Yla, she is fine. She left for the world of po some time ago. Considering she was able to make it unscathed, she is no doubt doing well in the city of Potarium."

The squealing of the old women trailed off into the distance, fading away from Cynkz's hand. The King leaned back a final time and looked at him.

"Cynkz, would you be willing to traverse the dark sea and go into Potarium? Perhaps you can find out what happened to their beloved Sister. You would also be granting me a small view into the realms beyond, so long as you have the thread with you."

"Of course we would!" Fiddle threw himself into the air, bounding over Cynkz's head and nearly taking the jester's hat with him. "Who would have thought our silly little adventure would take us so far, huh?"

"You cannot go, Fiddle," the King said, a caring undercurrent following his otherwise imposing voice.

"What?" Fiddle stopped, his face heavy and worried.

"Muns, creatures of the dark, they cannot go beyond Munderworld."

"But I... Why..." Fiddle slumped, his eyes looked back and forth, trying to come to grips with what was to come.

"Why can *he* go? What makes Cynkz so special that he has to leave me behind?!" Fiddle's tiny claws were pulled into tight fists, his hands wringing as he threw his tantrum.

"That is what I would like to find out," the King said.

Fiddle and Cynkz looked at one another in disbelief. Their eyes sparkled against the ominous light of the abyss as they attempted to restrain their emotions.

"Cynkz, you are awfully quiet and observant, despite the circumstances," the King said. "You will be perfect. I have no issue letting you travel forward."

"Will I ever get to see my friend again?" Fiddle said as he turned to look at his father with teary eyes.

"There are ways to keep in touch with him while he is in Potarium. Worry not. Though it may take some time."

"That's good." Fiddle turned back to Cynkz. "It's a shame. We went through all of that just to be separated. I can't remember the last time we were apart for very long."

Cynkz smiled, in part in an attempt to hold back the flow of tears with a tightened cheek. He leaned forward and placed a soft hand on Fiddle's coarse shoulder, gripping it tightly.

"This journey is still ours, my friend," Cynkz said. "I will find a way to keep in touch, and we will continue this quest together."

Fiddle remained still for a moment, then slowly drifted into the jester's chest and wrapped his small, wiry arms around him as best as he could.

"Fun, fun, fun, for the man and the mun, right?" Cynkz said.

Fiddle looked up, his own face tightened into a teary ball. "That's right, and you know what?" Fiddle backed away and spun in the air. "We'll get my brothers and sisters, THE Sisters, Orla and Kadd, and we'll have a big fancy council that will watch over you! You will be like a missionary! Cynkz, the Realm Walker! The Dark Leaver! The Munder Vassal!"

"Where are you getting these names from, boy?" the King huffed.

"I don't know. I'm just creative, I guess." Fiddle shrugged.

Cynkz turned his attention back to the dark deity, his expression pressed into a stern look, as if bracing for something to come.

"It's settled, then," Cynkz said. "I will venture forth and find out whatever I can. My first priority will be finding Yla."

The King readied his arms. "She may not be quite what you are expecting. Be careful, jester. And hold on to that ring. If I can recognize its craftsmanship, she certainly will."

"Of course. What should I expect in Potarium?" Cynkz asked.

"All you need to remember is this: the tower cradles the heavens. Go there, as high as you can, and you may find everything you are looking for."

"Noted. And thank you."

"Hmph," the king scoffed and smiled. He spread his arms and every layer of his wings out into the abyss. They disappeared into the blackness as they stretched into infinity. A peculiar circle of darkness began to form below the King's form. As it spun and clashed against the realm's menacing light, the soft hiss of ocean waves could be heard ringing from its center.

"Do not thank me yet. Your journey is far, *far* from over."

Cynkz looked into the portal. The swirling froth of ocean water splashing against its edges was oddly soothing, not unlike the faint stardust that flowed from the thread. He looked back to the reflective eye. His eyes moved slowly across each of the realms and rested when he saw Dulrot, the mountains and cliffs that he liked to perch upon to gaze at the night sky. He worked his vision back down to see the Sisters standing together, their quarters much messier than before. Orla peeked over their shoulders.

Cynkz met the eyes of his friend, who was trying to sneakily wipe away tears.

"Well, what's an adventure without a little risk, eh?"

The two were able to get a good, long look amidst the silence. They shared a warm smile with one another, and Fiddle was able to gather the strength to say goodbye.

"Yeah, I suppose you're right," Fiddle said.

Cynkz turned and began to drift toward the portal. He stopped just before entering its border.

"Go forth. All things within the dark ocean eventually find their way to Potarium's shores," the King said, maintaining his stance, his focus on maintaining the rift.

Cynkz looked on for perhaps a moment too long, then drew in a deep breath and threw himself into the raging, ethereal waters.

As soon as he was through, the Munder King lowered his arms, and the portal slowly collapsed. Fiddle finally let loose the breath he had been holding for too long before whispering a final few words.

"Stay safe, Cynkz."

As the imp drew back, he looked up to notice his father was relaxing, his head seated comfortably upon his mighty palm.

"So, about my siblings…"

Author Bio

Kyle Sorrell, also known as "Pendoodle," is a fantasy author based out of Northern Florida. Having grown up with countless fantasy and sci-fi influences, as well as a lifelong obsession with video games, he loves to stitch together stories of odd elements dipped in the weird and the wild. He was born on a naval base in a watery town in Japan and grew up a multiracial child, working different jobs—from assistant plumbing to theme park caricatures to truck driving. You can catch sneak peeks for his next crazy idea, or just the occasional illustration, at his personal website at pendoodlez.wordpress.com.

Book Club Questions

1. Which realm in Munderworld was the most interesting?
2. Which realm in Munderworld was the least interesting?
3. Which of Cynkz's transformations was your favorite?
4. Did any scenes stick out to you in particular?
5. Who was your favorite character?
6. What was your favorite sentence or line of dialogue?
7. Did this book impact your mood? And if so, how?
8. What surprised you the most in this story?
9. Did this book remind you of any other books?
10. Are you interested in finding out where the story leads to next?

11. What lingering mystery do you find the most intriguing/has the most potential?

12. Would you read another book by this author?

13. Was his prose unique or were there any influences that came to mind as you read?

More books from 4 Horsemen Publications

Fantasy

D. Lambert
To Walk into the Sands
Rydan
Celebrant
Northlander
Esparan
King
Traitor
His Last Name

Danielle Orsino
Locked Out of Heaven
Thine Eyes of Mercy
From the Ashes
Kingdom Come
Fire, Ice, Acid, & Heart
A Fae is Done

J.M. Paquette
Klauden's Ring
Solyn's Body
The Inbetween
Hannah's Heart

Lou Kemp
The Violins Played Before Junstan
Music Shall Untune the Sky

R.J. Young
Challenges of Tawa

Valerie Willis
Cedric: The Demonic Knight
Romasanta: Father of Werewolves
The Oracle: Keeper of the Gaea's Gate
Artemis: Eye of Gaea
King Incubus: A New Reign

Kyle Sorrell
Munderworld

SciFi

Brandon Hill &
Terence Pegasus
Between the Devil and the Dark
Wrath & Redemption

C.K. Westbrook
The Shooting
The Collision

Nick Savage
Us of Legendary Gods

PC Nottingham
Mummified Moon

T.S. Simons
Antipodes
The Liminal Space
Ouroboros
Caim
Sessrúmnir
The 45th Parallel

Ty Carlson
The Bench
The Favorite
The Shadowless

Lightning Source UK Ltd.
Milton Keynes UK
UKHW012047310123
416284UK00025B/151/J

9 781644 507322